Pieces

Of Me

BY NICKY SHANKS

Pieces of Me

Copyright © 2018 by Nicky Shanks.
All rights reserved.
First Print Edition: December 2018

Limitless Publishing, LLC
Kailua, HI 96734
www.limitlesspublishing.com

Formatting: Limitless Publishing

ISBN-13: 978-1-64034-497-6
ISBN-10: 1-64034-497-7

Dedication

This one is for all my tattooed bad boy loving fans out there. Those who know what they want and don't let anything stand in their way to get it. You inspire me the most.

Chapter One

Cinnamon and Whiskey

The air is thick with cigar smoke as it hovers over the backyard full of pretentious people...well, that and fake, over-the-top laughter. I can't believe I let myself get talked into coming here—this isn't my scene by a million miles. Now, my sister, Caitlyn...this is *her* scene. My gaze darts around the crowd as I try to make a solid escape plan, but all I can see is Ralph Lauren pleated pants and too-short cocktail dresses. The scents of several expensive perfumes mix together, and the potent cloud engulfs every space I run to.

"Hey there, sexy—where've you been hiding?" Caitlyn's friend, Sam, pokes my side and raises his eyebrows in amusement at me. "I wouldn't want you to lose your way around this place. You smell incredibly *delicious,* by the way." His low growl near my ear makes my stomach clench just enough to feel like I'm going to vomit. I can't stomach him; he's a six-foot tall walking hard-on, and he loves to

1

flirt with anything that walks on two legs with boobs…especially me.

"Where's Cait?" he asks. The lumpy shape of his nearly shaved head makes me think of pinholes. They open and close to let out all the hot air when he speaks. His cold, gray eyes are like small daggers that try and pierce every female he comes across. He flashes his creepy, crooked smile, which makes me shiver just enough to remember why I can't stand him.

I shrug, and chills run down my spine. I know I'm being watched by someone other than Sam—I *feel* it. The backyard is packed with people, so of course someone else is *looking* at me, but this is different. Someone is wrapping me in a more intense cocoon of paranoia than I normally have.

The stray ends of my long, chestnut brown hair fall from the pins holding the thick mess up as I shake my head at Sam. "I'm not her keeper; you should go and find her yourself." I inch away from him, but he yanks me by my waist. He holds me flush to his side, his fingers rubbing circles on my hips. I feel someone's frustration suffocate me; I push Sam away for the second time, and his eyes turn dark.

Sam nods at someone across the backyard and sucks in air through his front teeth. When he looks back at me, he assesses my body before locking his creepy gray eyes with mine. "You know, underneath all of your quirks and bitchy attitude is someone I can see myself sleeping with."

Oh, gross.

I push him off before I gag out loud. "Go away."

2

He laughs off my rejection and pushes me back with gusto, almost knocking me into the bushes. I can't see Caitlyn anywhere, so I grab a glass of champagne from a passing waiter's tray—*then another*—and dart through the sea of people. They're blocking the way back into the house, and all of my quick exits that I planned out before are now gone.

It isn't enough for Caitlyn that we're on completely opposite ends of the popularity spectrum—which doesn't bother *me*, but she'll never let me forget it. It's like she always has to one-up me, no matter what the circumstances. I don't remember most of my childhood with her, and the parts I *do* remember are confusing and pointless.

I started expressing concerns about my memories to my parents last year. Even though I don't remember it, I'm told I was in a car accident that gifted me with retrograde amnesia a few months before I started noticing signs that things didn't feel right. Whenever I try to recall a memory that someone in my family describes to me, there's nothing there. Everything before moving to Silver Lake is just…*empty*.

According to my parents, the headaches started after I left the hospital; they'd bring me to my knees at first. After a few months—and after we moved to northern California from Washington State—they died down. I still have them sometimes, but physical therapy wasn't really helping, so I never went back.

The dreams, meanwhile, started after we moved to Silver Lake—dreams so vivid that they'd haunt me for days. That's why I started asking questions about my missing memories. That…and the lack of pictures on our walls. No family portraits, no birthdays or Christmas dinners…*nothing.*

Maybe I don't remember anything about my life before a year ago, but my family does. Why wouldn't they want any reminders of it? My mom told me it's so I don't feel bad about the holes in my memory, and I guess I get that, but…the whole situation gives me a funny feeling, like I'm missing something *else*, too.

I know it doesn't make my family feel very loved to know I don't remember them or all the wonderful things they surely have done for me. I *do* feel bad about that. So now, instead of reminding everyone that I feel like a stranger in my own body, I say nothing and let the tension slowly build inside like a ticking time bomb.

"*Livvie*!" Caitlyn calls for me in her squeaky voice. "Livvie, over here!"

I don't want to look.

I don't want to look.

I don't want to—

"Hey, didn't you hear me?" Her sharp, fake fingernails dig into my skin. I swear I can feel the blood trickling down my arm. "Where are you going in such a rush?"

I hand her the two empty champagne glasses and smile the fake smile that she taught me. "Home." I shake my head. "I don't belong here."

Caitlyn frowns and tries to toss her bleached hair over her shoulder in annoyance. It amuses me when she does this, because her hair is shoulder-length and there's nothing to toss. "These *things* are important, and I attend to represent *our* family. We just moved here—we need friends." Her lips smack together, and the stickiness of her lip gloss makes a wet, sloppy sound. I laugh to myself, thinking it looks like glue. "You know what? Never mind. I don't expect *you* to understand."

"We moved here *months* ago." My entire body is numb as she walks away from me and re-joins her group of friends, picking up where she left off and laughing along with them. I would never, *ever* tell her this, but I desperately want that to be me. I don't have a lot of friends—no one that ever sticks around long enough to be *called* a friend, really—and while she's out there putting her good name to use, I'm stuck in between two brick walls, going nowhere fast.

She *is* right about one thing: I don't understand what she means about "family." How can I, when I hardly feel right about calling her my sister?

Caitlyn looks back at me and squints her eyes in anger, silently demanding me to leave.

Fine.

"I'm going," I mouth and pick up another glass of champagne, letting the bubbly liquid fill my throat before putting the empty flute back on the waiter's tray. The room starts to spin a little beneath my feet, but not enough for me to ask Caitlyn for a ride home so I have to listen to her complain the entire way. I manage to make it outside of the mansion before collapsing onto the damp, manicured grass with my head in my hands. I have no idea where I left my purse with my phone and keys, but it doesn't matter. I can walk home from here—all seven miles in these heels, if I have to.

"I would ask if you're okay, but that seems like a silly question," a deep voice rumbles above me. It amplifies inside my head, bouncing around the walls and making me dizzier than the champagne. "So I'll ask a different question: may I help you up?" The smoothness of his voice excites me and lights a fire inside of my stomach. I trust this person with everything inside of me, and I haven't even bothered to look up. Now I *know* I'm drunk; my thoughts make no sense.

A hand reaches down into my field of vision, but I shake my head and swat it away. "No thanks."

The long breath he lets out amuses me. I've managed to somehow annoy him without even looking up. The uneasy feeling he's having is bleeding into the air; he seems restless, like he can't stand still or something. Is this *his* house? Maybe he's pissed because I'm sprawled out, drunk, on his lawn?

"Suit yourself, but I think that the gentlemen looking up your skirt could use a break, don't you?" The world spins as I try to peek up through my messy hair. A group of older men stare at me from a few feet away as I feel the breeze between my legs; I snap them together. I groan and try to lift myself up, the champagne rushing to my head again. "Whoa, there, Bug," the man says, leaping toward me and holding out his arms. I fall and hit something hard, but I'm not on the ground.

I smile into his chest over his dress shirt, completely unaware of how much makeup I'm smearing on him. "Yum, you smell like cinnamon and whiskey." My mind races as my weight sags against his body. There's something igniting about his aroma—it's making my head spin even faster as he holds me.

The man laughs a deep, smoky laugh and brushes my hair from my face so he can get a better look at what he's getting himself into. "Let me take you home. You're in no condition to drive anywhere." I'm so dizzy that I can't think straight, but I know that Caitlyn will *kill* me if word gets around that her sister left the upper-class social mingle with some strange man. Ever since we moved to Silver Lake, it's like she's become an entirely different person...well, as far as I can remember.

"My sister," I mumble. "She's here."

More people stop to look at us, wondering what my problem is and sticking their noses up at me once they realize I'm just a little too drunk— something that regularly happens at these events when someone with a problem attends, I'm sure.

But I don't have just *one* problem.

I have *dozens* of them.

"Olivia!" Caitlyn scolds me as she rushes to us; her judging eyes cut right through me. I'm thankful for the warmth that my savior is giving me. I feel myself smile and snuggle into the man's chest, breathing him in and brushing her off. This only makes her stomp her feet harder on the ground in protest. There's something about his warmth that makes me feel safe and guarded, like I fit perfectly inside his grasp.

Her breathing hitches when she notices the person holding me. "*Jake?*"

Jake.

Jake *smells* good.

Jake *feels* good, too.

Caitlyn panics. "Olivia, come here—I'll call Dad to come and get you." I don't know if it's because I'm drunk or delusional, but the fear in her eyes sends chills down my arms.

"Is this one of your non-exclusive boyfriends?" A hiccup escapes my lips. "This one smells good."

Jake snorts. "I'll take her home…I'm headed out anyway." He starts to move his large body backward, away from her. She tries her best to suck him back in, her fear circling us, but he doesn't back down, and he doesn't surrender me to her.

Caitlyn nervously giggles. "Um, I can ride with you if you want. She's my *sister*—I *am* responsible for her. What are you even *doing* here? It's a really long way from Seattle."

"The same thing you are, I imagine," he growls. "How did *you* get into this party, anyway? I don't remember seeing your name on the guest list when I RSVP'd."

"We came with a friend. Sam Collins…do you know him?" Her eyes narrow. "He's probably looking around for us right now, to make sure we're okay."

Even through my haze, I hear the threatening tone in her voice. "Can't say that I do," Jake says. "Maybe you should run along and find him—I'm sure he'd *love* to show you off."

She reaches for me, but he turns away. "Jake, I

8

really think I should call my dad."

"I can handle it—I don't need you to tag along." He snorts and tightens his grip on me. My insides throw a little victory party as her mouth turns down into a slight frown. He holds my body upright against him as Caitlyn glares at my limp frame. "I'll take care of her, I promise."

"I'll just call my dad; he can come and pick her up, Jake." Caitlyn's repeating herself now, her voice getting higher and higher in pitch, frantic.

Why doesn't she want me going with him? Not that I really care as I snuggle further into Jake's chest.

He squeezes me tighter. "Like I said, I'm already leaving. I'll get her home. Don't worry, okay?" He starts walking down the yard, toward the lot full of parked cars, with my body still pressed against his. His cinnamon breath fills my nose, and his chest is so warm I could fall asleep on it if I let myself totally relax. But he *is* a stranger, and I *am* drunk. I should be way more anxious than I am.

"Hey, don't fall asleep, okay?" he whispers into my hair, now matted with sweat and probably reeking a little of cigar smoke. "I'll get you home." He gently places me inside the front seat of a gray Mercedes, straps me in with my seat belt, and quietly shuts the door. The headrest feels so good as I relax and listen to him get into the car next to me. "Where do you live?"

I scoff. "I'm sure you already know."

Jake pulls the car out of the lot with ease. "What's that supposed to mean?"

I feel sick.

9

"Nothing." I smile and open the window to breathe in some of the crisp, September air; I try to follow the trees as we pass them. The leaves are turning now, from green to red and orange, and it makes me smile because no matter how many memories I lose inside of myself, the changing of the seasons will always stay the same; it'll never betray me. I love the feeling that you get when the world gradually turns from summer to autumn. The smells and the sights and the temperature change make me feel a little less broken inside.

"I'm Jake, by the way." He rolls my window up from his side, his shoulders shaking as a cold chill apparently passes through his body. "And it's freezing, so let's just shut this."

I feel my face flush. "Sorry, champagne makes me *really* hot." I tuck my hands underneath my legs and sigh. "And thanks for the ride. Caitlyn likes to show everyone that I'm just a piece of gum stuck to her shoe any chance she gets."

"Well, I wasn't going to leave you a mess on a stranger's front lawn, now was I?"

I rub my forehead. "I guess I had a little more champagne that I probably should've."

"A little?" He laughs, and I blush for the millionth time. "I watched you guzzle down about six flutes, Bug."

I'm not quite sure how I feel about him watching me—or the weird nickname he's given me. *Bug?*

I *know* I've seen him before, somewhere, but I'd remember meeting someone like Jake around Silver Lake, for sure. Now that I finally have enough courage to look directly at him, I see where I wetted his dress shirt with my sweat-soaked hair and where the grass stains on my dress got his dress slacks dirty. I still feel the liquor in my blood, but there's something that pulls me toward him and calls for me.

Olivia. Olivia.

Not to mention he's absolutely *gorgeous*. He's concentrating on the road, so I have time to look him over a little soberer than before. His short, copper-blonde hair clings to his head from the evening's dew, but the top has longer curls that almost fall into his eyes. His jawline is long and joins his strong chin, a defined Adam's apple moving subtly beneath his skin. His narrow, pale brown eyes sit underneath straight and thin dark brown eyebrows. I can almost reach out and run my finger along the bridge of his nose; it's perfectly shaped and straight as it leads down to his full top lip and even fuller bottom one. A tingling sensation fills my stomach and creeps lower, so I snap my legs shut to try and drown it out.

"Can we get some coffee? I don't want to go home just yet." I smooth out my short dress, the one that Caitlyn *forced* me to wear. "I left my purse and phone at that party. I guess now would be the time to murder me if you were going to. I have no weapon or any other way to defend myself."

Jake shakes his head. "Do you always think the worst?"

"Yes."

"Why?" The city comes into view, and a Starbucks passes us by; my mouth waters, but the car lurches past it, and I frown. "What's so bad in your life that you think that way?"

A low groan comes from my throat. "I just want some coffee, not a lecture."

"I just want to get to know you, not any attitude." He pulls into a small coffee shop parking lot. "It's not every day I get to save a beautiful damsel in distress sprawled out on a wet lawn."

"Oh, you're just laying it on *thick*, aren't you?" I laugh. "I'm not *that* drunk, sorry."

Jake's brown eyes look hurt as he searches my face for answers. "I think you have a common misconception that all men are the same."

I stare at him, blankly. "That's because they *are*."

"So any man would've picked you up, offered to take you home?"

"Yes, they would. Although you *are* the first guy that hasn't tried to get under my dress, so I thank you for *that*." My words slur as I open the door, letting myself out. "But the day *is* still young." The parking lot spins; I manage to stand and brace myself as I hear his door slam shut.

Jake looks angry as he races toward me, making sure I don't fall on my face and hurt myself. "Let me help you," he growls in my ear, putting his arm around my waist like Sam did and tugging me into him.

Cinnamon and whiskey.

I smile and breathe in deeply, nearly unable to stop myself from standing on my toes and planting one on his lips out of curiosity. He pushes me inside and places me at a small, secluded table.

"Don't move. I'll get the coffee." He eyeballs

me, and I suddenly feel like doing what he says. I'm in no position to argue anyways, not with someone who has saved me from embarrassment in the upper-class Silver Lake community. When Jake comes back, he hands me a large, steaming mug, and I smile.

"Americano." He blushes and sips from his own mug, something dark and rich. "I hope you like it."

It's just the only coffee I order, that's all.

"How do you know my sister?" I look around the small coffee shop, noticing two women around my age eyeing us and drooling over Jake—even with me sitting *three feet away from him.*

Jake puts his mug down. "I'd rather not talk about her."

I snort and sip more of the deliciousness inside of the mug. "If you know Caitlyn, you know that I *don't* like to talk about her."

The corners of his mouth twitch as he thinks of an answer. He just looks so damn...*sad*. "What I want to know is where you've been hiding." Watching him lick the coffee from his lips is intoxicating. I'm sure that I'm staring as he sucks his tongue back into his mouth and smiles. "But yeah, anyway, I've known Caitlyn for a long time."

"Then it actually makes sense that we haven't met before." *Even though it feels like we have.* My teeth find the inside of my cheek.

"How so?" Jake's smile broadens, and it makes me feel even more jumbled inside.

Annoyed at the fact that I can't stop looking at his wide smile, I gulp down more coffee before I can keep making a fool of myself. I swallow the hot

13

liquid and wince at the heat in my throat. "I don't try and make it a point to meet her friends from that part of her life."

His eyebrows rise in intrigue. "That part of her life?"

I finish the coffee and lick my lips; Jake puts up two long fingers in the air, motioning for the barista to bring me more. "You know, cocktail parties and charity balls and black-tie parties and fancy barbecues in rich people's football field-sized backyards. She's putting herself into a world where she doesn't belong." I watch his thick thumb rub the handle of the mug and think about what his fingers would feel like on mine. There's no doubt he's attractive—every woman in this place can *feel* the sex appeal dripping off of him like wax off of a burning candle. The barista skips to our table and refills my cup, looking at Jake the whole time.

Jake thanks her and hands her a tip. I feel so self-aware that it's haunting me. I'm not looking for whatever he's trying to give me—or *take* from me. He finishes his mug and denies a refill from the woman. I feel the breeze of the door opening and cross my legs harder, suddenly remembering that I'm in a short, black cocktail dress.

His eyebrows furrow. "Everything okay?"

"This dress isn't appropriate for a coffee shop." I tug the bottom of the dress down and hope I don't pull the top of it down with it. "I forgot I was wearing it."

He stands up and moves his chair next to me, blocking me from anyone's view before he throws his suit jacket over my shoulders. "There, now no one can see your *inappropriate* dress." I try to move my chair a little away from him, but he continues before I can. "And can I just say...that dress isn't appropriate for *anything* outside a man's fantasy, Bug."

I melt all over the floor without him realizing it. I try not to notice the pet name he's created for me, even though a chill runs down my spine every time he says it. My hips are sore from squishing my legs together so hard, so I relax and try my best not to think about it. I notice him staring at my mouth, his hungry eyes fixed on my bottom lip, and I feel so self-conscious that I look away. "Don't do that," he murmurs. "Don't look away—I see you in there somewhere."

After nearly spitting out the rest of my coffee, I wipe the excess off my lips with a napkin. "What do you mean, you see me in here somewhere? Of course you do. I'm sitting inches away from you."

"You know what I mean. Don't be difficult."

My head spins. "I just need to get home and get some sleep."

Jake looks hurt that I didn't return his flirty banter. "I'll drive you."

"No, I can take a cab." I stand up, desperately wanting for him to stop me. "You've helped me enough. You're a nice guy, Jake."

"I don't mind, really."

"Please..." I hold my hand out to stop him from standing up. "Just let me go."

Jake thinks for a few seconds until he relaxes back in the chair; he presses his lips together, seeming to think carefully over his next words. "If that's what you want."

I nod. "I'm sorry about you having to save me; that's not the kind of person I am."

"Exactly what kind of person are you, Olivia?"

There's a moment where I think I can sit down and tell him everything. It would be nice to talk to someone for once that isn't biased about helping me remember things they think are important.

"I'm not sure."

"When can I see you again?" Desperation fills his voice, and it makes me sad. I honestly had *no* intentions of seeing Jake again, but something keeps drawing me back into him and his sad, light brown eyes and permanent frown.

"Olivia, I just *found* you—I need to see you again." The magic in his voice almost uplifts me. The hope that seeps through his mouth suffocates me, but I don't say anything before walking away from him to find a cab outside.

He follows me outside loyally. "Here, at least take this." A twenty-dollar bill is wrapped up in his fingers, and he doesn't let me jerk my hand away. He places it firmly in my palm before turning to hail a cab for me. I hop inside and don't say a word as he vanishes into the distance.

The whole ride home, all I can think about is the way he handled me when I fell and the flirty smiles that spread across his juicy lips whenever I blushed. His entire presence is so easy to be around that I find myself wondering if I should have stayed with him at the coffee shop.

It hurts to think as hard as I have been lately, but I search my mind for some sliver of a memory of him and find nothing.

One thing is for sure.

Even if I *don't know Jake, he definitely knows me.*

Chapter Two

Unicorn

"You should've *seen* her, Daddy."

My head is pounding as I wake up to bright sunlight and the familiar screeching sound of Caitlyn's voice downstairs, whining to our parents about how *horrible* it is to be in public with me. It's not exactly a basket of roses for me, either.

I hardly remember the cab ride home after I left Jake behind. I managed to shimmy out of the cocktail dress, now lying on the floor, and put on leggings and a t-shirt before passing out. I touch my lips and think about the dream I had—*the champagne-induced dream*—of Jake and me in some pretty steamy positions that make me blush even now.

"She literally almost passed out on the lawn!" The twinge in her whine heightens, and I feel her disappointment even from a completely different level of the house.

"Caitlyn, worry about yourself, okay? I don't

know why you even went to that party," my dad says. I hear the strain in his tone as he tries to hold back his anger. "Honestly, when are you going to grow up and realize our lives are different now?"

Hearing this makes my eyes pop open. There have been a few times when I caught my dad, mom, and Caitlyn talking about something intense, but whenever they realize I'm listening, it always stops. This time, I don't move a muscle or even breathe, just in case. I want to know what they're hiding from me; I want validation that my dreams are real and there's something they aren't telling me.

"I can't babysit her anymore, and I shouldn't have to! Not to mention who she left with—"

"Who did she leave with?"

She whimpers; the position she's put herself in now isn't as bad as ones she's put herself in before, but still…Dad can be pretty intimidating sometimes.

"Jake Redding."

He slams his newspaper down on the table, making me jump. It gets eerily silent, so I decide that I better get up and face the music before Caitlyn shoves her foot any deeper into her own mouth.

"Caitlyn, it's time to get on board with this or else."

"Or else, *what*?"

He mumbles something, but I can't hear what he's saying. She starts her waterworks and searches the house for Mom. Her sobs flit around the floor beneath me, and my mom's quiet voice tries to comfort her. This gives me an advantage—I can avoid them when I finally start padding on bare feet down the stairs and into the kitchen.

"Hey, Dad." I yawn and pick out a coffee mug, smiling to myself as I think about Jake and his Americano lucky guess. I wonder how he knew that was my favorite kind. It makes me think about his juicy bottom lip turned up into a mischievous smile, and I scold myself for obsessing over him. "I guess you've heard what happened yesterday, then."

He nods and picks his newspaper back up, not interested in having this conversation any more than I am. "You know I heard, you little eavesdropper. Is that true, who you left with? That part is the only one that concerns me."

"Jake? I didn't know his last name until now."

His eyebrows rise, and he looks slightly over his newspaper, just enough for me to notice, but then snaps his gaze back to the open pages. "Well, just be careful." His teeth grind together. This reaction is something I'm used to when my family gets into situations they don't want to talk about. Usually, it's just a hard subject change, but now Dad just starts to ignore the conversation completely.

"I don't plan on seeing him again, so it's really not a big deal." I find some Pop-Tarts in the cabinet, my stomach growling as I quickly open the package. I sit down next to him and pick up the comics. We read in silence except for the sounds of me chewing the breakfast goodness.

"You know, who I come home with won't be an issue when I move out." A bit of Pop-Tart falls from my open mouth, making Dad shake his head. "I have enough money saved up to get my own apartment."

"If you're ready to move out, you're welcome to do so. Your mom and I have always told you that."

"No, you've told me that recently. Who knows what you told me before my accident?"

Now that I've mentioned the accident, Dad gets uneasy. He doesn't like talking about it, mainly because I start asking questions he doesn't want to answer.

"Olivia," he warns me. "I'm not having this conversation again. Have you been talking to Dr. Ross about your dreams?"

"Yes."

"What does he say?"

For the record, I hate going to Dr. Ross. He's the therapist they stuck me with after I started expressing concerns about dreams and headaches I started having after the accident. I'm forced to see him two times a week for an hour each time. It's not exactly what I'd call fun.

"He says it's my brain's way of trying to heal. That the memories aren't really mine."

His newspaper goes back up like a shield. "He's the one with the degree, honey. I think he knows more about it than we do. If he says the memories aren't yours, why do you insist that they are?"

The doorbell rings, and neither of us volunteers to go answer it. He's done with the conversation and goes back to reading the newspaper. We're both hoping that Caitlyn or my mother will answer the door instead. I smile as I read a comic about a dog who's always getting himself into trouble, totally unaware that anyone else has entered the house.

"What are *you* doing here?" Caitlyn growls from the living room. A deep voice mumbles something back, but I'm not committed to listening to my sister flirt with some random guy in our foyer. I pull my legs up and tuck them underneath me in the seat; my dad shakes his head because he hates when I do this. "…Oh yeah, sure. She's in the kitchen—it's through there," my sister snaps at the visitor. A breeze wafts through the kitchen, and I feel him before I even look up.

Jake.

He smiles warmly at me from the doorway and then notices my father—he tucks his charm back into his pocket to use on me later. "I thought you might want this back." He smirks and holds up my clutch from yesterday…complete with gold sparkles, booze smell, and all. His dark maroon pullover sweater clings to his defined chest as he shakes the bag in mid-air. The space between his lips broadens as he chuckles at my embarrassment.

I start coughing, signaling for him to stop talking. "You didn't have to do that…I could've gone by there later."

"Well, a simple 'thank you' would suffice."

My father snorts behind his paper, and I glare at Jake, who isn't as amused. "*Thank you,*" I say with zero enthusiasm as I stand up, forgetting that I'm in pajamas, and go to snatch the purse from his hand. He looks down at me, his copper blonde curls shining in the daylight; he pretends to hold onto the purse with more strength than I have, pulling me closer to him.

"Can I take you to breakfast?" The spice in his

voice showers over me, making my knees a little weak as he lets go of the purse and forces me to take a few steps backward.

"I've already eaten, thanks." I shake my head and brush past him, hoping he'll just take the hint and leave.

"What is it about me that repulses you so much?" He walks after me, no rush in his steps. "I'm not sure what you've been told about me—"

I whip around and glare at him. "No one has said anything to me about you, if you must know. You don't repulse me—I said thank you for the purse. What else do you want from me?"

"Breakfast, I'm hungry." He pouts, and I have to admit—it's *adorable*. The soft, short curls on top of his head make me shiver where I stand. I want to wrap my fingers around them and lose myself in his pouty bottom lip.

He also makes me want to scream my lungs out. "I've eaten already…"

The low growl that comes from his throat is exciting and terrifying at the same time. He rubs the bridge of his nose and forces a smile. His once-warm eyes are now stoic and cold, chilling me to my core; I wish I'd shoved socks on my feet now that my entire body is covered in chills. "Okay, so you've eaten already. When *can* I see you, then?"

"You see me right now, don't you?"

That wasn't the right thing to say at all.

"You're frustrating as hell—do you know that?" His intensity is overwhelming as he towers over me, but I have no intention of backing down from his demanding stance. Caitlyn stomps down the stairs and eyes the two of us, placing her body close to mine but far enough away to keep from brushing arms with me accidentally. Even though Jake and I are steaming at each other, she turns to look at me like he's not even still in the room.

"Livvie, can you help me pick out an outfit for my date with Sam?"

Taken aback by this sudden interest in allowing me into her room, I brush her off when she tries to snake her arm around mine. "Maybe you can ask Jake for his opinion," I offer.

"I don't have an opinion about her body or what she wears."

Caitlyn snickers. "Yeah, *now,* maybe."

Jake notices my eyes grow wide and turns to my sister, clenching his already tight jaw. Almost laughing—*because why wouldn't they have been together*—I clap my hands together sharply and sigh almost a little too loudly. "Oh, were you two *together*? So *that's* why you seem so familiar to me. You were one of Caitlyn's flings, right? Well, *Jake,* don't you want to take a trip down memory lane with my sister? I'm sure you two have more in common than you might care to admit."

His eyes darken as he barely opens his mouth to growl back, "Oh, do tell, *Olivia.* Like what, exactly?"

I bite my bottom lip and push his frustration away from me as quickly as possible. I bet he likes to suck me into his controlling whirlwind because he can tell I like it a little. "Like me, for example. I don't want anything to do with either of you right now." I blow out a deep breath, push my long, chocolate-brown hair behind me, and walk away from the confused pair without a second thought or regret. There's no way in hell I'm going anywhere with someone who dated—*and probably slept with*—Caitlyn. That's not my type at all.

"I'll pick you up at seven for dinner." His voice booms up the stairs, but I just give him a backward wave. The purse is still clutched in my hand as I shut my bedroom door and go to the window. I wait a few minutes to see him walk outside and stop, playing with his phone before standing in front of the gray Mercedes parked in the driveway.

"I'm coming in!" Caitlyn yells but doesn't knock. This is something she does regularly...when she needs something from me. I cringe when I think about the last time she burst into my room and told me she was dragging me along to that stupid barbecue.

I throw a pillow at her but miss. "Get out!"

Caitlyn rolls her eyes—heavy with eyeliner even this early in the morning—as she marches across the room on perfectly tanned and waxed legs and collapses into the small, black armchair by the bookcase. She scans the shelves for something in her wheelhouse to read. I don't subscribe to whatever female swag magazine she reads, so she gives up and crosses her arms over her chest, waiting for me to speak first.

"He's *all* yours." I walk toward my closet, looking for a clean pair of jeans. I hardly want to sit here and argue with her about someone I have no interest in. The last thing I want is her sloppy seconds.

"Oh, I'm not here to talk about that." She opens a *Rolling Stone* magazine from the bookshelf. Her nose turns up when she sifts further through it, but it makes me smile just the same. "Jake Redding is trouble—what does he even want with you? Has he said anything?"

I slam my closet door and throw a pair of decent jeans on my bed after sniffing them to make sure I could still detect laundry soap. "Can you stop with the drama, Caitlyn? I just said he's all yours. What more do you want from me? I have no interest in dating someone that's already been contaminated by you."

She hardly realizes that I'm insulting her, because in her world, she is the Queen and all of the little peasants don't matter. "I want to know why he's picking you up for dinner at seven."

I take my leggings off and put the jeans on, replacing my t-shirt with a brick-red v-neck while she waits for me to answer. "I don't know, Caitlyn." I sigh and find some sneakers under the bed, sliding them on my feet. "I'm not going to dinner with him. You can go if you want."

She squeals and claps her hands together. "You should just call him and cancel if it doesn't matter to you." I groan, making sure she knows I'm annoyed, but the Queen doesn't care.

"I don't know why you even care. Didn't you already get what you wanted from him?"

"I don't know what you're talking about." She laughs like I should be as impressed with her as she is and tries to toss her hair behind her shoulder. It's like a comforting, repetitive motion for her. She still doesn't confirm her involvement with him. "Jake Redding is sort of like a...*unicorn*."

I laugh instantly. "A *unicorn*? Oh, this'll be good."

"No, seriously. It's pretty intense to be near him; I won't lie about it. He's strong-willed, and he knows what he wants, but he gets a little scary sometimes." Her fingernail taps on the now-closed magazine in her lap. "You can feel it, right?" Caitlyn smacks her glossed lips and shakes her head, not waiting for my answer. "He's the mysterious Redding boy, after all."

"Why's he so mysterious? Seems to me he just doesn't want to play your little high school games." She stands up, knocking the magazine to the floor and not even blinking an eye to the mess she's made at her feet.

"Well, Jake is the oldest of the Redding boys: There are four. There's Jake; he's twenty-five. Tyler is twenty-four, Noah is twenty-three, like you, and Grant is twenty-one, like me." I try to pretend like I don't care, especially since she still feels the need to remind me of basic facts about myself, like my age, as if I'm *completely* mentally incompetent. "Their mother, Mary-Anne, is a socialite, they come from old money, and Jake is the only Redding boy that you hardly see at any social functions or in any pictures. He doesn't like the spotlight—he actually hasn't been seen or heard from in over a year."

"And that makes him mysterious? Hardly." I turn my back to her, but I'm interested in the conversation now. "How do you know so much about him?"

"I mean, duh, it's not that hard. Anyone who's smart enough to use the internet can dig up dirt on someone."

A light turns on inside my brain—why haven't I thought about this before? She notices the new glimmer in my eye and realizes she's messed up.

"I don't even care. I don't want him—you can have him." I cringe at the fact that I basically just treated him like property from a board game, but I have to make her feel like I've moved on from my idea.

She forces a giggle and skips out of the room, not bothering to pick up the magazine that she let drop on the floor. I don't even worry about saying anything as I pick it up and look around the room, pocketing my phone. I finally find my car keys underneath a pile of scrap pieces of paper in my purse, which I use to write down thoughts whenever I get them, in fear that I might forget *everything* by the time I reach thirty. Napkins, receipts, fast food bags…whatever I have at the time. I smile when I start to read some of them and place them gently on the dresser. I glance up at my reflection in the mirror, staring back at me with what appear to be knowing eyes.

"What?" I say to it, shrugging. "I'm not *that* big of a mess."

"You're going to be late for Dr. Ross if you don't get a move on," my mom says from down the hallway. I glance at the clock next to my bed. She's right; I have twenty minutes to get to his office, and it's fifteen minutes away. My shift at the YMCA starts not long after my appointment, so I find my backpack underneath a pile of clothes. After throwing my charger and some notebooks into it, I zip it up and race down the hallway, kissing my mother on the cheek as I pass her by.

I half-expect to see Jake's gray Mercedes blocking me in the driveway; I daydream about his big hands wrapped around my waist and his cinnamon breath as he kisses me. Before I see it, I step into a hole that my mom has dug into the ground for a seedling, and my ankle twists behind me in searing pain. I manage to stand and climb into my car without alarming anyone—I just wanted to go to work and leave this entire morning behind me—but my mind keeps racing back to Jake and everything sinister I can think about him in a fifteen-minute drive.

I hardly remember driving to Dr. Ross' office as I pull into a parking spot and take my time turning off the car. Each path I take in my mind when I think about Jake…they all lead to the same exact place, the same thought:

Jake is part of me.

Chapter Three

The boy

I hate the squeaky leather sofa that Dr. Ross makes his patients sit on. It's hard and plastic feeling underneath me; it's probably another way for him to annoy the people who come to him for help.

Like me.

I stopped talking in our appointments a few weeks ago when Dr. Ross—a sixty-something man with a gray ponytail and full beard—told me flat out that my dreams and slivers of memories aren't mine, and I'm creating them to fill a void inside of my soul.

"So, Olivia…" He starts with this same speech every time just as he sits down across from me in his comfy-looking armchair. "Have you been having any more dreams?"

I shake my head and stay silent.

"Are we spending this hour in silence again, then?"

Somehow, I don't even blink—that would be some form of reaction that I can't afford.

"Olivia, I can't help you unless you talk to me."

"I *did* talk to you." I'm fully aware that I've broken my code of silence against him just to defend myself. "I told you *everything*. I told you about the dreams I've been having; I told you about the people in my dreams and every detail about them. You said I was making them up inside my head."

He nods and scratches something on a yellow notepad. "And you still think I'm wrong?"

"I *know* you're wrong."

His pen moves faster. "Can you tell me how you know that?"

"I just know, okay? I don't care what you say— you're wrong."

He holds up his hands and waves me down. "Okay, let's say that I'm wrong. I'm open to exploring that option if you are. Can you tell me what it is about these dreams that makes you believe so strongly that they're yours?"

What a stupid question.

"They're coming from my brain."

"Yes, but…is that the only reason you think so?"

There hasn't been a second where I even thought I would open myself up to Dr. Ross again, just to get pushed back down. Still, he's the only person still willing to listen to me, and I have to take what I can get.

"I know they're my memories. They feel too real when I wake up for them not to be. Something isn't right, Dr. Ross, and I have to figure out what it is.

31

Maybe it's because I can't remember anything from before the car accident, and it's my way of filling in the blanks, but I don't really think so. I can't explain it, but...there are things that just...feel right."

He writes quickly on the notepad while I speak. Once I stop, he lays his pen down on the pad, and his narrow blue eyes look up. "Why don't you close your eyes, lean your head back, and take me through the dream like we would do before?"

I take a deep breath and exhale slowly before leaning my head back on the sofa so I can let the rest of my body relax. Dr. Ross counts backward from ten slowly, and by the time he hits one, my body is slumped on the cushions and I'm nearly snoozing away. This is one of the few places that allows me to relax enough to trust that someone won't snatch me in my sleep and I'll wake up without any memories at all.

"Okay, start from the beginning..."

***

Big red and white moving trucks take up the entire circle drive. There are dozens of men running around in brown jumpsuits with the words "Seattle's Best Moving" on their backs in bold, black letters. One man is ordering them around; he's pointing and barking at his men.

"Work faster and smarter! Faster and smarter!" His spit launches into the air around him.

I'm off to the side, where I've found a spot near one of the trucks in the grass to play with my dolls.

Their names are Eliza and Mary, and I can't remember when I got them, but I know Santa brought them to me years ago.

It's warm outside. Unusually wet and warm. Muggy. It's May, and the spring rains have already started to retreat for the summer heat. Things are strange and fuzzy inside my head—it's hard to focus.

"There you are!" a woman shrieks behind me before plucking me up from the ground. "I've been looking everywhere for you! Where've you been?" Her voice sounds funny. She's not from around here; her accent sounds like Mary Poppins. "Your mother has been ill about you!"

She takes care of me, this woman. I can't remember her name.

"Come on." Her strong grip wraps around my tiny wrist. "You'll get lost in all this ruckus. Are you hungry, dear?"

My stomach rumbles as soon as the woman stops to look down at me. Her eyes are big, round, and golden brown. They make me feel warm and loved despite the stern look on her face. I know she cares about me, but I don't know who she is.

"Where did you find her?" A tall man bends down in front of me once the lady closes the front door of the enormous brown house behind us. "Where've you been, love?"

His accent is the same as hers, only a little rougher. "I don't know," I say. I'm not scared or sad; I feel nothing. The man accepts my answer as gold and winks at me, patting my head. His long, spider-like legs stand back upright, and he frowns

33

at the lady still holding my arm. "You'll do good to keep track of her, won't you, Miss Claudine?"

Miss Claudine. That's her name. She's my nanny. But who is he?

"I will, sir." She flicks the corners of her mouth up into a smile. "I was taking her in for lunch."

The man nods and moves to the side, smiling at me as the lady gently pushes me past him. Miss Claudine was the one who told me we were moving here; she's the one who flew on the plane with me, and she's the one who gave me candies when I started to cry.

Yet I never hear anyone say my name in these dreams.

Miss Claudine sits me on a chair in the kitchen, then rummages through some boxes to produce a clean plate and utensils. "These will have to do for now."

"Can we order a pizza?"

Her peachy cheeks brighten. "I think that would be just fine for today."

Our moment is broken by the sounds of children screaming and playing outside. I race into the living room to find the source from the open windows. Dozens of children, big and small, run wild around the yard of the big blue house across the street. Kids zip around each other, tossing footballs and throwing water balloons.

"Can we go over there?"

Miss Claudine puckers her lips. "We can't just go barging into someone's party, sweetheart."

"It's a kid's birthday party."

The look she gives me tells me that she's giving

in. "All right, then. Off you go to crash another child's birthday party, you little social butterfly." She laughs and follows me from the house and back into the front yard, where fewer movers are flittering around.

My stomach hurts from the nerves of not knowing anyone at the party and getting caught, but I pluck courage from somewhere and wear it proudly as we march across the street and enter the backyard of the party house with our heads held high.

Miss Claudine is able to snag us some birthday cake and grape soda, which makes her feel triumphant and useful. Loud music is playing over dozens of speakers around the extravagantly decorated backyard, and kids are everywhere I look.

"And who is this?" A woman stands next to the table we've sat down at to eat. "I don't believe I've met you. Are you in my son's class?"

Miss Claudine blushes red. "Oh, I'm sorry." She sticks out her hand for the woman to shake. "My name is Claudine, and we've just moved in across the street. We didn't mean to crash the party."

"No, please don't leave. You're welcome to stay and enjoy the party. Why don't you run along with the other children and play, dear?"

The two women stare at me, so I leave my half-eaten birthday cake and grape soda on the table and walk away so they can talk in private. The garden paths I find myself on wind around the backyard, and the screams get louder and things start to crash to the ground.

"That's my piñata!" a boy shrieks.

I push a few bushes aside and see dozens of kids helping themselves to the contents of a broken piñata while the boy who'd just spoken stands with his hands in the air. There's nothing he can do but watch his birthday fun being stripped from him by a litter of his savage friends. The bushes crinkle beneath my feet, and it catches his attention, but I manage to step back from them in time so he doesn't see me.

A stone bench sits on the other side of the clearing, so I sit down and bring my knees up to tuck them under my chin while I wait for Miss Claudine to find me again.

"Hey, who are you?" The boy's voice finds me. "I don't know you."

He walks into the clearing and crosses his arms over the chest of his blue t-shirt.

"I'm moving in across the street."

"Why? What happened to Todd and his family?"

I shrug and look at the ground. "I don't know who that is. Sorry."

"Why are you so sad?"

"I'm not sad."

The boy laughs, and his feet shuffle closer to me. "You look sad."

"Mind your business."

"This is my *party!" He laughs at me again. "You're pretty frustrating."*

I hear my dad call my mom that all the time. A warm feeling washes over me, and I know the dream is going to end soon—it happens every time. The boy smiles at me; his white-toothed grin gives me good feelings inside.

"I'm eleven today."

"Happy Birthday."

He's tall for his age but bossy too. When everything around me starts to fade, I bring my eyes up to meet his so I can hold onto him for a little longer. He's the first person that's entered my dreams that's given me this feeling.

"You and I are going to be best friends," the boy announces with a smirk, shoving his hands into his pockets. "You'll see."

"I don't even know you. How can you know that?"

He sits down on the gravel path in front of me. Miss Claudine calls my name in the distance, but time's already run out.

"I just know."

Chapter Four

Pizza, please

Tongue-and-cheek is always the best way to solve a problem.

The cheap, scratchy paper wrinkles in my fingers as I read the words over and over again. I never really believed in fortune cookies and their magic powers like everyone else. The thought of my entire future hanging on the balance of some pre-printed, mass-produced stale vanilla cookie is laughable.

Then again, I'd believe just about anything right now.

"What's yours say?" Brant, who's on duty in the weightlifting rooms today, hovers over me and snatches the paper from my fingers. "Oh, *man*. You know you're supposed to put the words 'in bed' after each fortune, right?"

I shake my head and reach up to re-do the messy bun that holds my tangled mess of thick hair in place. I don't care what he's talking about. I just want to eat my lunch in peace and obsess about what I don't know about my past and why Caitlyn hates Jake so much. I don't care what anyone says; I know I'm right about this.

"No, I didn't know that," I dryly say, but he doesn't catch my hint and go away.

"Yeah, so it's 'Tongue-and-cheek is always the best way to solve a problem...*in bed*.'" His smile matches his mental age, and I want to vomit. I can't break free and run, though—he's in my area, and I can't leave the front desk. "Get it?" Brant snorts, and I can't help but crack a smile at his stupidity. I actually like him a little—in a platonic way. He's fresh out of high school, eighteen and bright-eyed, something I'm definitely not. I can never tell if he's flirting with me or he's just plain clueless, but either way I'm in no way interested.

"Go away, Brant." I pretend I'm annoyed. "You're immature."

He winks at me and smacks the desk before turning to walk away, his tanned muscles bulging from the ripped tank top he wears. "Yeah, but that's why you *love* me, Liv." He pockets my fortune and waves at me but doesn't look back. I have a few hours to kill before I can go home, and my lemon chicken is cold and rubbery, so I toss the takeout container and open up a new browser on the desktop computer. Googling my name, my parents' names, and Caitlyn's name turns up absolutely nothing. It's almost like none of us even *exist*.

"So much for that idea." My whisper turns the air bitter.

I barely notice that I'm five minutes late shutting the front desk down when Brant's exhausted voice wafts down the hall. "Hey, get your head out of the clouds. It's after seven already." He yells so I'll shut off the lights in the weight rooms and he can go home, too. I rush through everything and grab my stuff; he waits for me as I lock the door behind us. We start walking toward my car, like we always do when he closes with me.

"Oh, hey, man. We're actually closed now, but we open at nine tomorrow, okay? You can come back then if you want to work out."

A weird feeling pushes through my body when I reach into my bag to fish around for my car keys.

"Yo, man, I *said* we're closed," Brant says, his voice getting louder. "Did you hear me? You need to stay back." I stiffen and fumble faster for my keys, though I can't tell what direction this mystery person is coming from. "Hey, look, don't come any closer, man…I'm *warning* you."

The fear in Brant's voice is finally enough for me to stop digging through my bag and look at the person he's talking to.

I gasp loudly and blush the hardest I ever have in my entire life.

Jake.

Jake is here.

Jake is here at my job.

He. Looks. Pissed.

I feel his disappointment from the few feet away we are from each other. Clutching my chest, I tap Brant on the shoulder and laugh nervously. "It's okay. He's here for me." Both of their sets of eyebrows rise in intrigue, and I realize what I just said. "No…" I shake my head, and my hair falls from the bun for the millionth time tonight. "I mean, I *know* him, he's okay. You can go ahead and go home, Brant."

"But—"

Jake clenches his jaw and glares at the poor kid. "She said to leave."

Brant isn't sure, but he eventually gets scared enough of Jake to bow out and practically run to his car across the lot. I shake my head at Jake and scowl; his temper is ridiculously out of control and seriously embarrassing to witness. "You don't have to be such a jerk. You *do* know that, right?"

"You were supposed to have dinner with me tonight." His voice is cool, and I can see the lost look on his face as he steps into the dimly lit space in front of me. "You should've told me you had to work. I would've waited and picked you up."

"Well, I drove myself, so that would've been pretty hard." I wink sarcastically and brush my body past his, touching his arm with my shoulder on purpose. "Thanks for running my bodyguard off; have a good night."

It isn't a surprise that his long legs catch up with mine in just a few strides, but then he turns me around and gently pushes me against the side of my blue, hand-me-down station wagon. I can feel his breath on my lips and they tingle; sparks of electricity run up and down each lip until he starts tugging at the ends of my hair and twisting them in his thick fingers.

"What am I gonna do with you, *Olivia*?" His whisper is rough and *dirty*. "You just keep trying to run from me, and I don't intend to let anyone keep you from me again."

I can't breathe. My throat is dry as he clutches the sides of my hips and holds me in place, exactly where he wants me to be. *What does he mean by someone keeping me from him...again?*

"You know, some guys *do* know when no means no." I breathe slowly. His eyes are hooded and on fire. "You'll have to excuse me if I don't want someone who slept with my sister, and trust me, that doesn't leave very many men left in a close radius."

Jake's full lips turn up into a smile. He's so damn close to me I can almost taste him.

Cinnamon and whiskey.

I let myself breathe him in, and the world melts into dark colors around me. "I *never* slept with Caitlyn...or wanted to, for that matter. I like my women feisty, disease-free, and strikingly *beautiful*."

"I don't care either way." I try and catch my breath, but his thumbs are pressing into my hips with frustration. His body is dangerously warm and inviting enough for me to want to throw it all out the window and let myself melt into him. "I-I need to go."

He glares at me and pulls away; the entire firework show stops cold. "Let me take you to dinner—you need to eat."

"Is that a *demand*? Caitlyn did say you are intense and demanding."

He keeps his eyes on mine and licks his full lips. The wetness that stays behind is intoxicating enough for me to *need* to taste it. "Can we stop talking about her?" he snaps. I'm a little uneasy about his temper—Caitlyn warned me about that, too—but I'm not going to say another word about her. I've made him angry and frustrated enough for one day; I at least feel bad enough about it to let him take me to one small little harmless dinner.

"Okay, pizza." I force a smile across my face. "Pizza, please."

Jake scoffs. "I can take you wherever you want, and you want *pizza*?"

"Are you a pizza snob, Jake?" I joke and poke his sides playfully; that's something my sister probably would've done, and that makes me feel ten shades of icky inside. "We can't be friends if you don't like pizza. That's like a number one rule for being friends with me."

He laughs, and I notice how light and airy it is when it's real. "It's a good thing I don't want to just be your friend, then." He opens the passenger door of the Mercedes and nudges me inside, closing me in and getting in next to me. "Are you afraid of me? I've been told that I can get a little intense lately. I recently lost something that meant the entire world to me, and it's been frustrating getting it back. I think I've been doing a decent job of keeping the heat down."

I want to burst out in laughter. "You could stand to turn it down a few more notches."

"Are you *mocking* me, Bug?" He turns to face me. I don't want to see if he's joking or not, in fear that he isn't as amused as I am. "I do think you owe me an apology, *Olivia*." The last few letters roll off of his tongue like sweet candy melting in his mouth.

43

"No one calls me Olivia unless I'm in trouble." I shake my head and look through my bag for my phone to send my mother a text telling her that I'm not coming home right away. After a few seconds of me ignoring him, he clears his throat. Our eyes meet; I blush something fierce, and he licks his bottom lip.

"You blush a lot," he teases me, and his eyes take on a playful sparkle. "I guess I'll let you slide on that apology."

"Apology in the form of what? Handwritten letter? Social media? Verbal?" I laugh and shove my phone into my jeans pocket. The weight of the car shifts, and I smell his cinnamon breath before I turn my head and see his body inches from mine again.

"Whatever you want."

I'm so nervous I might actually lose all body function. "I'm sorry I made fun of you." The words stumble out of my mouth, and he draws back, amused that I've managed to make my way out of that one with grace. There's a challenge in his eyes as he drives us away from the parking lot, my car fading in the distance.

"Where are you kidnapping me to?" I try and lighten the mood, and he smiles from the side. "I mean, you basically *are* kidnapping me."

Jake pulls the car into the parking lot of a brilliantly lit café almost an hour later and pushes the shifter into park. "Since you act like a child most of the time, I can safely say I agree with you about the kidnapping part." Pouting, I push open the door and let myself out, not waiting for his lean body to catch up to me so I can try to make it inside before he does. The hostess that greets us, a really tall and thin black-haired girl, looks at me with knowing eyes.

Even strangers can see right through me.

"Why are we in Garden View? Are you taking me to Seattle?"

He chuckles. "Not unless you *want* to go to Seattle, but that's still almost ten hours away. What's in Seattle?"

"Well, hello to the both of *you*." I half-expect to see cigarette smoke come out of her mouth, from her stale, scratchy voice. "It's been a long time. Table for two?"

I feel Jake behind me, close enough to touch me. "Yes, Abby. Is my usual table free?" His arm slides around my waist and rests on my hip bone, exciting me in every way imaginable. I like when he touches me, though I wouldn't admit it out loud. There's something soothing in the way he handles me; he doesn't need a map of my body to know exactly where things are.

Abby motions for us to follow her, and he gently pushes me ahead of him, like he's protecting me from some weird freak attack from behind.

Or like he thinks I'm going to run from him.

"A pitcher of raspberry iced tea, please, Abby," Jake says, and the woman nods, running off to do what he asks. The café isn't a hole-in-the-wall; there are socialites having cocktails with their girlfriends in designer clothes and handbags and businessmen having nightcaps and trying to pick up the socialites for a last-minute booty call. They're all off in their own self-soaked worlds, and here I am: alone with the mysterious and super intense Jake Redding.

He thanks Abby for the pitcher and pours the liquid into my empty crystal drinking glass first, then his own. "Thank you for coming here with me. This place holds a lot of memories for someone I used to know."

"*Why* am I here?" I feel the words jump from my tongue, maybe a little angrier than I originally intended. "What exactly do you want from me, Jake?"

My outburst doesn't make him happy. His long, square jaw tightens, and it's like his eyes pull mine into him against my will. I can't look away, and this makes him smile; the dark stubble on his jawline and chin glistens under the café lights, and I find myself wanting to kiss the corners of his thick, frowning mouth.

"And what exactly is it that you *think* I want from you?"

I snort. "Don't answer a question with a question."

"Don't ask me questions that you don't want the answer to, then." He stands his ground as a waiter comes up to us, and my mind races so fast that I barely hear him order a gourmet chicken pizza for us.

"Is she okay? Does she need some water?" the waiter asks Jake, mildly concerned by the paleness of my face.

"She'll be fine." Jake waves him off. "You'll be fine," he says again, this time to me directly. "Just relax and enjoy the time we spend together; I told you what I want from you."

"Jake, I'm not looking for anything that you want."

He sips his iced tea and smirks. "What is it that I want that you can't give me?"

"I don't know! You won't give me straight answers—it's annoying!" I yell/whisper at him, and this time he looks a little annoyed by my tantrum. "I only came here with you because I felt bad for blowing you off and you made your little weird puppy-dog-Jake face. I don't want a boyfriend or anything else right now. I have way too many things going on—"

"Like what?" He takes another sip of his iced tea and raises his eyebrows.

My mouth stops moving. I can feel the word vomit rising in my throat; it's burning my tongue, and I fight with everything I have to keep my story to myself. I don't need his pity looks or a Prince Charming riding to save the day in his gray Mercedes.

I just want to be able to breathe without feeling like an imposter.

"Jake…" The sorrow in my voice fills the air, and his eyes soften with sadness for me. "There's just things going on for me right now that take up too much of my time. I'm not looking for anything else more than friends, I guess."

"So you said." He smiles, and I get a glimpse of his bright white teeth as he rubs his jaw. When he leans his tall body toward me over the table, he's still only inches from my face. I smell the cinnamon like it's bursting from sparkling capsules around my body. "I think you need to relax. It's only pizza." He leans back in his chair, his dark blue sweater clinging to his chest as he breathes in and out.

He can breathe freely because he can be himself...I never thought I would be jealous of a blue sweater.

"Tell me something about yourself that no one else knows." His rough thumb runs along his bottom lip, wiping off the excess iced tea from his mouth. "I want to know everything I can about *this* you."

I snort. "*This* me? You met me yesterday, and I was a drunken mess on a stranger's lawn in a too-short, too-tight cocktail dress. That's *this* me."

Jake licks his lips, and I feel weird in my stomach. I can almost feel his lips on mine, and I touch them to make the tingling stop. "I like that dress," he says.

I feel the heat rush to my cheeks, but I can't hide it from him. I have nowhere to run. I bite the inner part of my cheek and force myself to look over at him. "I'm a mess, Jake. I have something wrong with me. Trust me, you really don't want me."

"Oh, but trust me, Olivia. I really, really do." He senses my hesitation and stands up, moving his chair next to me, like he did at the coffee shop yesterday. "You may not understand it right now, but you'll see just how much I really do want you."

I want to scream loudly and tell him about my memories.

...or the memories that aren't there.

What would I even say?

"I'm a complete mess. I can't remember anything before moving to Silver Lake. Nothing is familiar to me, not even my own family. Sometimes I dream about another life, a life that isn't mine, and it feels more inviting than this life ever has."

He takes my hand, and I let him hold it gently in his; he laces our fingers together, and his smile coats my insides like warm maple syrup. "Don't you know this is real life?" I laugh and place my other hand over my mouth. "I'm not normal; there are things about me that I can't explain. I'm a mess, but I don't need you trying to fix me."

Jake nods, and the waiter brings our pizza. It smells so delicious that my mouth waters when I get a whiff of it. He has, once again, ordered my food and drink for me and gotten my tastes spot-on, like he knows *exactly* what I like. "I'm not trying to fix you. It's actually quite the opposite."

I look down at the steaming perfection on my plate and lick my lips, ready to devour every inch of the cheesy, gooey masterpiece inches from my mouth.

"I need *you* to fix *me*."

Chapter Five

Blue sweaters and promises

I know for a fact that my jaw is on the floor. I feel it against the cool hardwood planks, lying against the part where people place their feet, scraping the dead particles of life across the rough surface without a care in the world.

Don't laugh, Olivia.

Don't. Laugh.

"I'm sorry." I hide the fact that I am *completely* amused at his confession. "You're saying that you want *me* to fix *you?*"

Jake rubs his chin. He's upset with me, but I have to admit: he does a pretty good job of taking whatever I throw at him. I'm not trying to be difficult, but I definitely have no intention of fixing someone else when the pieces of my own life feel like they're permanently in shambles.

"Olivia, say something, please." He grunts and looks around the café, noticing the women staring at him without shame. He hardly cares as his eyes quickly find their way back to mine. His hand is still glued to mine, and he squeezes, *hard*.

The air is dry and scratches my throat. "I have a lot going on in my life, and I don't have room for you."

Jake takes another sip of his tea. He glances over at me and ignores my hesitation; he's so comfortable around me that it's surprising. "What's so complicated in your life? Do you want to talk about it?"

I say nothing. The way his sexy jaw tightens and his brow furrows when he thinks I'm considering it is sexy. Still, I remain where I stand before.

I want nothing from him.

He caresses my palm with his thumb like it *belongs* there. As I realize we're still holding hands, my cheeks flush with heat. I expect him to call me out, but instead, he smiles and lets go of my hand so we can eat the deliciousness in front of us. I'm not the girl who picks at her food, even in front of someone, so when I inhale two slices of the pie and gulp down half of the raspberry iced tea in my own glass, Jake looks at me with amazement. I like the silence between us; I'm able to relax with a large, protective cushion beneath me.

"More iced tea?" the waiter asks, but I wave him off and feel the flush on my face again.

"The check, please." Jake locks his eyes on me. That's something I find odd about him; I've noticed he won't look *anyone* in the eye but me. Not even Caitlyn…each time they squared off, he still didn't look her directly in the eye.

"Ready?" He takes my hand into his and pulls

me out of the chair, making it a point to slide his arm around my waist and squeeze as he leads me back to the car. His massive pride wraps me in a cocoon, and everyone feels it when we pass them by.

Instead of opening my door and helping me inside of the car, he spins me to face him. Jake towers over me, his cinnamon breath dangerously close. I allow it to take over my body and make me weak. His body *slowly* pushes me against the side of the car, and he lowers his full mouth to my ear to whisper, "I want to take you somewhere else...will you go with me?" His bottom lip brushes my skin, and I'm about to explode all over him.

Jake pushes back the hair falling around my collarbone and grazes his lips across the bare skin, sending my spine into a frenzy. I shiver where I stand. I'm frozen underneath him, tucked into a blanket of immobility; it feels so good that I don't want him to stop. His chestnut eyes are glowing when he looks into mine; he's so messed up and lost that he might be even worse off than I am.

That still doesn't mean you have to feel sorry for him.

"Please come with me?" He kisses the tip of my nose gently, melting whatever defense I have left.

"You're...*intense*." I blow out a gentle breeze of air and watch his curly hair move from the wind. My entire body *vibrates* underneath his; he's still pinning me against the car, and I wonder what passersby might think about us. "*That* was intense."

The fullness of his bottom lip is tucked in as he gently nips at it with his teeth. I see something dark poking out from the collar of his sweater, so I raise my hand slowly and pull the fabric down, seeing the black lines of a tattoo underneath my fingers.

"Well, well…" I return the fabric to his neck. "…tattooed *and* bossy. It looks like you might be too much of a bad boy for me, Jake Redding."

He growls. "Again with the assumptions about my character and intentions." His thumb finds my bottom lip and slides across it. The roughness of his skin excites me. "Are you sure you want to go with me now that you think that?"

I want to wrap myself around you and never leave your damn side.

"I'm not scared of you." I duck out from his grasp. The moment's broken as he opens the door and helps me inside. We ride in calm silence back toward Silver Lake; I see the things around us vanish, and we pull into a dark, empty parking lot. "Okay, I'm scared a little now." I fake a smile and try to tuck my fear at the back of my mind.

He laughs and pulls me out of the car, placing my body in front of his. Kissing my forehead, his body lowers in front me slowly. I feel his grip around my leg, taking off my shoes and socks and leaving me barefoot and confused. Both pairs of our shoes litter the front seat, and he takes my hand, pulling me behind him through the cool sand of the beach.

"We won't be bothered here. I know who owns this beach." He grabs a few blankets from a small building we pass on the way to the water. He places them on the sand, and I know he wants me to sit down next to him, but now I actually *am* afraid.

I don't want to fall for him.

"What are we doing here?" I sit a full arm's length from his grip. He opens his arms wide and leans his head back, breathing in the crisp September air, and it makes me smile. I feel his release, letting go of everything and just...*being*. I envy him too, because the more I see the happiness grow on his face, the more I become jealous that all of my problems are piled too high on my shoulders and it's impossible to escape.

Not remembering an entire life can do that to a person.

"Tell me what you're running from." His deep voice vibrates my eardrums. He pulls my body close to his, with no warning or permission. "And I'll tell you what I'm running toward."

I don't want him to know.

Keep it together, Olivia.

"I'm different." I might as well start crying again and give him a better show of just how much of a mess I really am—maybe that will finally scare him off. "I mean, I can't remember anything."

Jake nods; he's *actually* listening. "Like you have a short memory? That's not so bad. There are some things in my life I wish I could forget."

My head finds my hands, and I cross my legs, tucking them underneath my chin in automatic defense. "No, I was in a car accident over a year ago, and I have amnesia. I had a pretty bad head injury."

"How do you know that?"

"My family told me when I woke up in the hospital."

"And you can't remember anything from before the accident?"

Embarrassed, my face flushes. "Nope, nothing before I woke up in the hospital. I don't even remember the accident."

His long arms pick me body up and place me against his warm chest; he cradles me like when he picked me up from the wet lawn. His heartbeat is directly under my ear, and it quickens as he holds me. "Don't ever worry about telling me your problems again, do you understand?"

I sniffle. "We barely know each other."

"Knowing someone for days or decades doesn't make them care about you any less."

I notice the tremble in his voice, and it takes a few minutes for things to warm back up between us. Since we've moved to California, I haven't made it a point to get close to anyone. Being with Jake is exciting and addicting, two things that are dangerous to mix.

The sun completely disappears, and the moonlight covers the sand around us. I let him nuzzle my body back into his because I need the comfort. His heart beats so fast that it pounds against my ear; I feel it reaching out of his chest.

"How many tattoos do you have?" I sleepily ask, and I feel him smile into my hair.

"A few. Would you like to see them?"

I yawn again and can't find the strength to move my head from his chest. "Are they in a decent place?"

"Most of them." He laughs, and I move with his chest like a wave in the ocean. "Would you rather see the ones that aren't first?"

I groan into his blue sweater. "You can't see it, but I'm rolling my eyes right now."

"Look," he says, rolling up the left sleeve of his sweater. "They're tasteful, I promise."

I lift my head and look at the skin on his arm. Several different designs cover his flesh on top of the hardness of the muscle he's purposely flexing. The one that catches my eye is a large tree on his forearm—broken and barren.

"What's this about?" I run my fingers over the ink, and I feel his body shake from my touch.

"You really wanna know?" His eyes fill with sadness as he looks from me to the tree. I nod and lean some of my weight back into him to calm him. His other arm slides around me and I hear him blow out a sigh. "It's a tree that sits on my property. It's dead now, but someone once made me promise never to have it cut down." I yawn and snuggle into his hands; it's hard to keep my eyes open and listen. "The tree got termites and I couldn't save it, so I got this so she would always have that tree in some way because she loved it, and I loved her." He's talking about a woman, someone he seems to still love deeply. "These tattoos that I have, they're like...*pieces of me*." He frowns, and I want to reach out to touch his face to erase his internal sense of destruction.

"Caitlyn did say you're the mysterious Redding boy."

"She doesn't know the first thing about me."

The snap of his voice tells me I've said the wrong thing.

"Why don't you like talking about her?"

His tongue grazes over his bottom lip. "I'd rather talk about you."

He puts his body next to mine and pulls me onto his chest, his heartbeat racing faster this time. I allow myself to lie with him as long as nothing gets out of hand, but the waves call me to sleep before I can worry about anything else in the small part of the world we live in.

Falling asleep on a beach with a man I hardly know.

That's the Olivia I've grown to be.

Regardless of who I *think* I used to be.

Chapter Six

The tree

What's that amazing smell?

Chocolate. Maple. Bacon. Coffee.

My teeth sink into the inner meat of my cheek. There's nothing more I love about the man downstairs making Christmas breakfast than the way he does things like this for me. I honestly don't know how I got so lucky; fate has always been on our side, I guess.

The tantalizing ribbons of explosive flavors fill the bedroom. He's lit the fireplace too; the room is toasty and invites me back to sleep before the snaps of bacon wake me back up.

Jake knows this is my favorite day of the year.

I smile into the comforter, keeping my love for him to myself. He gets me, inside and out—he just gets me. Anyone else would've frowned at the number of gifts I've stuffed under the Christmas tree—but not Jake. He ran out at the last minute, drove twenty miles, just to make sure I had enough wrapping paper for everything that littered the living room floor.

His heavy footsteps trudge up the stairs. I close my eyes quickly and let the rich smell of freshly brewed coffee excite me. His weight moves the mattress as he sits down at my thighs, rubbing his hand up the curve of my ass.

"Merry Christmas, baby," he whispers.

"Merry Christmas to you, boyfriend."

Stretching, I wrap my fingers around the fabric of his t-shirt and pull him down to meet my lips. He tastes like cinnamon, and it's the best kiss I've ever had. Jake smiles against my lips and slides his arm underneath me, pulling me from the comforter and onto his lap facing him.

"Just like I like you, awake and straddling me."

"Is that so?"

A growl rumbles in his throat. "And screaming my name."

My skin is on fire. His fingers grip the flesh of my ass with one hand; the other hand brushes hair from my collarbone before pressing his hot lips against me. In seconds, he's ripped off his t-shirt and returned his lips to my flesh; he trails them up the side of my neck and stops behind my ear.

"Run away with me."

His fingers behind me are only inches from pushing the fabric of my panties aside. His hot lips part mine, and his tongue runs along the top of mine.

"And go where?"

"I don't care, let's just fucking go."

His hands run up my back; he pulls the tank top

over my head and throws it on the floor next to the bed. My bare C-cups bounce with their newfound freedom; his reddened lips find the soft flesh in between them, suctioning the skin into them. The way Jake handles me—the real way he handles me—keeps me needing the release.

"Baby, I'll go anywhere you want. Let's just go and never come back."

My fingers grip his copper blonde hair, tugging it back as he moans. His fingers move closer to the edge of my panties.

"We've talked about this. You'd miss it here."

"I can learn to live with it."

"This is our home; I don't want to leave. We belong here...together."

The instant I press my lips against the stubble of his neck, his body shivers. His fingers push the fabric aside and press into the wetness that's been waiting for him. He moves his fingers around in circles against the swollen peak of my clitoris.

Jake is motivated by sound and touch; the deeper my moans become, the faster his fingers work. His teeth gently close around my left nipple when it becomes easier to access after I tip my head back and explode all over his hand.

The silk of his boxers rubs against my wrist as my arm snakes behind me and opens the front flap. The familiar warm flesh that greets me is hard to wrap my fingers around the entire way I pull it from its cage. I have to lean sideways to grab a condom from the bedside table, and the sight of the silver package excites him even more. Jake's breathing quickens every second that ticks by and I've got a *hold on him; when he can't take much more, he grips my sides to lift me up.*

"I love you more than anything I've ever loved before." His chestnut eyes burn into mine. "I'll never love anyone like I love you."

My thighs prepare themselves as he wraps his arms around me, pounding his hard flesh in between my legs. Wrapping my legs around him for stability, our moans intertwine and we become one. He grips the roundness of my ass and bucks me up and down until my eyes roll to the back of my head. My toes start to curl as he swiftly turns me around and releases me onto the bed.

Leaning my body back up, I kiss his flat stomach and trail my lips up and down his v-shape. Each time my lips meet his flesh, he shivers and lets out a small moan.

"You make my fucking head explode."

The giggle I let escape my lips sets him off. Jake pushes me on my back and spreads my legs as far as he can before pushing his hard dick back where it belongs. The sweat that drips from his body sizzles against my hot skin; it takes a few minutes for everything to come back into view and my heart to slow down to a normal pace again.

Collapsing next to me, Jake kisses my bare shoulder and laughs. "You've won again. We're staying here."

"I'll always win. You love me too much to let me loose."

Nuzzling against my neck, he smiles. "You're right about that."

Snow blows against the bay window. He

hesitates to let me leave the bed; I wrap a blanket around my body and crawl into the window seat. "It's snowing. My tree won't survive the winter."

My favorite maple tree—that once stood proud, vibrant, and tall in the backyard—was one of the main reasons I asked Jake to buy this house. I would imagine children playing around it, chasing each other and laughing until they gasp for air.

Now...it sits broken and barren.

Jake comes to me, sliding his body next to mine. "I know you love that tree."

"Are you sure it can't be saved?"

The bigleaf maple's naked branches weep to be saved.

"I'm sure, baby. I've asked six professionals who all say the same thing."

Accepting his answer for the ninth time he's told me, I let a tear fall down my cheek. "I know you think it's silly...you think it's just a tree."

Jake smiles wide as he brings his thumb to my cheek and wipes away the hot tears. Letting me melt into him, his arms wrap around me for comfort.

"I know what it means to you."

"Promise me you'll never have it cut down."

Jake kisses my head and wraps his legs around mine.

"I promise."

Chapter Seven

Run

My eyes flick open, and the waves softly crash in front of my body.

What the hell was that?

Clearly, the dream I had was some sort of adaptation of my version of what sleeping with Jake would be like. I'm sore from the way I slept and the cold morning air is nipping my skin where the blanket isn't covering me. I close my eyes because I'm still tired; I don't want to wake up yet and face whatever's going to come after this. Especially having a dream that isn't mine—it *can't* be mine. There is no way I could remember Jake's tattoo, let alone some tree in some random backyard. The dream I had must have been because it was the last thing he said to me before I fell asleep.

It has to be.

My left arm swings around my body, searching for more blanket, but all I find is another equally as cold being behind me. His arms tangle around me

63

and he softly breathes in the scent of my hair from behind. I open one eye, trying not to move and wake Jake up, noticing that it's now daylight. Birds chirp around us cheerfully—mocking me as I twist my face in horror at the thought of what I've done to myself. I focus on the extreme need to untangle myself from his tight embrace and run.

Run. Run. Run.

This isn't me; I don't fall asleep on random beaches with random guys. I scoff and mock them from afar while I sit in the corner and try to figure myself out. I don't need this drama, but here I am— putting myself right in the middle of something I shouldn't be in.

"Good morning, Bug," Jake says into my mess of brown hair, burying his nose deeper into it. "It's freezing out here. Are you cold?"

I pretend to still be asleep because I don't know what else to do. I feel him slowly brush my hair from my face and his eyes burn into my skin, making sure I'm not awake. He picks my body up from the blanket we lie on, carrying me gently to the car and putting me in the back seat. I wait a few minutes for him to get into the car and drive away, careful on the turns so he doesn't wake me.

Do I let him know I'm awake?

What's he going to do when he gets me home?

His phone rings, and I don't open my eyes to interrupt a chance to eavesdrop on his call. "Yes?" His voice is tired and quiet; it takes a lot of concentration to hear what he's saying.

"Yeah, I'll be there soon."

"I know what time it is."

"I *said* I would be there soon."

"I have to do something first, but it won't take long."

"I'm at the beach. Can you meet me at my hotel?"

"I know how far it is from Seattle."

"Yes, I'm with her."

"You can't possibly understand."

"Okay, I'll see you soon."

"Yeah, you too."

He clicks the phone off, and his gaze lights my skin on fire again; I feel him looking at me through the rearview mirror, but I can't bring myself to open my eyes. It isn't until the car comes to a stop, and he opens the back door before he hovers over me, picking me up again.

Is he going to dump me on my doorstep?

My eyes snap open immediately. "Put me down." He nearly jumps out of his skin when he hears my voice. He doesn't do what I ask, so I wiggle my body to make him lose his grip and let me fall to the ground with a loud thud on the pavement. I make a soft grunt and rub the hip bone that's broken my fall.

Anything is better than being left on a doorstep.
Thrown out like trash.

"What the hell?" Jake growls. I wiggle free from his grasp again, nearly smashing my face against the brick walkway leading to the front doorstep that he stands on. "What the hell is wrong with you?" Jake's fingers shake a little and run through his hair as his eyes examine my body to make sure I'm not hurt.

65

I'm hurt, but not physically.

"I have to get inside." My shrill voice makes the air colder around us. "Thanks for bringing me home and thanks for dinner." I know he's confused; there isn't anything I can do about that right now. I don't know who he was talking to on the phone, but it sure doesn't sound like he's single enough to be falling asleep with me on a beach.

"Olivia, talk to me." His voice isn't enough to make me turn around. I told him I'm not scared of him and I meant it; although, I might be afraid I'll fall into his bad boy, covered in tattoos, sexy grin and cinnamon and whiskey trap, only to be left in the cold alone.

Not today, Jake Redding.

The mysterious Redding boy.

He grabs my arm and turns me around to face him, anger and hurt in his glassy brown eyes. "Help me out here. What's going on?" His full lips quiver; it's hard to tell if he's just angry because I'm denying him what he wants or if he's scared he'll lose me when I walk through that front door.

He never had you, Olivia, remember that.

"I have to go, Jake, so thanks for dinner and the whole," my hands find the space between us; I separate the thick air that sticks between our chests, parting it like dark smoke, "listening thing."

"Don't run from me."

I turn my body around, quick and annoyed. It's a little amusing—since he *towers* over me—but I stand my ground and clench my jaw the same way he does. "I'm not running. I'm saying goodbye. Have a good day." I blink a few times, watching his face redden and the fire in his eyes burn brighter. "I need you to just get into your car and go home, Jake."

"I'm not going anywhere until you tell me what the hell happened between last night and now. How did we get to this?" His voice is layered with agitation and fear. Quickly, my head spins with bits and pieces of Jake flushing through my mind. I'm seconds away from telling Jake about my dream when I see the living room curtains open and then close again even faster. My dad opens the front door and steps outside, noticing the verbal attack stances we have.

"Everything okay out here, Liv?"

"It's fine. I'll be in soon." I know that even when he goes back inside, he's still watching us. Jake rubs his chin and lets out a long gust of air, and the sadness creeps back into his eyes. "Help me understand what's going on here. *Please.*"

"I was awake for your phone call in the car. I'm not interested in being the other woman." My teeth grind together, sending a pain up my jaw that makes my vision a little blurry. "I *warned* you, Jake. I told you I'm a damn mess. I'm not looking for anything but the memories I'm missing, and you charmed your way in there. I knew this would happen."

He hovers over me. "You knew *what* would happen?"

For the first time in months, my head starts to pound with searing pain behind my eyeballs like so many times before. The stress I'm putting myself through is bringing the headaches back again—with a vengeance.

"This." I smack his chest lightly. It pushes him back a few steps for some safe distance. "I have a hard time trusting people. I'm not intentionally pretending to be someone I'm not, but it's really confusing when someone comes into my life and keeps more secrets from you."

Jake keeps his sadness tucked into his heart, but he lets just enough of it seep toward me to make me feel even worse. "That was my mother on the phone." His voice is fragile; I've succeeded in hurting his feelings. "I'm late for a meeting with her and our family lawyer. That's why she's so upset."

I'm going to vomit.

"Please...don't run from me," he whispers into the breeze. The air catches my ears, tickling them as his words slide down into my chest. "I don't know what else to say other than, just...don't run from me."

"I'm not running from you. I need to focus on myself."

He's only inches from me now, pulling me into him. Jake buries himself in my hair and squeezes my body tight.

Cinnamon.

"You have to say the words." My throat closes, and I can't breathe. "*Say it*, Olivia."

This is so weirdly soothing that it freaks me out. Part of me wants to wrap my arms around his neck and take him inside to heal his invisible wounds, but the other part of me—the *sane* part—knows that's beyond normal and not a healthy thought to even entertain.

I need to find out the truth about my accident.

I can't have distractions.

"I want you to go, Jake." I say the words and watch his face crumple with a thousand deaths. "This isn't a *goodbye*. I just want some rest, okay?" I sigh, upset with myself that I have singlehandedly messed up someone's day. "I'll call you later, okay?"

"Okay." He kisses my cheek and walks back to the car, slowly pulling back onto the road. I wave at him before closing the front door behind me and blowing out all of the air I've been holding in.

"You sure you're okay, Liv?" my dad asks when I take in another deep breath to replace what I just lost. "What was all that about? Did he say something to you? What did he tell you? Where've you been all night?"

I wave him off, but I make sure he's aware that I'm annoyed with his obvious dislike for Jake Redding. "Nothing, just drama. You know I don't do drama." He chuckles, and his gaze returns to the television show he's watching. He pretends horribly that he's even still interested in it as I walk upstairs to my bedroom. I collapse onto my bed, still in my work clothes, and I swear I still smell Jake's spicy cinnamon breath.

I really want him.

I really, really want him.

And that's really, really not okay.

Something feels unlocked inside of me when I'm near him—like I'm level on the ground, both feet planted, and I'm literally not afraid of anything getting in my way.

I don't have to work again until tomorrow

morning, so I feel safe enough to curl into the blankets and try to sleep away what just happened.

The tree. The ceiling is the only thing I can stare at in the darkness above me, but all I see is that tree, illuminated in my mind like a glowing rope of turquoise glitter.

Jake. I manage to surprise him in ways that I didn't even know I could, and he's just so...*relentless*.

I have to close my eyes and sleep Jake away.

It's going to take more than one night to forget about Jake Redding.

Chapter Eight

Mother

Jake

I need to punch something.

No, I need to *kill* something.

It tears up my insides to know how badly she's hurting. I want to *murder* the next hard surface my fist can slam into.

The Mercedes screeches to a stop in my hotel's circle drive. I let out the air I've been holding in since I walked away from her. She still frustrates me more than anyone. Still, she's twenty-three and figuring herself out, and here I am, twenty-five and chasing someone who doesn't even fucking remember me.

Oh, but I have my mother.

"Nice of you to finally join us, Jacob," my mother scolds me as I enter my hotel suite. My name rolls from her tongue like a snake's hiss, and I have to loosen the collar of my wrinkled shirt.

"It's a half-hour drive from Silver Lake."

"Yes, I'm aware. We were already near here on business, so you're lucky we could meet you here instead of Seattle."

She nods toward Neal Franklin, our family attorney, so he can start his boring presentation. He's been trying to solve my mother's money issues for three months. I notice her glance over at my choice of clothing and shake her head in disapproval quietly. The sooner Neal starts, the sooner I can bail and go back to Olivia. It's still so fucking weird to call her that. My heart is tugging me away from reality; it's crazy how much a person can make you fall in love with them—*twice*. I can't stop thinking about her and the way she blushes when I touch her or the goosebumps it gives her when my breath tickles her skin.

Her smooth, pale skin.

Her long, silky milk chocolate hair.

Her round, wide brown eyes.

The attitude she gives me *still* turns me on.

Olivia. Olivia. Olivia. Olivia.

I want her so bad it's killing me inside.

She has to remember *something*.

I've looked for her for over a year; she was being kept hidden from me so close but so far away.

Why are they letting me see her now?

Why are they lying to her?

She knows she's not who they say she is.

I don't care. She belongs with me…I have to make her see that somehow.

"Jacob? Are you listening?" My mother glares at me. "It's not an appealing trait to gaze off in space chasing dreams that aren't real anymore."

I'm cursing her in my mind for speaking about Olivia like that. "I'm here. Go ahead, Neal."

Neal looks at me wearily but continues, despite the dryness of his voice. "So basically, you're the only one with a trust fund left, Jake. You've hardly touched it since you turned twenty-one." His cough is dry and gross as I picture clouds of germs filling the air around me. "If we were to liquidate that, your mother won't be totally out of debt, but she'll be close enough not to lose the house."

"So sell the house." I snort. "Sell the cars. Sell the vacation houses." I wave my arms around in the air.

She nervously laughs. "I thought you were okay with this. Need I remind you of how I got into this mess in the first place?"

"I'm fine, Mother. Go on."

Neal blabs more about interest rates and loan repayments; when he stands up to shake my mother's hand, I know it's finally over. It'll only be a few minutes before I can race to the car and drive back into Silver Lake, hoping she'll want to see me even after she made it clear that she needs space.

You're gonna fucking run her off if you don't back the fuck off.

"Okay, so I'll run some numbers and get back with you, Mary-Anne. Jacob, it's always a pleasure to see you, son."

My mother goes into the kitchenette to take our cups and saucers to the sink while I show Neal to the door. I hope to put myself on the same side of it as he is when he leaves.

"How much will I have left?" I ask in a low voice; Neal knows I wasn't listening in the meeting. "Out of my trust fund, how much?"

Neal looks sick. "Nothing, Jacob, you will have virtually nothing. All you'll have is the revenue from your businesses. Even though that's substantial, it's nothing compared to what you have access to now."

I want to grab Olivia so badly right now and hold her tight to make my pain go away. "So between you and me, what do *you* think is in my best interest?"

My mother clinks dishes around in the kitchen, so Neal knows that we're safe to speak freely. "As your *family* lawyer, I say do it so your mother doesn't have to sell everything and be the laughingstock of Seattle." His eyeglasses fall down a little on his nose. "But as your *friend*, I say don't. This isn't your problem, Jake. You should sever your ties now and just live your own life free from this."

"You know I can't leave her behind. I spent an entire year searching for her. She was in fucking California this whole time." My lips stick together like glue at the thought of leaving Olivia behind.

"I don't know, but do you want your mother to drag you down with her? She had millions of dollars at her disposal and chose to invest in some crazy places. No matter who convinced them or who coerced them into signing, your mother knew what she was getting into." His eyes lock with mine; he's scared for me. "I think you should walk away. That's what I would do if I were you."

"Walk away?" I look around for anyone lurking. "I love her. I can't leave her behind."

Neal sighs and pats me on the shoulder. "Then take her with you, kid. I'm sorry to say, though, you don't belong in Seattle anymore." He's right; I can't give my mother everything I have to get her out of debt. I need that money to start a new life in a new place.

With Olivia.

I'm still not used to calling her that.

"What did Neal say?" my mother says behind me, and I turn to face her. I know she can see it in my eyes that I'm having second thoughts.

"I'm not going to do it, Mother. I can't give you everything I own to help you with your mistakes. You're going to have to crawl out of this one on your own."

She isn't surprised. "Jacob, you have forgotten that it was *your* advice that led me to investing so much money with Michael Cervase. Now you are telling me you won't help clean up the mess you created? I'm leaving—we are done here. If you won't help your family, we don't require anything else from you, like always."

I think about Olivia.

I need to see her.

She fixes me every single time this happens.

She knows what to do; she knows how to love me.

At least...she used to.

"We are done now, Jacob. Don't come back to Seattle."

"Goodbye, Mother."

The air is getting colder each day September grows older, but I don't mind; I like the nip of cold air against my skin. It helps me remember that I'm alive as my feet pound on the pavement of the parking lot and I throw myself back into the driver's seat of the car.

Olivia.

Answer the phone, Olivia.

"Jake." Her voice is sleepy. "I thought I told you *I* would call *you*?"

"I need to see you." I clench my jaw. "Now."

Olivia yawns into the phone, and I smile, thinking about her hair falling around her pink, blushing cheeks. "Demanding as always."

"*Please*, Olivia."

"You just left a few hours ago. I need room to breathe."

"I know I'm smothering you." Desperation drips from my tongue and falls in my lap; I'm a few short words away from crying.

"Oh, Jake—"

I cut her short; I feel like I'm losing her again. "I *need* you, Olivia." I know she can feel the darkness in my voice, because it's suffocating me just by opening my mouth. She's always been that person for me, the one that always steers me in the right direction. I've been so lost without her that I can't tell which way is up anymore. The anger inside of me rises, and I'm about to lose control. I've been trying my best to manage my rage, and when I saw Olivia for the very first time, I felt like my chains had broken free and I could finally just…*be.*

Be free.

Be careless.

Be myself.

"Are you okay?" I hear her shuffle around in bed. I imagine her tangled up in the sheets; I never thought I could be jealous of a bed before. "Did something happen?"

I want to tell her anything she wants to know.

But I don't want her to run again.

I need her to trust me first.

"I just…I need you."

A few long seconds pass, but I won't give up. She's never going to see me as anything but what she wants to see: a guy that's going to break her heart with his demands and his bad boy ways…and sad tattoos and memories that I can't share with her until I talk to the people lying to her alone.

"Come over."

That's all it takes for me to hang up the phone and hit the gas pedal.

All I can think about is grabbing her and never letting her go.

She isn't going to be apart from me again.

Chapter Nine

Addicted

Olivia

"I just really needed to see you—don't start yelling at me," Jake growls as soon as I open the door and let him inside the house after he called. His frustration pins me against the wall and holds me there; the two of us have some unspoken, terribly wonderful moment between us. "I wasn't imagining things at the beach last night. You were mine, and it felt real."

Well, come on in and make yourself at home in my heart, then.

I swallow without making a weird noise as he stares me down. His eyes are bright, and it's hard to keep his gaze without blinding myself. But I do it anyway—I keep my brows furrowed the same as his so he can see that I won't be giving into whatever he's trying to sell me: whatever words he's going to try and sneak in to put me under his spell.

"We met two days ago—"

"Please don't act like there wasn't something there last night. Don't do that to me," he pleads and raises his right arm onto the wall, resting it near my head. He never breaks eye contact with me as his shadow towers over my body. "*Please*, Olivia."

"You're *scary*." I nod toward the living room where my dad is still watching television and no doubt eavesdropping in on our heated conversation. "Let's go upstairs, okay?" I run my finger along the stubble on his jawline before I even realize what I'm doing. I instantly know I shouldn't have touched him like that. He's just so *overbearing* that touching him sometimes dominates the corners of my mind.

You don't even know him! You met him two days ago! You don't have time for this! Don't you want to find your memories?

I swat my thoughts away and push him into my bedroom, shutting the door behind us. I feel his warm hands on my shoulders, twirling my body around to face him before the door even clicks all the way closed.

"I can't let you say no to me. There are reasons I can't let you go. You just have to trust me." He lowers his gaze to my hands, picking them up and pulling me closer.

"I don't know anything *about* you!" I whisper angrily.

He takes my face into his hands, kissing the tip of my nose. "You want to know something about me? I am so completely fucking addicted to you and everything *about* you." He laughs at my hands, now swatting him away from me. "I can't think of anyplace I would rather be than right here, watching you get so irritated over nothing."

"And you. Don't forget my irritation toward *you.*"

"Insult me all you want, Olivia. I know the truth."

I finally pull a pair of clean jeans from the basket and wonder if I should just go ahead and pull off my sweats to change or wait until he leaves. "And what *is* the truth, Jake?"

What does he seem to know about me?

Jake scoffs and leans back onto the bed; he has no intention of moving or elaborating on any irritatingly addicting roped piece of information he's sprinkled on the ground like bread crumbs for me. "I just mean I can see through your tough exterior."

I see the exhaustion in his eyes; he did sleep on a beach overnight, after all. I do things silently around the room, and each time I sneak a glance over at him, his eyes are drooping lower and lower. Finally, I hear his light snore from across the room. I'm able to pull a blanket over his large body enough to keep him warm. When he slowly breathes out, the light blonde curls float in the wind on top of his head. Suddenly my bedroom door flings open, Caitlyn chatting loudly on her phone as she enters.

I shush her and wave my hands in the air. When she sees Jake sleeping on the bed, her eyes widen, and she hangs up on whoever she's talking to. "Is that…?"

"Yes." I glare at her. "Leave him be. He's tired."

"From *what*?" her voice squeaks, and she looks sick. "Did you two…?"

"No, of course not. What do you want?"

"I can't believe he's sleeping in your bed." She frowns and lets out a small snort. "What did you do to him?"

"I didn't do anything to him. Get out." I wave her off. "You're going to wake him."

She snickers and says, "Yeah, wake the *beast*."

I stop in my tracks and look at her, wondering why she would say something like that. "What is your problem with him? Did he break up with you or something? I never did ask the details of your relationship." My teeth grind together, and her body squirms a little in her stance. "I want to know what you know, Caitlyn."

"Jake and I never dated." Her small voice wafts toward me as she sits in the armchair across from the bed. "We just don't really see eye to eye on a lot of things, that's all."

I've had enough of the elusive comments from both of them. "Are you talking about a woman? He mentioned something about being in love with someone before. He talked about her when I asked about his tree tattoo."

This time, she doesn't try and hide her cringing at the information I'm giving her. I don't say anything as her eyes dart toward Jake's still body and narrow angrily at him. "I dated his brother, Noah. That's how Jake and I know each other, okay? Olivia, really, let's just leave the Reddings out of any conversation we have from now on."

"Fine, then let's talk about me."

"What about you?"

"I want to know what you're hiding from me."

Caitlyn sighs. "Livvie, we've all told you over and over: we're not hiding anything from you. It's getting really old having someone call you a liar every day." Her voice is matter-of-fact. "What makes you so sure the dreams you have are real, anyway?"

"I just *know*, Caitlyn."

"Stop trying to fill a void with anything you can hold onto."

I don't stop her as she stands up and leaves the room, leaving a hollow, deafening sound where she shoved another subliminal message into my brain.

"What was that about?" Jake asks, but his eyes are still closed when I turn to face him.

Now is the time to come clean with him about exactly what's so different about me. "She thinks what everyone thinks, that's all."

"What does everyone think?" He sits up and pats the bed next to me.

I sit down. "That I'm crazy."

"Why do they think that?"

"If I tell you, you'll think I'm crazy too."

Jake laughs loudly. "Olivia, trust me…I *won't* think you're crazy."

Maybe it's the light in his eyes or the fact I can't trust anyone else, but I collect my thoughts and sort them out.

I'm ready to tell him everything.

"I told you about my accident." He nods, and I continue, "but I didn't tell you everything else. At first, after the accident, I was having blinding headaches and couldn't even get out of bed. Then the dreams started. They were patchy, and not a lot made sense. Actually, still nothing makes sense…"

Jake's hand finds mine, interlinking our fingers. "Take your time."

"The dreams I have, they feel real…I don't know how to explain it. They're mine from a different lifetime."

"Like a past life?"

"No, like from before my accident. They're the memories I'm missing."

Jake tries to process the information without looking at me with pity—the look everyone else gives me. "You think your missing memories are coming back to you in dreams?"

My body tenses when I notice the tone of his voice. "I told you that you'd think I'm crazy."

"I *don't* think you're crazy." He moves closer to me and rests his forehead on mine. "Have you talked to your parents about it?"

"They're the ones who sent me to a therapist twice a week." I notice the time on the clock beside the bed. "Which I'm going to be late for if I don't get a move on. My appointment's in half an hour."

Jake's eyes light up. "I'll drive you since your car is still at work."

"If you'll drive me to work in the morning, I can just pick it up then."

Before I say anything else, he's jumped up and extracted his car keys from his pocket. Putting my bag over his shoulder, he takes my hand and promptly leads me down the stairs and out into the chilly September air. I have to direct him through the Silver Lake streets to get to Dr. Ross' office; the smile he's wearing is the brightest I've seen on him yet.

He parks the car and turns it off, ready to settle in and wait.

"You're staying out here, right?"

Jake takes his hands off the steering wheel. "I don't want to overstep. Do you need me to come in?"

"No, I'd like to go in alone." My body relaxes. "That sounds great, actually."

"I just want to get to know you, Olivia." Jake runs his thumb along my knuckles. "There's something about you...I'm addicted to you."

"So you've said."

I have five minutes before my appointment starts, and I realize that Jake knows all these things about me—or lack of things—and I hardly know anything about him. Putting my dreams and lost memories on hold, I scan my brain for something to latch onto.

"How was the meeting with your mom?"

He frowns. "My mother is broke and wanted me to fix it for her." I know it might not be any of my business. He looks at me with broken eyes; I can't help but automatically be on his side. "I won't help her. She'll bankrupt me, and where would that leave *my* future? I have big plans for the future I want." His full lips curve into a smile while he daydreams about something brilliant. "If I didn't know better, I'd say *you* were trying to get to know *me*, Olivia White."

I blush. "Oh, my first *and* last name. You must

mean business."

"Oh, I mean business." He shakes thoughts from his head onto the blanket in his lap. "I mean serious business when it comes to you."

"It scares me when you're so intense like that." I blush, not thinking before I speak. "We just met, and you're so...*into me*. It's just a little much to get used to, not to mention I have *zero* business trying to help fix someone when I'm a mess myself."

Jake places his palms into his lap. "There are things about me that I'm not proud of."

My chest tightens, and I can feel a panic attack rising in my throat. Jake places his fingers around my knee, and the panic bubbles away until I can breathe freely again.

"Olivia, I would never do anything to hurt you, but you do have to trust me." The words that trickle from his throat sound so final that it's hard to argue with them at all. I have a burning feeling crawling down my throat that Jake is right.

How can he be right?

I know he's completely into me, like he's found his trifecta of love at first sight: the perfect woman, flirty banter, and instant attraction all wrapped up in one little Olivia White. I bite my lower lip thinking about his rough hands clutching my sides, picking me up and holding me against the wall earlier downstairs. I feel a twinge in the pit of my stomach as I watch his lips move while he speaks; I still feel the electricity they provided against my collarbone and his hot cinnamon breath on my skin.

"Olivia?" Jake's face is alight with laughter. "Don't you need to get inside?"

I blink a few times, his raised eyebrows coming into focus. "Oh, yeah. I better go."

You can use this to your advantage…

Before I leave the car completely, I turn to catch his eyes with mine. "Can you help me find out the truth? It would mean spending more time with me and being the only person I trust."

"Find the truth about your dreams?"

"I know I'm not who people say I am, Jake. I'm going to prove it."

He sighs and rubs the bridge of his nose. "You know I'll always do what I can to help you, Olivia—"

"But you don't believe me."

"It's not that I don't believe you—"

"*Do* you believe me?"

Jake takes a long look at me before backing down. "I believe you. If you say the dreams are real, then they're real."

"So we have a deal? You'll help me?" I lean my body farther into the car, keeping my breath in time with his. "This is a one-time only deal, take it or leave it."

His whisper pushes against my breath. "Deal."

"So it begins," I say and take a deep breath, leaning back into my own personal space. "Piecing together my existence."

Piece by piece.
Brick by brick.
Lie by lie.

Chapter Ten

Lacey

"Welcome to your second session of the week, Olivia." Dr. Ross pushes his glasses up the bridge of his short, stubby nose. "I'd like to talk more about the dreams you've already had in the past next week, if that's okay."

The leather sofa squeaks under my weight. Dr. Ross takes my silence as some form of non-verbal agreement, and honestly, it doesn't surprise me. I'm sure that once I left his office yesterday, he couldn't wait to call my parents and tell them about the crazy things I said in my session.

"If you're up to it, I'd like to try a mild form of hypnosis."

My eyes widen. "You want to hypnotize me?"

"If that's okay. You're twenty-three—you don't need parental permission."

Taking my phone from my pocket, I quickly send Jake a text asking him to come inside. The receptionist speaks to someone, and Dr. Ross gets up from his seat to see what they're talking about in the lobby. When he returns, Jake follows him into the room, and I blush.

"What's wrong?" He sits down next to me.

Dr. Ross sits back down in his chair and crosses his arms. "Who are you, son?"

Jake holds his hand out for the doctor to shake. "Jake Redding."

"Well, Jake, as I was saying to Olivia before she texted you for comfort." Jake looks back and forth between me and Dr. Ross. "I wanted to try a new approach to her session today. I'd like to place her in a mild hypnosis, one that she can easily come out from."

"Will it help her remember anything?"

Dr. Ross nods. "It could put her in a level state where her mind unlocks itself enough, yes. Although, Olivia, you might not be able to speak during the hypnosis, but you can most certainly have visions."

"Are you sure I should be here?" Jake whispers.

"I want you here. I can't do that alone. No offense." I blush at Dr. Ross. "I'd like Jake to stay."

"I have no issues with that. You'll get better results the more relaxed you are."

It takes five minutes to get everyone positioned in the room where it makes the most sense. I lie on the squeaky leather sofa with Jake at my head and Dr. Ross sitting next to me at my knees. He speaks to me, but it sounds like he's farther and farther away; he counts down from ten, and something makes me feel like I'm floating in mid-air.

Like I'm outside my own body.

"Concentrate on the first thing you can hold onto," Dr. Ross says. "Focus and choose your memory. See what your mind can unlock for you and the sounds around you."

The sounds around me.

Dr. Ross talking.

Jake's heavy breathing.

The clock ticking across the room.

The squeaky leather—

***

She screams.

I hate it when she screams at Daddy like that. I don't know why she hates us so much; he gives her whatever she wants, and it's still not enough.

"Let me go!"

A door slams.

"Fucking open the door!"

Daddy hardly ever curses.

"I hate it here! Why couldn't we just stay in L.A.? You told me our lives would be better here, you fucking liar!"

"Sabine, calm down! I can't control what people say here, just like I couldn't control them there. If you don't want them talking about you, don't give them shit to fucking talk about!"

Sabine. I always thought Mommy's name was pretty, just like her. I love her long, dark hair and how she brushes mine before bedtime. That was before we moved here. Before I met the boy across the street and before the yelling started.

"You have a daughter that needs you, Sabine.

You can't just walk away."

"I never even wanted her! You forced me to have her, Michael!"

Michael is my daddy. He's tall and strong and plays tea parties with me whenever he's home. He works a lot, and Mommy leaves a lot, so usually it's just Miss Claudine and me in this big, empty house.

"You're right, I did force you to have her. I wasn't going to let you kill my daughter!"

"I fucking hate you!" Mommy screams, then her voice gets louder. I hide in their closet because it's the first place I can run to before I'm seen. "Michael, don't fucking touch me!"

Bang!

***

My eyes snap open, and tears run down my cheeks. Jake strokes my head and looks worriedly down at me, but Dr. Ross starts clicking his timer again and counting down, forcing me to return to my dreams.

***

Soft music plays, and people mull around like zombies in our living room. It was my eleventh birthday yesterday, but no one remembered. Well, no one except the boy across the street. He sent me a birthday card and a bag of Hershey's Kisses.

Dad shoves his hands into his pockets and talks somberly to a pair of older women. They hug him and pat his shoulder, comforting him.

I don't think I've ever been this sad in my entire life.

I loved Miss Claudine like a mother. She basically was my mother since my real one never acted like it. Dad loved her too—maybe not like he loved my real mother, but he loved her like his family, and that's exactly what she was.

"Hey." The boy from across the street leans down and smiles. "Are you okay?"

I can't speak.

"Can I hold your hand?"

He takes it without consent, but I don't mind. His brown eyes look like acorns.

"You're going to get through this," he says and squeezes my hand. "I'm going to help you."

"Why?" Tears stream down my face. "You don't have to."

The boy across the street takes a tissue from his pocket and wipes the tears from my cheeks. He moves next to me and wraps his arms around me, hugging me close.

"Yes, I do."

Dad walks to us. "Lacey, come. Miss Claudine's sister, Natilda, wants to speak to you." He pulls me up from the seat, but the boy from across the street doesn't let go of my hand until he has to.

"Will you be here when I get back?"

He smiles before Dad pulls me away completely.

"I'll never leave you."

***

"Give her some space to let her come back," Dr. Ross tells Jake. "Olivia, find the sound of my voice and clear your mind."

The room comes back into view, and Jake's more worried than before.

"Your eyes."

Jake's eyes widen with fear. "What about them?"

"How do you feel?" Dr. Ross cuts in. "We're out of time, but I want you to sit as long as you need to get straightened up. Did you have any visions, Olivia?"

I sit up on the leather sofa and put my hands between my legs.

"My name is Lacey."

Jake coughs into his hand. Dr. Ross scratches a few notes on his notepad and nods like I'm speaking, but I'm not.

"I didn't get my last name, but my name is Lacey, not Olivia."

"Okay, what makes you think this?"

Anger bubbles in my throat. "Because a man in my dream called me Lacey."

"A man? Who was this man?"

"My father. His name is Michael, and my mother's name is Sabine."

Jake swallows so hard I hear it. "I think she's had enough for today, don't you, Doc?"

Dr. Ross closes his notebook and smiles at me. "You did very well today, Olivia. We'll pick this up next week at your first session."

Jake rushes me out of the room before I can demand to talk about this any further.

My name isn't Olivia.

I'm Lacey.

Chapter Eleven

Mockingbird

The world is a crazy place. It can change the person you are into someone you never thought you would be before you even realize it. Most times, it's too late to change yourself back. Some moments I look around and think—*think hard*—about each piece of the puzzle of life that has led me here.

I only really have one piece of myself.

I know I am *not* truly who people say I am.

"It doesn't make sense. I Googled the name Olivia White and found nothing. I need to know my real last name so I can find the answers I need." I let Jake drive me to work the next morning because my car is still parked outside the YMCA. I'm on lifeguard duty today for the morning water aerobics classes, which doesn't even need a lifeguard at all, really. He yawns, and I can tell that the lack of sleep is really catching up to him. "Don't you work?" I not-so-subtly ask, wondering what he actually does during a normal day.

"Don't you worry about me. I'll do some work when I drop you off."

I prod him further. "Doing *what*, though?"

Jake's *handsome*, especially rugged and unshaven like now. I'm not exactly short, but the way he towers over me is exciting; the outline of his defined chest beneath his navy sweater and motorcycle jacket tantalizes me, and I want to run my fingers through his hair.

Stay on task, Olivia.

Lacey.

My stomach drops.

"I own a few small businesses around Seattle." He wiggles his nose at me. "I actually work for my money, if that's what you were wondering. I don't take what isn't mine."

I blush because he's caught me being judgmental without trying.

"Just wondering, that's all." I make it a point to quickly change the subject. "Thanks for the ride." I let myself out of the car as he parks next to mine. In three seconds, his grasp is around my wrist, pulling me back toward him like clockwork.

"There you go, running away again," he snips at me with a cool voice. The parking lot is loaded with cars, but we're alone outside. "I thought you were going to stop all that?"

"You believe what you want to believe." I don't want to argue with him—there's nothing to argue about. "Have a good day."

"Don't Google yourself."

"Bye, Jake."

His lips turn into a thin smile, and he forces

himself to take a few steps back. "I'll text you later," he grumbles and gets back into the car, peeling out of the lot before I can argue.

"He just keeps surprising me." I head inside toward the dressing rooms to change. This has been the most challenging few days of my life, with a man that I hardly know but I feel like I've known my entire life. Being with Jake is real and easy; I don't have to choreograph my moves around people I don't remember at all.

And his eyes look like the boy across the street's eyes.

Stop it. Don't go there, Olivia...Wait. Do I call myself Lacey now?

How do I know I'm not *really* going crazy? I need solid proof that these dreams are real. Hold on. What did Caitlyn say the other day?

It's not hard to do a simple internet search on someone.

Someone like Jake Redding.

The lifeguard bathing suit is a comfortable one-piece built for modesty. I'm thankful for that since I have trouble seeing my reflection these days, not recognizing the person staring back at me with borrowed eyes and a stolen frown.

I wave at Brant, who's teaching a group of sixty-something women how to use the water to exercise. I stifle a laugh when he makes a horrible face at me.

"Hello, ladies." My voice carries across the water. I wave at them, giving Brant a thumbs-up before heading toward my chair in the middle of the walkway next to the pool.

A cool breeze wafts around me, and I think it

might be Jake running back to see me—maybe even secretly hope it is. When I don't smell the cinnamon radiating from him, I frown and turn around to see Sam's smug face smiling at me. "Well, hey there, babe." He winks and puffs his chest toward me, a litter of snickering friends several feet away from us.

"*Sick.*" I gag. "Don't bother me, Sam. I'm on duty."

Sam laughs in a high-pitched tone, making sure his friends hear every word he says to me. "Are you serious? What, one of the old ladies is going to slip and need you to rescue her? Come on, Liv. I just want to talk to you."

I narrow my eyes when the slimy words ooze from his lips. He holds up his hands in surrender. "Fine, I'll leave you alone. I just came to see what the deal is with you and that guy from the party, anyway. I hear he's bad fucking news."

The chair is cold when I sit down; my legs shiver more from the way Sam makes me feel than the cold surface beneath my bare legs.

"What do you mean? Hey, come back here!" I yell, and his smile widens when he turns to face me.

"I noticed that he dropped you off. Was that your walk of shame?" Sam's voice rises back up enough for the group of friends to hear. "You should've given me a chance. Should have moved on me while you could, but now you aren't even on my radar."

My laugh billows through the hall. "You were *never* even on my radar. I hardly remember you exist at all sometimes, really."

"What did you say to me?" he growls and walks back a few steps, realizing that he was about to launch himself at me. Before he does something he'll regret, clouds shade his eyes and he sneers at me. "I'd be careful who I piss off if I were you. I know a lot of secrets about *a lot* of people. Your family has deep roots, remember that." He narrows his eyes in warning before smiling toward his friends and walking out of the hall with them.

"You just *met* my family!" I holler at his back.

Brant makes his way toward me after getting his students out of the water; his tan chest glistens under the water droplets left on his skin.

"Hey, you okay?" He ducks down so he can see my face. "Screw that guy. He's a jerk." He smiles and puts his wet arm around me, leading me back to my chair. "I don't have another class until eleven— do you want a soda from the machine? My treat." He sings the last part, and it makes me smile.

"Fine, thanks." I wave him off, and when he leaves, I'm alone in the pool area.

The silence echoes off the walls, and I close my eyes to think.

What did Sam mean about knowing secrets?

Does he know things about me*?*

"Here you go." Brant hands me an orange soda and sits on the concrete next to my feet. He places his now-warm body against my leg like a puppy dog, sipping his grape soda in a few complimentary moments of silence. "I don't like seeing you sad, Livvie."

"I told you to stop calling me that. I thought we agreed."

He shakes his head, and his sunshine-colored hair falls around his forehead. "Nope. You're stuck with it. Might as well embrace it, *Livvie*." It amuses him when I groan and tug my leg away from his arm. "So that guy from the other night, he was pretty…*intense*, right?" Brant gulps and stares up at me. "Is he your boyfriend?"

"Jake and I are just friends."

He accepts my answer and doesn't press his luck with any more questions; we sit in silence and make slurping sounds while we drink our sodas. After ten minutes of no conversation, I can tell that he's bored enough to make up an excuse about checking the locker rooms, and he leaves me alone again.

The water inside the pool is calm and bright blue. It reminds me of a pool from one of my dreams. My eyes widen as I replay a hot summer day inside my head: my small hands and short legs run around a lush, green backyard with someone chasing me, and I scream in delight as they pick me up and twirl me around. When the strong arms put me back on the ground, I look up and expect to see my father staring back at me, but instead, it's a man I don't recognize. Behind him sits a long, elegant pool with bright blue water just as calm as the pool in front of me. The memory is so real that I can feel the warm sunshine on my face and the damp, thick grass beneath my bare feet as the man frowns toward the pool and a woman sits on the edge with a tangled mess of brown hair—like mine—and large sunglasses.

***

"Sabine. Your daughter is home from summer camp."

My mom's lips are chapped and bright red. Her skin looks rubbery and gray; six weeks ago, before I left for summer camp, she looked healthy and bright. Now, she's a ghost.

"Hi, Mom." I wave. "I made something for you."

She ignores me—her usual—but I dig inside the makeshift craft bag and pull out a headdress made from multi-colored feathers and ribbons. I take two small steps forward and hold it out for her.

"Sabine," Dad warns her. "Take it."

Mom's chapped lips snarl. "You fucking take it. I don't want that shit."

She talks about me like I'm not even here.

Dad grips my shoulders and turns me around. For as long as I can remember, he's done this when she's hurt me, and this is how he eases my pain. Focusing on his steel gray eyes, the sorrow I feel when I think about my mother hating me fades, and his smile warms my heart.

"Daddy loves you." He kisses my forehead and takes the headdress from me, putting it on his head and shaking his body comically. "What do you think?"

"You look fucking stupid. Take that damn thing off, Michael."

He ignores her and dances around the backyard with me. I've missed our backyard; the summer camp in Wyoming didn't have the plush, mossy green grass we have here. I missed Dad, too, and I always miss Miss Claudine when I'm away.

"Where's Miss Claudine?"

Dad frowns. "Miss Claudine isn't feeling well, Lacey. We need to give her time to rest."

Mom laughs loudly. "She has fucking cancer, Michael. Tell her the truth." She pushes her sunglasses on top of her head, making her dark hair fall around her sunken face. "It's better you know this now and he doesn't put fantasies in your head, Lacey. Miss Claudine is dying. She's gonna die. We all die someday. I'll die, Dad will die...you'll die."

Dad sighs and pats my back. "Not for a long time, okay?"

Mom snickers and puts her glasses back on her face. She wobbles when she stands, and I notice she looks like a skeleton with skin draped over it. This is the first time she's spoken directly to me in months.

"Life isn't gumdrops and lollipops. Life isn't fair. Remember that."

***

"Hey, it's time for you to go, right?" Brant says. I jolt back into the reality where he's standing over me, his face twisted in confusion. "I've been saying your name for like thirty seconds...are you okay? Do you want me to call your mom or dad to pick you up?"

My head is pounding so hard that there's two of him.

I fake a small laugh to show him that it isn't a big deal. "No, of course not. I'm fine. I just need to take a nap, that's all." I don't allow him any time to bother me with more questions before I quickly wave at him and disappear into the locker room to change. I text Jake to meet me at my house as soon as possible. I'm able to get in and out within minutes, long before Brant even has the time to catch up to me. I notice him in my rearview mirror as I pull out of the parking lot; he shakes his head and shoves his hands into his pockets in defeat.

When I pull into the driveway, Jake is already waiting for me.

"What's wrong?" The fear in his voice is crystal clear. I clutch my forehead and stumble out of the car; Jake catches me before I hit the hard ground. "Olivia? Talk to me…what's happening?"

"Headache."

He breathes in deep and holds it. "What can I do?"

No one is home as he carries me toward my bedroom and gently places me on the bed. His long fingers stroke my hair as his quick heartbeat near my chest helps me concentrate on something other than my throbbing head.

"I have medicine on the dresser. Blue bottle."

Jake jumps up and retrieves the bottle, putting a white pill in my hand and snatching the bottle of water on the bedside table. The pill goes down easy, and I know it takes ten minutes to start working, so I start singing inside my head like I always do.

"Better?" His fingers run through my hair. "You looked like death, Olivia."

"It feels like that sometimes." I crinkle my eyebrows and place my head on his chest. The super-speed rate his heart is pounding feels good against my temple. "I've gone blind before when this happens; the doctors all say it's just part of the head trauma. Eventually they'll go away."

"Seeing you like that scared the shit out of me. Are you sure you don't need to go to the hospital?"

The medicine starts to kick in, and the headache slowly drifts away. There are so many things I have to do. Tell Jake about Sam. Google Jake's name. Find out my real last name.

"Jake, I have something to tell you."

After pulling me down next to him without warning, his broad arms tighten around me, and my ear presses against his heartbeat again, rapidly growing stronger and faster. "You remember Sam Collins, right?" I wait for his skin to grow hot with rage. "He said some things to me at work today that were really odd."

Jake's voice is breathy and light when he parts from me and finds my eyes. "Like what?"

"He said he knows secrets about people. He mentioned my family having deep roots." Jake doesn't look as worried as I am. "Are they even my family? Maybe I shouldn't even care."

His fingers find a few stray ends of my hair. "Of course you should. They *are* your family, no matter what you find out."

The way Jake touches me is nice. His rough and warm fingertips slide across my skin like they know every inch of the map of my body. I find myself reaching toward the collar of his t-shirt, pulling it down and looking at the dark marks of memories on his skin. The tree memory rattled me at first, but once it settled in its home inside my mind, there was no going back. Each time I think about it, it *feels* real, and for the first time in a long time, I have a memory that I can truthfully call my own.

"What's this one?" I run my fingertip down the edge of a partial tattoo that is being hidden by the upper sleeve of his t-shirt. "Is this a bird?"

He smiles with delight. "That's a mockingbird."

I push the fabric of his sleeve up over his right shoulder blade, and his skin shivers as I graze it with my fingertips. The massive mockingbird reveals itself, and my smile widens with its bold presence.

"That's my favorite bird, the mockingbird," I whisper, watching the goosebumps rise on the surface of his skin where my breath trails upward.

"It's fate," he whispers. His lips find the space where mine are, and he tugs his lower lip into his mouth with his teeth. He finds my chin with his fingers and pulls my face near his. I can faintly smell the cinnamon embedded inside him. "Olivia—"

"I think you need some sleep." I kiss his forehead quickly and jump from the bed before he can catch me. "I'm going to take a bath—get some rest." The bedroom door nearly slams behind me, but I don't care.

There's a bathtub with my name on it.

Whatever my name really is.

Chapter Twelve

Intruder

Jake's phone rings, and I hear him answer it all the way from the master bathroom. This is the only bathroom with a large enough tub to stretch out in. My legs feel good soaking in the soapy bubbles around my body.

His voice is muffled; I can't make out exactly what he's saying, but his deep voice carries easily. He searches the house for me and gets closer, his words come into focus, and I hear his side of the conversation clearer.

"No, everything's in my name. Nothing is in her name."

My body squeaks against the porcelain as I try to lean closer toward the open door to listen better, covering my body with the bubbles in case he finds me and comes barging into the bathroom without notice. We are *nowhere* near the point of seeing each other naked.

"I said I'm not doing that. No need to bring it up. I'm not leaving her behind. Meet me at my hotel in thirty minutes."

"Meet me at my hotel?"

He's in my parents' bedroom now. His body comes into view, towers in the doorway, and his lips spread into the sexy, wicked grin I've come to know him for. I completely forget that I'm in the bathtub—*naked*. Jake hangs up his phone without saying goodbye and doesn't wait to be invited inside the bathroom; his boots cross the door frame, and I know that if he doesn't turn back soon, there's no telling what will happen. I watch his eyes dim; he's looking down at me like I'm a wounded gazelle and it's a hungry lion's lucky day.

"I have to leave for a little while." He bends down to my eye level. "There's a few things I need to take care of. Can I come back later?"

I manage to push some of the bubbles over my chest again, trying to cover as much skin as possible. "You go and take care of your business. I'm not going anywhere."

"You better *not* go anywhere." His eyes narrow across the bubbles. Jake realizes that this is all I can give him as he kisses my forehead and looks down at the bubbles covering my body. "You know I can still see right through those, right?" He winks, jumping out of my grasp before leaving me alone in the bathroom and letting me drift off.

***

Sunlight.
It's already daylight?
How long have I been staring at the ceiling?

After we ate pizza and unpacked a few boxes with immediate needs in them, Mom and Dad went to bed and Caitlyn left with some people our age that she met when she and Dad got the pizza.

Me? I didn't bother putting a sheet on the mattress. I didn't even bother putting my bed together at all. It got cold halfway through the night—when I heard Caitlyn finally stumble in—so I found a blanket in my boxes. After taking the tags and binding from it, I realize it's brand new and never been used. It doesn't have that worn feeling, like my body fits perfectly inside of it.

I use it anyway.

The pillow I find is the same way; I'm so exhausted that I don't even bother caring.

Until now.

Ripping through the boxes, everything I pull from them have price tags on them. Bedding, clothing, toiletries, accessories: they're all brand new. Why would I have all brand new things? Did I not own anything before my accident?

I have to know why I can't remember anything.

My eyes close, and I stand in the middle of the mess I've made.

I'm so alone.

"Livvie!" Caitlyn screeches. "Are you awake?" She barrels through the bedroom door and frowns at the mess surrounding me. "What the hell happened in here?"

"Nothing is mine."

Her eyes widen. "What do you mean? Those boxes had your name on it."

I point to the piles of new things on the floor.

"Everything is brand new. Why is everything brand new?"

She doesn't hesitate to giggle. "Mom and Dad bought us both brand new things before the move. Don't you remember?"

I hate her when she does this. It's been eleven days since I met her, and I literally have only been able to stand her for a few short moments of it. Where the hell did she come from? She can't be my sister; she's nothing like me.

Is she?

I don't even know anything about myself.

"Livvie? You okay?"

"Just go away." I start throwing things back into boxes. When she leaves, I can breathe again. When I started asking questions in the hospital—I only remember two out of eleven of them—no one had any clear answers. They evaded me; nothing made sense to me, and I recognized no one. They told me they're my parents and my sister, and I have nothing to prove otherwise.

No memories.

Nothing.

It takes a few hours to unpack the room. There's a lot of yellow in here. Do I like yellow? I gather the tags and take them downstairs to the trash bin in the kitchen. Mom dances with her earbuds in; she's putting dishes away like a symphony. She notices me and jumps, clutching her chest. "Olivia, you scared me. How long have you been standing there?"

"Just a minute."

"Is your head feeling okay? Any pain I should

know about?"

"No, I'm fine."

"Have you unpacked your room?"

"I just finished." The tags make a swooshing sound into the trash bin. "I just came down to throw the tags away."

Mom quickly smiles. "You can help Dad in the living room."

I can take a hint; she wants to be alone. I find Dad in the living room, and he's unpacking the television and surround sound.

"Where are all the pictures?"

He looks up and shrugs. "What do you mean?"

"Pictures...family pictures. Where are they?"

"Oh, they're in a box around here somewhere. Some of our boxes seem to be missing, actually...Hopefully, our pictures aren't one of them."

My eyes narrow. He knows I don't believe him.

"Have you unpacked your room?"

"Yes."

Dad nods and scratches his head. "You should find Caitlyn and help her. I'm sure she's taking her sweet time."

Again with the brush-off.

Brand new things.

No family pictures.

People I can't remember.

...I'm in trouble.

***

The water starts to cool down about an hour after

Jake leaves. The bubbles are nearly gone when someone comes through the front door, slamming things around. The towel I brought with me wraps around my body snugly, just enough for me to race back to my bedroom. I shut and lock the door before being seen. Whoever came inside has now broken a glass of some sort, and a wave of fear rushes over me.

If it were my parents, they wouldn't be making that much noise. Even though Caitlyn gets bratty most times, she wouldn't be breaking glass without so much as a girlie squeal. And Jake wouldn't be downstairs—he would be here with me if he had come back already, so my stomach drops when I go through the suspects and find nothing that would make sense.

Someone is in my house who shouldn't be here.

Panic sets in my bones, and I run deeper into my bedroom to towel dry so fast I think my skin is going to rub off. As I quickly dress, I notice my phone on the bed where Jake's body was lying only an hour or so before. Should I call him? I don't even know if there's someone really intruding in my house. It could be nothing at all. Now, someone stomps up the stairs with heavy boots and opens doors just to slam them seconds later, making no sign of stopping or slowing down their search of the house.

The doorknob of my bedroom moves, and I let out a small squeak. My phone shakes in my hand, and Jake's number is the last one to pop up.

"Hey, I'm almost done, okay?" He answers with such charm that it's hard to remember the terror that could be on the other side of my bedroom door waiting for me.

"S-S-Someone's in the house," I whisper, cupping my hand over my mouth to muffle the sound further. "I was in the bathtub, they came in breaking things downstairs, and now they're upstairs, outside my door. I don't think it's my parents or Caitlyn. Can you come back?"

Jake's breath hitches as I hear him start running. "I'll be there in five minutes." His voice is hard and angry. "Call the police and have them get to Olivia's house right *now*," he says to someone before shutting a car door and starting the engine. I hear the tires of his Mercedes burn out against the pavement. "Olivia?"

I say nothing and hang up the phone, hoping that all the noise I just made didn't trigger the intruder toward me. The doorknob moves again, and this time, I know they're trying to get into my bedroom.

Trying to get me.

"I know you're in there—I see your feet from underneath the door, little bird," a man says from the other side of the door. I look down at my bare feet, wiping the droplets of water from my eyes to see better. "Come out, come out, wherever you are." He laughs the most horrible, smoky laugh I've ever heard.

I really wish Jake would hurry as the man pounds hard once on the door, turns the knob, and opens the door...slowly. He broke the lock easily, like he knew exactly how to hit the wood to snap the latch. *He's done this before.* My eyes widen as I back away toward the wall.

The man steps inside and looks around the room, then his eyes glue on me. "You all alone in here, little bird?" His balding head turns just to make sure someone isn't waiting to pounce on him, like he's ready to pounce on me. "Well, well, looks like it's my lucky day. You *are* all alone in here."

"What do you want?" I yell. "I don't have anything of value in here."

His feet scrape across the floor; I smell the alcohol on his breath so strongly that it makes me sick to my stomach. "Oh, I beg to differ, honey. *You* are the highest value item in this whole place." He walks to me, and I can't move; I can't fight back. He takes a chunk of my hair and tugs on it; the sensation isn't welcoming. "Stand up, girl. I just want what I was promised, and you're going to help me get it."

"I highly advise that you let her go." Jake's eyes are bloodshot and dark as he looks at the stranger who has a tight grip on my head. "Let her go before I kill you."

The man laughs but knows that Jake can snap his neck with barely any effort by the looks of the two of them and their physiques. I wish that he would just push me toward Jake and run, but he pulls a knife from his pocket instead and puts it to my throat when he stands me upward against him. "I'll slice her fucking throat open if you take one step closer, kid."

Jake growls. He wants to move forward to save me but doesn't; he can tell that this man is telling the truth. "Give her to me and take what you want from here. We'll leave, and you'll never have to see us again."

The man laughs loudly. "I want my money. The girl's just insurance to get back what I was promised."

"W-What were you promised?" The knife presses into my throat. I look at Jake's sad eyes. He can't take his eyes off of the man long enough to share my fear until I whimper softly when the knife presses deeper into my thin flesh. He sees that I'm scared; he smiles at me and puts a little ease into my veins, like he's telling me to relax inside my mind.

The man scoffs and presses the knife so hard into my throat that I feel a trickle of blood dripping down my neck onto my t-shirt. Jake's body trembles with rage. "I was promised money was hidden in this house. I was also promised no one would be home."

I feel so dizzy that I'm going to pass out as he pushes the knife harder into my neck, and I can now feel the sting of an open gash. If he pushes any more...

Jake clicks his tongue against his teeth. "Looks like someone lied to you. You've got the wrong house. Who told you this information?"

The man says nothing but throws me on the bed with such force that I nearly bounce back up and into his arms again.

"It's your lucky day, after all," he snarls, holding the knife toward Jake. "Let me pass."

Jake snorts; the anger in his body radiates through the room. I want to close my eyes so I don't see the things he's going to do to him. I silently wish that he'll just let the man pass and wrap me in

113

his arms until my parents come home.

"It may be *her* lucky day, but it isn't *yours*." He lunges at the man. The knife gets lost in the scuffle; I can't see it anymore to even pick it up to help. I yell Jake's name loudly; he doesn't look over as he pins the man on the floor, repeatedly punching his face even when the blood stains his hands and the man becomes unresponsive.

"Jake, *stop*!" I run over to him, restraining his arm from bringing down another blow. "You're going to kill him. Please stop."

The look of horror in his face when he sees the fear I have for him is heartbreaking. "I should kill him for what he's done to you." He looks back down at the man. I take his head into my hands and hold him to my chest so he can hear my heartbeat. The blood that trickles down my neck onto my t-shirt makes him bite his bottom lip until it turns white.

"Jake, please," I beg. "Let him go."

Finally, Jake does what I ask. The man is bleeding on my carpet with his eyes closed, but I see his torso moving up and down from shallow breathing. Jake stands up and wipes his forehead with the sleeve of his shirt, ashamed to look at me.

"I would've killed him if you hadn't stopped me. He was hurting you." A tear falls from his eye. "He shouldn't have touched you like that." I don't say anything as I cradle my phone in my shaking hands.

"Are you afraid of me?" he whispers.

"No." I try to find a smile stashed somewhere inside of all of the chaos. "You saved me—*again*."

Jake's lips curve into a smile as the man stirs at

his feet. Before either of us realize what's happening, the silver flash of the knife digs into Jake's side. He looks at me with sadness as I scream his name and he falls to his knees. The man runs from the room, and I hear yelling at the end of the stairs as someone tells him to get on his knees and put his hands over his head.

"Up here!" I yell so loudly the room shakes. "Someone help us! We're up here!"

A few men in uniform come running into the room and call for an ambulance, allowing me to put Jake's head in my lap and stroke his hair. He smiles up at me like nothing is happening around us and we're alone.

"You just got stabbed and you're *smiling*?" I shake my head through the stinging tears in my eyes.

He laughs then coughs, careful not to move too much as the movement agitates the knife still embedded in his abdomen.

The paramedics come into the room, followed by my parents, who look so horrified when they see the blood on my carpet I think they might faint.

"Livvie, what happened? Why is there a man in handcuffs downstairs?" my mother screeches and then runs for me, pulling me into a bear hug. "And why is there blood all over your floor?"

My dad pats Jake on the shoulder once they get him on a gurney. "Hang in there." He looks at the paramedics and keeps his hand on Jake's shoulder. "Will he be okay?" One of the medics speaks with him about Jake needing small stitches as my head starts to split in two with searing pain again.

The police question us after Jake gets his stitches and refuses a trip to the hospital. We both had the same story, and my parents and Caitlyn heard every word of it. When all the first responders have gone, Mom shuts the front door, and her eyes fall on Dad.

"Who would tell a junkie that we had money stashed here?"

Dad sighs and rubs the bridge of his nose. "I don't know. Maybe it's a prank?"

Caitlyn snorts. "That's a messed-up prank."

Jake chimes in. "Maybe they just had the wrong house. You guys just moved here a year ago, right? Maybe they thought someone else lived here."

When Jake's eyes meet my father's, they nod slightly at each other and then quickly look away in case anyone sees them and whatever message they're sharing in their minds.

They *know* each other.

They're both holding a secret.

A secret that I intend to find out.

Chapter Thirteen

Smack

For three days, Jake has been in my bed. His large body snuggles underneath my pale-yellow comforter; his long legs almost hang over the end when he relaxes.

The first two nights were peaceful. His light snoring was a welcoming sound to me when I crawled into the armchair to pretend to read. For the first time in what seems like forever, I don't have to worry about his obsessive pull over me. Or even how sometimes he makes me feel like I'm the only person in the room—*naked and exposed*.

"I still don't see why your boss won't give you any more time off," Jake pouts. "I mean, someone close to you was *stabbed*, and you need to be here for me, right?"

I hold my breath. I thought he was going to say something leading in a different direction, but Jake's feelings for me aren't so obvious anymore. Before zipping up my sweatshirt, I shake my head

117

and smile. I remember to grab a band to tie my hair up before I leave. "I told you, Rosemary isn't exactly the warm-and-fuzzy type. She only let me take the first two days because my mom talked to her."

"The woman runs a YMCA, for Christ's sake," he scoffs. "Isn't a major job requirement to *be* warm and fuzzy?"

I have to admit, being Jake's friend is easy— much easier than I thought it would be. He's actually funny when he tries to be. He's also someone that doesn't like talking during movies…I had to find that one out the hard way.

"Look, Jake…" I sigh and zip up my bag, throwing it over my shoulder in hopes that he'll take me seriously. "My mom and Caitlyn are here to tend to your every need. Just make sure you text my mom first if you don't want Caitlyn in bed with you by the time your painkillers kick in."

"As if I needed *that* reminder."

I feel a little guilty that I'm racing off to work when he's still pinned to bed; I've been shut up inside for days, and I need to be alone to Google Jake's name. "Okay, I'll tell you what: tonight we can watch whatever movie you want."

"Whatever I want?" His interest is piqued, and I instantly regret what I've just said. "Okay, fine, when do you get off work?"

"Six. I work an early shift today with Brant." The glare returns, but I smile and wave anyway, rushing out of the room before I'm forced to have the conversation that's brewing in his mind.

He thinks I won't come back.

The air is getting colder the closer to October it gets. I welcome the crisp flicks of icy air against my skin. I think about how off-track I've gotten—I was supposed to be researching Jake's name and looking for the truth about my memories. Of course, Jake getting stabbed set me off a little; I make a mental note to start researching at work the moment I get there.

When I slam the car door behind me in the YMCA parking lot, Brant smiles and waves at me from the entrance doors and hurries me inside, out of the cold.

"Well, I don't think too many people are gonna wanna swim today, do you?" He snickers at his own joke. "I'll change into my suit anyway."

"I don't need to see your abs, Brant." I let him take my jacket for me. "Why don't you just close the pool and work out?" He hangs the jacket neatly on the rack near my desk and frowns.

"There's more to me than just working out, Liv." His voice is sad and weak. "Is that all you think I'm good for? Someone nice to look at with no brains?"

"Whoa, where is this coming from?" I hold up my hands in defense.

A mischievous smile creeps across his face. "I'm only kidding, Liv. You should've seen your face, though. It was pretty good." I groan and sit in my chair, ignoring him until he finally takes the hint and walks away. I'm not sure if he went to open the pool or not, and I hardly care. On a usual Wednesday, the building is a ghost town. I open the doors and let in the first few early morning studs so they can cram in their workout before going to their day jobs.

I spend half an hour searching Jake's name and sifting through pictures of his brothers and his mother. I even see a few of him at various events, but not nearly the same as his family. I don't learn much about him other than exactly what Caitlyn told me before.

I guess she was right about the simple internet search.

After I finish watering the plants in the reception area, the bell for the front door rings.

"Well, hey there, *gorgeous*. Have I told you that you're the sexiest of the White daughters? Not that it's enough for me, but—" Sam's slimy voice oozes, and I feel the stings of ice in my veins as he gets closer. "—you know, you're not good enough for me anymore now that you're fucking that no-name riff raff. You're tainted goods now, baby."

Smack.

It isn't that sentence that makes me turn around and slap him across the face—it's my newfound courage. Something I didn't have when my attacker lunged at me. Once my hand follows through with my heart, the sting on my palm is probably nothing compared to the red mark across his formerly smug face. Sam stands in front of me, stunned and gradually getting angry.

"Don't you *ever* touch me again," he snaps, getting close to my face. "Or someone kidnapping you will be the *least* of your worries."

"What did you say?"

His laugh is dark and scary. "I'd watch out if I were you, *Olivia White*. You never know what's behind the next corner for you." Before I can ask him what he means, he's escaping toward the weight rooms, out of eyesight.

Hours pass before I think about Sam again; I figure he must have slipped out the back door because I didn't see him walk past me again. Then Brant saunters toward the front desk with a pizza in his hands.

"Pepperoni and extra cheese from Sal's...you *know* you want some." He winks and opens the box in front of me on the counter. The steam tickles my nose. "I'll only share with you if you forgive me for earlier."

I lick my lips. "Okay, I forgive you." I snag a slice from the box. The warm, gooey goodness melts in my mouth as Brant and I eat in silence. I watch him pull two bottles of water from the mini-fridge in the lobby, and he hands me one.

"I know sometimes I can come on a little strong with people," he says after gulping half of the bottle. "I just didn't grow up with a lot of positivity around me, and I overcompensate by just being...*extra*." I don't know anything about his past, only that he recently graduated and moved from the Midwest somewhere the day after he walked across the stage.

"It's fine. You just need to learn how to be aware of other people's emotions." I smile because he really is just a sad, lonely kid. "I like being your friend, Brant. You're a good person, you have morals and values, and you're pretty funny sometimes."

"I am?" His eyes glow like Christmas lights.

I meet his eyes and give him a look to calm down. "*Sometimes*. Just be yourself, the best version of yourself that you want to be. Don't be someone just because another person thinks you should be different, okay?"

"Whoa, Liv." His voice is a little weak. "That's pretty deep."

I take a small, white piece of paper from my desk and hold it in the air for Brant to see. "Fortune cookie, about six months old." The both of us start laughing hysterically, and I have to close the pizza box so we don't snort all over the rest of the food. I feel the desk vibrating, and Brant points toward the computer, where my phone is ringing.

"Your boyfriend is calling you." He stifles his laughter. "I'll let you get that. Do you want a soda?"

I shake my head and pick up the buzzing phone. "No thanks. I'll say goodbye before my shift is over." I wave him off and hit the answer button on the screen. "I haven't even been gone for five hours and you're already calling me. What happened?"

Jake's deep voice is sleepy, and his words are slurring, like he'd taken a painkiller and it's already starting to take effect. He chuckles, and I hear his body shuffling around in my bed.

"Is it so hard to believe that I miss you already? Can you come back now?" His yawn is loud.

"You know I can't come home. I get off work in three hours…can you wait for me?"

His deep laugh tickles my insides, and I blush, looking around to make sure no one's watching me lose my cool. "You know I'll always wait for you, Bug."

"Okay, get some sleep."

"I'm serious. Why don't you take me seriously?" I wonder if I should hang up and let him fall asleep, hoping that he won't remember anything when I get back home. I know that's a long shot, so I bite my bottom lip, listening to his plea for me. "I just wish that sometimes you remembered, you know?"

I suck in air, nearly choking. "Remember what?"

"Nothing. I should sleep now," he quickly says before clearing his throat. "I'll see you later, okay? Be careful on your way home." He hangs up without saying goodbye or anything else remotely close to making me feel better about the elusiveness he just displayed. I always feel like Jake knows something I don't, like he knows my life better than I do, and that's scary, not to mention impossible.

Still, I can't shake what he said for the rest of my shift. The clock slowly ticks the time away because it knows I'm itching to get back to Jake. I decide that I'm going to straightforwardly ask him what he meant by that, even though I know in my heart of hearts that he's going to evade the question and act like he doesn't remember.

I just wish that sometimes you remembered.

I wave goodbye to Brant; he stays behind to talk to some of his friends, and the cold air rushes through my bones the moment I step outside. The parking lot is still fairly empty; the after-work crowd hasn't shown up yet. As I shuffle my feet toward where I parked the car and search my bag for the keys, I don't see him until it's too late.

"I bet you think you're smart, don't you?" His growl meets me before I see him. "You're going to pay for humiliating me in there, Liv." Sam's eyes are dark and cold—no one's around for me to yell for help. The anger in his eyes alerts me that I'll need some. He steps closer, and a wicked smile paints his strained lips. "You don't have anyone to save you now—where's your boyfriend when you need him? He's saved you once from a bad guy, but can he save you twice?" Sam licks his lips, and I want to gag, but I keep my distance.

"What do you want from me, Sam?" I whisper. Fear warps my voice as it leaves my body and circles around him.

He laughs, and it makes me feel gross. "You know what I want from you."

"You can go to hell if you think you're getting *that* from *me*." I grit my teeth and plant my feet on the ground firmly. If he thinks that I'm going to let him attack me without a fight, he clearly doesn't know me like he thinks he does. A stranger in my home is one thing, but for Sam—someone I know and have despised since the day I met—defending myself isn't going to be the issue here. "You better let me pass, Sam. Let me get into the car and I won't tell anyone that you're threatening me."

He laughs loudly, his eyes darting around the parking lot as if he's seen movement. "You have quite an imagination, Liv. Come here or you won't like what happens to you if I have to chase you."

"What's going to happen to her?" Brant says, placing his hand in mine from behind. I want to cry; my entire body is shaking so badly that I'm finding it hard to stand and support my weight. "You know, I've seen you harassing her for weeks here, and it stops now. I've already called the cops, so I guess you have two choices: either you can get into your car and leave her the hell alone, or you can go to jail when I hand over the security videos of each altercation you two have had at her place of employment. My advice? I would run."

Sam snorts and lunges toward me, trying to push Brant away. They get their arms tangled, and Brant pins him onto the ground with a few quick wrestling moves. Once the police cars zoom into the parking lot, Brant and I talk to them, and they take Sam into custody. He volunteers to take me home, and I realize that once again, I let someone save me.

"Thanks for taking me home, Brant." My voice is weak. "Jake isn't going to like what happened. Maybe we should just keep it a secret for now."

"Is he your boyfriend?" Brant's voice thickens. "I mean, seriously, is he?"

I shake my head, but he doesn't look over at me. "No, he's not."

"Then why do you care what he thinks?"

I don't answer him, and I think about what I could say without lying to myself the next time someone asks me this question. I can't explain it to anyone without looking completely insane, but Jake and I just...*belong*.

"I think you should tell him. Don't keep secrets," he says as we pull into the driveway of my parents' house and the curtains in my bedroom sway with force. "Plus, he'll wonder where your car is and why I'm dropping you off."

"Yeah, I didn't think of that."

"Hey, can I tell you something?" he asks before I

can open the door and escape. He doesn't wait for me to answer. "I just think you should know, you're a great person too. I mean, you deserve the best, and I just want you to make good choices for yourself, you know?"

I chuckle. "Fortune cookie?"

He sadly shakes his head. "No, I just don't want you to forget yourself in the process of trying to find someone else."

I hear Brant's words ring through my head as I watch him drive away.

I can't forget myself if I don't know who I am.

No matter how fun it is to pretend for a little while.

Chapter Fourteen

What if...

I hear Jake's rapid breathing as I step into the bedroom; he pretends to be asleep, but I heard his feet shuffling around the room on my way up the stairs. After a few minutes, he stretches and yawns, flashing a fake wake-up smile.

"That's a pretty amazing image to wake up to." The boyish charm he tucked into his pocket is making its way back. "How was work?"

Brant told me I shouldn't keep secrets, but I didn't agree to that. "Uneventful...pretty boring, actually."

Jake isn't buying it. "Then why did that kid drop you off? Where's your car?" His voice strains as I curse Brant under my breath for being right about how Jake would react. "Did your car break down? I knew I should've offered you to drive mine."

I hold my hands up to stop him. "Calm down. Nothing happened."

"*Something* happened," he growls, and his intense eyes lock with mine. "You can't lie to me. I

127

know when you're lying."

"How?" I sigh and sit down next to him on the bed. "Fine, but before I do, you have to promise me two things. First, that you won't get angry." His eyebrows raise, and I quickly continue. "Second, after we talk about it, we move on and go back to finding out the truth about me."

The wheels turn inside his head while he listens to my demands. The angst that he has toward me is like being burned by a match. When he slowly closes his eyes and holds them shut for a few moments, I know he's silently agreeing with my stipulations.

"Okay, remember Sam? He sort of…attacked me at work today."

The fire in Jake's eyes drills into my soul. "Tell me you aren't serious."

"He came in this morning and started shooting off his mouth. I lost my cool and slapped him across the face. He was waiting for me after I left work and tried to attack me, but Brant sort of showed up and saved me. I wasn't in a safe state to drive, so he brought me home in his car."

The redness of Jake's face extends to his neck, and his eyeballs become bloodshot the moment when he gets a really good idea about what I'm saying. I half-expect him to blow up with rage, but his hand finds mine instead and squeezes it. His eyes are misty as he tries to hide his gaze from me.

"Are you okay?" I ask, but he doesn't make eye contact with me as I lift my gaze to find his. "Jake?"

"Are *you* okay?" The raspiness in his voice makes me squirm a little as he holds my hand tightly in his. I find myself falling into wonder inside my mind. I wonder what he's like when he's alone...I wonder what he likes to do with his free time, and I'm still wondering why he wasn't sleeping before he started staying here.

Before I know it, his full lips find mine, and he presses them together. It takes a few moments before I latch onto his mouth and deepen the kiss he's started. I should be thinking about the effect this kiss will have on his feelings for me instead of how soft and exciting his lips are against mine. Even his tongue tastes like cinnamon as it ribbons around mine like a symphony, and his hands travel along my jawline and on the small of my back where they rest like they're home.

Like he knows the road map of my skin.

I let Jake kiss me because it feels good to have someone want you—even if you indulge in their emotions a little too deeply. It isn't like I find him unappealing; in fact, it's quite the opposite. I've been fantasizing about him since the moment I met him, and to say that the dreams are wild would be a *serious* understatement.

I slide my hands up his long torso, over his hard chest, and rest my nails softly in the hot skin of his thick neck when his body completely freezes and he pulls his lips from mine in frustration.

"I can't." He lowers his head. "I'm sorry." The lump in my throat swells when he looks back into my eyes. I literally feel his pain through his chest.

"Jake," I breathe his name, and my fingers find his face. "I thought you wanted this?"

"You have no idea how badly I fucking want

this." He feels his lips with his fingers; they hover over the same spots where I sucked his lips into mine. "I just don't want you to lose focus on your quest to find the truth. I know how much it means to you."

From the moment our lips touched, I felt something shift inside of me, and it grows larger and larger like a bubble in my stomach.

"I won't." I blink a few times and think hard. "How is it that you know me so well?"

Jake sighs and brushes hair out of my eyes. "What if I told you that I've known you for most of your life?" The words that he paints in front of my eyes captivate me enough to follow along with his illusion. "What if I told you this isn't the first time we've kissed or held hands…would you believe it?"

"I've dreamed about you."

His eyebrows rise. "Like a memory dream?"

"It was right after you told me about the tree tattoo, on the beach. I dreamed about a conversation we had about the tree after we…"

Jake's eyes flash with curiosity. "After we…what? Had sex?"

"Something like that. I know it's from talking about it before I fell asleep. That memory wasn't mine…that memory wasn't real."

The frustration leaks from Jake's skin and wraps me inside of it. It's suffocating me as steam rises from his ears. "What if it *was* real? Why are you so adamant that your other dream memories are yours but not this one?" His voice booms through the bedroom as his breath hitches. "Why isn't being who you are now enough?"

"Because I don't *feel* like myself!" I scream at him, and my eyes widen. "I haven't felt like myself in a long time…I don't expect you to understand." I lower my voice and fold my hands in my lap. I want the fight to be over with. "It's like I'm a stranger in my own skin, with shattered memories of someone else's life."

The air between us is tense now. He raises his hand and places it on my shoulder in comfort. "I think you need to rest," he says in his deep voice, laying my body down next to his without any protest from me. "You need to talk to your parents," he breathes into my hair. "Make a list of everything you want to know and ask them."

I let myself get lost in his warmth as sleep finds me and carries me off somewhere far, far away where no one else can hurt me.

***

"Happy Birthday, Lacey." Dad's gray eyes flicker from the dancing flame of the solitary candle shoved into the chocolate cupcake in front of him. "How does it feel to be fifteen?"

"The same as fourteen, I guess. I still can't drive or do anything sixteen-year-olds can do."

Dad laughs and pats my leg. "Don't wish your life away, sweetheart." The accent Dad carries with him has lessened since we moved to Seattle, but it's still there. It's British—just like Miss Claudine's—but I've never asked him where he's from, and he's never given me any indication he wants me to know. Our relationship is strictly on a need-to-know basis, and he's been pretty hands off the last few years.

Since Mom disappeared.

I think that maybe he's starting to hate me like she did, too.

"I'm headed out for a business dinner." He notices my eyes when I look at the clock on the wall that reads nine p.m. "Can you take care of yourself and not open the door for any strangers?"

"I'm fifteen, Dad."

He rummages through his wallet and slaps a few hundreds on the counter. "I might be gone a few days, so make sure you get to school on time and don't step out of line. I'll have someone drop in and check on you. If you need more, use your credit cards."

"Where are you going? I thought it was a business dinner?"

I hate when he does this. Every time he walks out the door like this, it makes me afraid that he'll never come back.

"It's a business dinner in Boston, honey. I'll be back in a few days."

He smiles, and then he's gone.

I'm alone in this big house again.

A loud knock at the door scares me out of my skin. Just after Dad told me not to open the door to strangers, then a stranger comes to the door. I grab my phone and, despite my heart nearly beating from my chest, walk to the front door.

Looking through the side window first, my heart jumps.

"What are you doing here?" I open the door and see his face. He hasn't spoken to me since I tried to

bring him home, but I made sure he knew I was still thinking about him—even if he wasn't thinking about me.

Jake looks like he's been crying; his eyes are swollen and red. "I'm sorry."

"For...?"

His long arms stretch across the open doorframe. "I'm sorry for being a jerk. I'm sorry for being someone you couldn't count on. I promised I'd always be here for you, and I haven't been, Lacey." He steps into the door, and the same feelings he's given me all these years come rushing back tenfold. "It's you."

I back away. "What's me?"

"You're my soulmate. You're the one for me."

I reach out and feel Jake's forehead. "Are you feeling okay?"

Jake takes my hand and pulls me close to him. The heat radiating from his skin wraps around me; his left hand slides around my waist while his right hand caresses the side of my cheek. My stomach is doing summersaults as Jake eases his lips down to mine and presses them together.

This is everything I've ever wanted.

He presses his forehead against mine. "You are everything to me, and I'm sorry it took so long to see it. I'm sorry for who I've been this past year, and I'm sorry I haven't been the person you need me to be."

"Jake, there's no way my dad will let me be with you."

He scoffs. "We don't need his permission."

"I'm only fifteen—we do need his permission."

"It's not like he's ever here. I just saw him come back and leave you alone again." He kisses me again, and it sends electric sparks down my spine. "You shouldn't have to be alone."

"I'm used to it."

"That's the problem." He brushes hair from my face. With his left hand, he pulls my right hand to his chest and presses it against his heart. "Can you feel that?"

"Your heartbeat?"

He nods. "You've made me see that I don't have to be that fucked-up person anymore, Bug. You're my best friend and the only person that truly matters to me. I'll wait for you, if that's what it takes. I know we're young, but..."

He tips my chin up to look deep into my eyes.

"I'm in love with you, Lacey Bug. I always have been...and I always will be."

Chapter Fifteen

Secrets

Jake

Fuck!

Where the fuck is she?

She told me she'd go home with him and then sneak out so we could run away like I've been trying to get her to do for two years. This time it's different; this time he wants her to change her name and identity so she can break ties with the fucked-up shit he's done and live a better life. He expects her to go live with a sister she's never met, her husband, and their daughter—all of whom she's never...fucking...met.

Not to mention he wants her to leave me.

I'm not letting that fucking happen.

"I love you, Jake Redding," she said to me before he pulled her out of my house. "When I come back, we'll run far, far away." She pressed her forehead against mine and forced back her tears.

"It's you, Jake. It's always been you."

That was hours ago.

My phone rings, but it's not her. "Noah, fuck off. I don't have time—"

"—Lacey's been in an accident. Your plan didn't work. They cut his brake lines, and she was still in the car, Jake."

I sit in an armchair in the living room before I collapse. "What the fuck are you talking about? She was supposed to call them after he left! They weren't supposed to cut his fucking brake lines!"

"I don't know what happened—maybe they changed their minds. She's hurt pretty bad...you better get to Seattle Grace."

Noah knows everything about everyone. If something happens in this city, he's the first person to go to for any details, so I know he's not lying. I hang up on him and grab my motorcycle helmet, shove it on my head, and squeal the tires of the Harley out of the garage.

All I can fucking think about is her.

I wasn't on board with her plan, but she'd had enough of her father trying to control her.

And I fucking love her. I'll do anything for her.

I hardly care about parking in an actual spot when I get to the hospital; the emergency room is full of people bleeding, peeing, and throwing up everywhere. The overweight nurse behind the check-in counter ignores me when I rush up and knock on the counter three times.

"I'm here to see Lacey Cervase."

She rolls her eyes. "Are you family?"

"Yes."

The woman checks the book in front of her. "Name?"

"Jake Redding."

"You're not on the list."

Fuck this.

I look down at her book through the window and see Lacey's name in room ER12. Not giving a fuck who'll try to stop me, I reach in and push the button to open the ER doors and let myself in. The nurse screams from her box, but I'm already searching for Lacey's room.

ER12.

Two police officers are standing outside, guarding her door.

"My girlfriend is in there—I need to see her." I start to open the door in between them.

"Only family allowed, kid." The officer on the left pushes my hand away. "And you're not."

"Lacey!" I start calling for her. "Lacey! Get the fuck off of me!"

The door opens, and a man comes out—a man I've never seen before. As the door slowly closes— and I see the love of my life wrapped in tubes and machines on a hospital bed—it never even occurs to me that it'll be the last time I see her.

***

There's nothing I'll be able to say to her when she finds out that I'm a fucking liar like everyone else in her life. For now, she's sleeps on my chest and dreams about a life that she thinks is better than what she's got now, but she doesn't remember the bad parts.

I make sure that I don't move my body so she won't wake up. This is the first time she's allowed me to get this close to her. It's been hell getting her to even trust me and not make the mistake of falling for someone else. She's mine, and no one else gets to know what her love feels like if I can help it.

Kissing her, though, that's something I've been *aching* for since the day I saw her on that lawn...for the first time in over a year. She was taken from me once, whisked off into the dark night without a single goodbye. They wouldn't let me see her in the hospital, and when I arrived home to an empty house, there was a note from Caitlyn, apologizing for deceiving me but saying it was for the best that they take the love of my life where she could live a better life...with people she didn't even know.

Even though I expected that Olivia wouldn't remember me, it still hurts to know she has no memories of me or the time we've shared. I don't know what else to do but make her fall in love with me all over again.

I wonder what she'll think of me when her memories do come back and she knows all the stupid shit I've done. It'll devastate her if she finds out the truth of how shit really happened.

I can't even be there for her like I need to be.

Like I *want* to be.

There used to be a time when she dreamed about vacations and college...getting the perfect gifts at Christmas for the people she loved. She loved herself, too. Now she's a shell of that person, and I don't know how to help her.

But I know that I want her back so badly that it's getting too hard to keep the secret I have been sworn to keep. I think about Sam and how much pain he'll be in once I call one of my brothers to take care of him. She doesn't need to know about that. I think about Tyler, Noah, and Michael, my brothers who all love Olivia too. Once they knew they had to keep this secret, the three of them couldn't handle it and scattered around the country like cockroaches and hid from her.

But I stayed.

I stayed because I love her.

Because I'm in love with her.

I've always belonged to her.

My phone lights up on the table beside me, and I manage to stretch my body to reach it, unplugging it from the charger and seeing Noah's name flash across the screen. All three of my brothers have been trying to reach me since I told my mother she couldn't have my money, no doubt in hopes that they can change my mind and talk me into it. I hesitate to even answer it, afraid of waking her, but as she opens her mouth and snores softly, I smile and hit the button to greet him.

"Noah." I hear his loud sigh. "If you're calling me to talk about money, save your breath."

"Hello to you, too," he says, out of breath. "I'm not calling about money, brother."

"That's good to hear." Olivia shifts her weight next to me; her eyelashes touch her cheek as she drifts back into her dream. She's always been amazingly beautiful. "Then why are you calling?"

For a few moments—*a short few moments*—I

139

ease my mind into thinking that my brothers aren't on my mother's side and it isn't four against one. "I just wanted to check on you. I heard a rumor that you've found Lacey."

I look down at her and smile. "It's not a rumor if it's true. Her name is Olivia now."

"Jake, you know that's dangerous, right?" he warns me. "How many times do I have to tell you it's a lost cause with her?"

"As many times as it takes." I tighten my grip around her body. "I'm not going to give up on her, Noah. Don't act like you want me to fucking leave her behind."

I hear him suck in air through his teeth. "You're not giving up on her if you move on, Jake. She doesn't remember you."

"Her memories are starting to come back, Noah."

"How?"

I hesitate; I don't like telling anyone more information than they need to know. "They come back to her as dreams. She knows something isn't right. She's not stupid."

Noah sighs. "You can't hold onto her forever—" I only listen to the beginning of his warning before I hang up on him.

He's wrong.

I *can* hold onto her forever.

And I *will* hold onto her forever.

Chapter Sixteen

Burning daylight

Olivia

Jake snoozes next to me, unaware that I've woken up in a panic.

He's the boy across the street.

Why hasn't Jake told me any of this?

It's not a coincidence that Jake found me...

He's been *looking* for me all this time.

I do my best not to wake him as my body eases out from his grip. I catch a glimpse of myself in the mirror before I leave the room. I've always felt like a stranger in my own body, and now that I've had that dream—amongst all the other crazy things that have happened lately—I *know* I am a stranger in my own body.

Lacey Bug.

My brain whirls as I take each step downstairs one by one, hoping that maybe they'll melt away and underneath it all will be my true life without

141

any doubts. The crazy part is…I *look* like my family. I look like my mother; Caitlyn and I have the same bone structure and body type, but my dad…I don't look like him at all.

"Hey, Livvie," Mom greets me as I enter the living room. She's sitting on the sofa reading a magazine, so I sit across from her and stare. She notices the ghoulish look on my face and frowns. "Are you okay? What did Jake do?"

My frown deepens. "Why does everyone automatically blame Jake?"

"For reasons you don't understand." She matches my annoyance. "You don't know him—"

I stand up and ball my fists at my sides. "That's what people keep telling me, but guess what? I *do* know him. I know that everything he says about loving me is true."

"Oh, Olivia, you're being swayed by puppy love—"

"*Stop it*! I know Jake and I were together before the accident! I know he lived across the street from me and my *real* family!"

She puts the magazine down on the table in front of her; as she sips her coffee, her eyes darken when they meet mine. "Just because you dreamed something doesn't mean that's how it really was. I'd appreciate it if you'd stop accusing all of us for holding you hostage in a life you don't want."

"I just want the lies to stop. I want to know who I am."

"You're Olivia White!" Her voice rises. "Anyone else is dead and gone."

"So you admit it? You admit to lying to me all

this time? Who the fuck am I? Who are you people? Jake knows you, so you must be someone he trusts, so why don't you trust him?"

"Excuse me." A tear falls down her cheek, and she gracefully leaves the room. I wait for someone to run in and scold me, but the only person that comes to find me is Jake.

He looks sleepy, his eyelids still drooping from lack of sound sleep, but he smiles at me anyway. "I felt you leave the bed...you okay?" He sits next to me and relaxes into my space. His long, heavy arm slides across my shoulder blades, and he pulls me into his chest. I wasn't lying to Mom; Jake's love for me *is* real. I feel it wrap around me like feathers every second of every day. I've never felt a love like this before, and it's annoying that my family is trying to take it away again.

"I remember you, Jake." His eyes widen. "I know who you are to me. You were in my dreams last night, and I remember."

"You remember what, exactly?"

My lips find his, and he welcomes me by squeezing my body against him. His arms wrap around my waist, and even if I wanted to, there's no escaping the long-awaited release Jake needs from me right now. His nose nuzzles in my mess of hair; I feel him smile against my ear. "This is fucking amazing. Are you sure you remember?"

Our eyes lock together. "Not everything, but enough. Jake..." My thumb caresses his jawline. "I know I'm not Olivia White. I want to know everything...and I want to know it now."

He wastes no time. "I'll tell you everything,

baby. *Everything*. I can't fucking believe this is happening right now." Tears roll down his cheeks, and he pulls me into him again. "Come with me; come home with me to Seattle."

"For how long?"

"Just a few days. When do you work again?"

"Saturday."

Jake sniffles and wipes the tears off his cheeks. "That's three days. We'll have plenty of alone time for me to explain everything. I have pictures, videos, and letters at my house in Seattle. Please come with me, Olivia."

"Isn't it an eight-hour drive from here? What about your hotel room?"

He lifts my body with ease and tugs me up with him. "If we leave now, we'll make it there by nightfall. I've already checked out of the hotel, and my things are in the car."

Jake leads me back upstairs so we can dress and get warm clothes on to venture out in the chill of the early October air. I dress myself, but I feel like an emotionless robot—there's nothing in this entire house that is familiar to me right now. So many questions are swirling around my mind; it's hard to catch one and keep it long enough to remember what I want to know.

The smile on his face says it all: *Jake is happy*.

No one comes into the room to stop us, but Caitlyn does meet us at the bottom of the stairs once we're dressed and ready to leave.

"Don't go." Her big olive-green eyes burn into mine. "Liv, don't go."

I snap my arm back from her grasp. "I told you

I'd find out the truth."

"I'll tell you everything. Just don't go with Jake."

"I'm going, Caitlyn." I shake my head, disappointment dripping from my skin. "Of all people, I expected at least you to tell me the truth."

"I told you what I was allowed to tell you!" Her small hand wraps around my wrist. "Jake surely isn't telling you everything. Please, can you just stay and let me explain the real story?"

Jake slides into our space, his eyes dark and scary. "Ready?" He looks at Caitlyn and frowns. "Do you have something to say to me?" She backs off a little and hangs her head. The bleached strands of her hair pale her nearly translucent skin even more. I've never seen her like this; she's not normally one to back down from an argument…especially if she feels that she's right.

"Don't run away with her." Caitlyn's voice is flat and strained. "Don't take her where we can't find her."

"We're just going to my place for some peace and quiet." His assurance blankets me now, too. "I promise I won't take her from you."

They're talking about me like I'm not even here.

"Jake—" She starts to lift her gaze to meet his, but again she backs down.

He tugs on my arm, and I go with him, briefly looking back at her longing gaze where I stood seconds before. I always thought I annoyed her, but she actually cares about me. It takes a while to process this new feeling.

Even though we drive straight through to Seattle,

I drift off halfway into our trip and have the worst dream I've had yet thanks to the impending headache starting to rattle my brain.

***

"I'm not going with you." Dad's face reddens as I stand my ground. "I don't care what you've done or what you've pulled Jake into. I'm not going. I shouldn't have to pay for your mistakes."

Dad's eyes are sad and dull. "You're right, you shouldn't have to pay for my mistakes. Unfortunately, you do*, Lacey. You're not safe here—not with me in prison."*

"I'll empty my trust fund and pay them off to leave me alone."

The woman trying to take me with Dad clears her throat. She looks like me and Dad; she shares the same gray eyes we both have. "Who the fuck are you?" I snap at her.

"My name is Carrie Stevenson. I'm your sister."

"I don't have a sister." I look at Dad, shaking my head. "This is what you've come up with to get me to leave with you? Paying someone to be my fake sister?"

"She's my daughter, just the same as you."

Jake struggles in the corner; he's being held back by two large men who look like professional bodyguards. "Don't fucking listen to them, Lacey! Don't let them take you!"

Dad sighs and pats my shoulder. "Honey, you're not safe here, not anymore. I promise that when you are safe, you can come straight back here...straight back to Jake."

I know *he's lying.*

"I'm not *stupid!" Spit flies from my lips. "I know you better than that. You want to control me. You want me to do what you want for* your *benefit. I'm not doing that anymore, Dad! I'm not a pawn in your little game...I'm not Mom!"*

Dad shakes his head. "Lacey, don't make me force you. The more time you spend here with Jake, the more danger he's in."

He's not playing fair.

My chest heaves up and down. "What do you mean?"

Jake grunts and struggles more in the men's arms. "Lacey, baby...please, don't listen to them."

"The people that are after me, they could be after Jake. The longer you stay here with him, the quicker they'll be able to find him."

"Jake wasn't part of this!"

Carrie crosses her arms over her chest. "It doesn't matter. He still worked for Michael. Lacey, please, we're trying to keep you safe. We're trying to keep everyone *safe."*

My eyes meet Jake's, and I know what he wants me to do.

He wants me to run.

"I want a minute alone with Jake, then I'll leave with you."

Dad, Carrie, and the two bodyguards look at each other, and Dad nods to each of them. "Three minutes. Say your goodbye and meet us outside."

Jake gravitates to me once everyone leaves the house. He frantically pushes my hair back from my face and kisses my cheeks where the tears have stained them.

"Don't fucking do this, Lacey. Don't get yourself into this. You run, okay? Run your fucking heart out. Call Noah. He'll find you."

I sob into his chest. "I can't leave you…I'm not leaving you. I'm going to stick to our escape plan."

He shushes me and strokes my head. "That plan is ages old. It won't work."

"I have to try." I press my lips against his like it's the last time I'll ever touch him again. "Meet me here in an hour; I'll be back for you. Then…we'll both run. Together."

***

When Jake wakes me, I see the sign for Seattle before the dizziness subsides and I'm able to force words from my mouth.

"Why would Caitlyn think you'd take me where no one could find me?"

His body tenses. "I don't know. She's crazy."

"Don't stop being the only person I trust."

A lightbulb ignites in his head. "I ran away with you once, a few years ago."

"What do you mean?"

He rubs the bridge of his nose; he's frustrated that I'm so persistent for information. "Your dad never wanted us to be together. So we ran away together and made it as far as Salem, and they found us."

"How could they have any say?" I bite the inside of my cheek.

He looks embarrassed. "You were only fifteen, and I was seventeen. They tried to charge me with some pretty fucked-up shit."

We pull into a long circle drive at the last house of the street we're on, and time stops.

I know this house.

It doesn't look cold and overbearing like the rest of the houses in the neighborhood; the three-story, red-brick structure invites me inside. My eyes scan each floor as if I can see into the windows, imagining what each room feels like to be in.

"Do you remember this place?" His voice is almost a whisper as he parks the car only a few feet from the red front door. I keep scanning the property; my head spins from how much I *think* I remember. "Come on." He sighs and unbuckles his seat belt. "We're burning daylight. I want to get the house warm enough to stay the night...I haven't slept here in months, so everything's turned off."

I let him untuck me from my seat once he walks around to my side and opens the door. It's crazy how much I know about everything and nothing at the same time. I smell cinnamon as he unlocks the front door, and I step into the huge foyer right behind him. His large hand finds mine and tugs me inside fully so he can close the door behind us.

To the left of the foyer is a large sitting room with white couches and a red-bricked fireplace; a golden-colored cage sits around the opening so the embers don't trail out when it's used. A fluffy white rug is spread out in front of it, and I imagine Jake and me lying in front of a roaring fire underneath several blankets. It makes me smile.

Through the sitting room, an archway takes you into the biggest kitchen I've ever seen. Dark oak cabinets line the wall behind the shiny, metallic stove, and the island in front of it matches the marble countertop perfectly. Everything looks so clean and untouched, like no one's lived here for a long time. Jake said he hasn't slept here in months...but it looks more like the house is brand new and was never touched at all.

My heart skips a few beats.

"Jake..."

He shakes his head. "Don't worry about it. I know you don't remember."

My eyes lower to the ground. "I *want* to remember." My gaze fixes on the window behind him. It leads to a lush, green backyard with a garden near the patio. I can't see the end of the property from inside the kitchen, but I can see the daylight fading fast along the tree line.

Jake's right. We're burning daylight.

"I just want answers. I want to feel free."

He takes my hand from behind. "You're free here."

"Every memory I have with you in it, you're the one person that always finds me in the darkness."

Jake smiles. "I've loved you from the moment I met you." He pinches my chin with his thumb and index finger. "There's nothing I won't do for you. Even bringing you back here so you can finally know the truth. I'm sorry I lied to you about who I was...I just didn't know how to help you."

Jake's right. He *did* lie to me, just like everyone else.

"I think it's a little different, maybe." My own voice surprises me. "Even though you had the same reason for lying—protecting me—you never acted like the dreams I had were crazy. You believed me and let me find my way."

He chuckles. "Even with so many unanswered questions and half-truths, you're still so optimistic about the outcome. Your light is one of the reasons I'm so fucking in love with you, Olivia."

Jake breathes my name, and I pull him with me as I gravitate to the fizzling sunlight in the backyard. The cool breeze tickles my skin, but I don't care. The door opens with such ease that it's hard not to want to drift into the fresh air. I feel like I'm walking into another world—and I would've believed it if his hand wasn't clutched tightly into mine, guiding me through my haze.

I breathe the October air deep into my lungs. "I'm ready to know it all now."

"Let's go inside; I'll tell you everything."

I reluctantly follow him back inside and into the living room so he can stall a little to figure out what to say to me. "I want to know it all. From the beginning. No more lies."

The war that wages in his head when he decides what to do makes me sad, but it's not enough to stop me from putting my foot down. He starts a fire in the fireplace, trying to stall long enough to start the story off right.

"Okay, I'm ready." His voice trails around his body as he faces away from me. "You have to promise me one thing, Olivia. Just one thing."

My body feels like lead. "What is it?"

When he turns to finally face me, tears stain his cheeks and his chestnut eyes are on fire. He takes his hands from his pockets and falls to his knees—he's weak, and I can tell this is going to be one hell of a story. He sniffs some of his sadness back into his body before forcing his eyes to meet mine again.

"You have to promise me that you won't leave me again when you find everything out."

"Jake—"

The growl that leaves his throat is alarming. "*Promise* me."

"I promise I won't run away screaming. Is that what you want to hear?"

He nods. "When you find out my part in this, you'll hate me."

"I won't hate you." My lips tense. "Why would I hate you?"

A long pause lingers between us, and neither of us dares to move closer.

"It's my fault you lost your memories."

Chapter Seventeen

Daddy issues

I know I'm glaring at him.

I feel the tension of the room suffocating me.

"I told some bad people where your father would be, and they fucked with the car, making it crash. You weren't wearing your seat belt, and Michael was…you smashed your head against the dashboard. I swear to God, Lacey…I mean, *Olivia*…I never knew you were in the car. I wouldn't have told them a damn thing if I knew you'd be there. When I found out what I'd done—"

I hold up my hand for him to stop. This is the first time he's slipped up and called me Lacey instead of Olivia. "Is that what our plan was?"

"Our plan…what? What do you mean?"

"Our plan, Jake. I dreamed about the last night we saw each other on the way up here. I know we had a plan. Was that the plan?"

Jake swallows and runs his hands down my arms. "The plan was for us to get the fuck out of here before any of this happened, baby. That was the plan. Nothing else matters beyond that." Inches from me now, his hand snakes around the side of my neck, and he smiles down at me. "You deserve to know the truth, and I want to be the one to give it to you. I know you inside and out, Olivia. I know the pain in your eyes, and I know the empty holes in your heart."

My eyes narrow. "I didn't realize I was so hopeless."

"Not hopeless." He smirks and runs his thumb along my bottom lip. "What do you want to know first? What haunts you the most? Let me guess. You want to know who your father is." Jake stands up and slowly moves to the sofa, where he plants me. "Michael Cervase was your father."

He finds my hand and squeezes it, keeping me grounded so I don't fly away. "I'm telling you the truth, Bug. Here." He pulls a few large photo books from the table next to him. "Look through these." He places the heavy books next to me and then the first one in my lap. I don't want to open it, but something inside of me is telling me that this is my only hope for knowing for sure.

I open the book.

The first picture makes me slam it right back closed.

"I-I d-d-don't want to do this," I stutter. "Jake, I d-d-don't want t-this."

"You don't have to do anything you don't want to do. Everything is up to you, understand?"

I take a deep breath and blow it out slowly before opening the book again. The first picture is the gray-haired man from my dreams, and he's sitting next to me at a fancy restaurant table. Our happy smiles don't look deceiving, but the pain in my eyes staring back at me makes me feel things deep inside my stomach. Picture after picture, it's the man and me with happy smiles and love in our hearts.

"This is crazy," I whisper and turn the next few pages.

"That's Michael; that's your dad."

I wet my lips. "I've never seen pictures of myself before the accident."

"What did they tell you about it when you asked?"

"They always told me boxes were lost in the move to Silver Lake, and all of our pictures were one of the lost ones."

The last half of the book are pictures of Jake and me doing romantic things together; we both look so happy that it hurts my teeth from it all being so sweet. He watches me closely as I get to the end of the book and close it, my mind straining so hard that it's giving me a headache. "These pictures are just confusing me more." I blink away a few tears.

The sofa that I've cuddled into is so comfortable that it makes me sleepy. Alongside the warm fire only a few feet from us, the entire day catches up with me. My eyes are droopy with sleep. I feel Jake's electric presence next to me, and I allow myself to be someone else—*somewhere else*—for the first time in a long time.

My fingers trace where his dark tattoos are over his sweater.

The dying tree.

The mockingbird.

I don't even care what my heart is screaming at me.

My mind wants to launch my body on top of his and latch on forever.

Examining his rough fingers as they tangle around mine, there's a tattoo on him I haven't seen before. I take his left hand and turn it over a few times in mine; he exhales slowly and kisses the tips of my fingers. "That's our promise to each other."

The infinity symbol in black ink wraps around his left ring finger.

As Jake thinks about the meaning behind this tattoo, he smiles, and his eyelashes touch his cheeks. "We were too young to get married—well, I was eighteen and you were still sixteen and too young—so I got this instead. You were against using a fake ID to get one, so you would draw it on your finger with a magic marker whenever it would fade. It was our promise to each other that nothing, not even infinity, would stop us from loving each other."

I frown at my naked left ring finger. "I'm sorry, I didn't know."

"I know you didn't, so don't feel bad. Maybe someday you won't have to draw it on, right?"

The warmth of the fire has won me over into exhaustion. "Hey, do you want to go to sleep?" His velvety smooth voice tickles my ears. "No one has slept in our bed since the day you…"

"Since the day I what?" My ears perk up a little, although sleep is still kicking me in the ass.

His arms are around me, pulling me into his chest while he stands up. "Since the day you left." There is so much sadness in his voice that it seeps into my heart as he sways with me in his arms. He treads up a large spiral staircase to the second floor in silence. We go through an enormous doorway, into a bedroom that looks like something straight from a designer catalog.

"Home sweet home." He gently puts me down on the soft, pale green comforter overlapping the king-size bed. "You still have some clothes here if you wanted to change."

This is so weird.

I feel like I belong here.

"That entire closet is yours, actually." His laugh thickens as my nerves go crazy. "I haven't touched anything since you left."

I breathe in deeply and walk toward the closet door Jake's talking about. I expect to open the door and see a few items left behind, but instead...it's a big enough walk-in closet to have a sofa sitting in the middle of the room. My lips turn into a frown as I scan the room and notice nothing that *looks* familiar to me. It's frustrating because I know these things belong to me; I feel it.

He notices my sadness, coming up behind me and wrapping his long, hard arms around my torso. "I don't need you to remember anything, Olivia. It's okay if you don't. I love you just the same."

A tear falls down my cheek. "How can you love someone I used to be? What if I'm not the same person?"

Jake twirls my body around and wraps me in a

bear hug; the hardness of his chest is welcoming, and his spicy cinnamon scent caresses my nose. "You're the same person, I promise. Just a different name." His lips quiver like they do when he's said too much. "You're kind and considerate, you love your family, and you're…" He looks down with a bashful smirk. "*Exciting.*"

I chuckle and place my palms on his chest; our gazes dance together long enough to make my insides melt. I see his full lips lower down to mine like it's in slow motion, and I let him press them together, sending waves of warm pleasure down my body.

"Wait," I murmur against his lips, "I want to talk about my father. Tell me more."

He doesn't act annoyed that I've broken our kiss; he's more excited that I haven't run away yet. He keeps one arm around me and leans to his left, opens the top drawer of a dark oak chest of drawers, and smiles. "You get changed and I'll tell you anything you want."

He kisses my forehead and leaves me to rifle through the closet. It's more of a room than a closet, and it makes me feel awkward just being in here; it's like I'm rummaging through someone else's things and Jake's cheating on her.

My stomach drops.

"Jake?" I call for him. "Can you come back in here?"

His copper blonde curls emerge into the room almost immediately; the look on his face is half-twisted in terror and excitement. "What's wrong?"

How can I say this?

158

"I, uh, well…" I feel the instant flush in my cheeks. "I just want to make sure you're not seeing anyone."

He snorts. "Besides you?"

I shrug. "I guess. You've never really mentioned it."

He sits on a bench across from the oak dresser and stares up at me with sadness shadowing his round eyes. "You're the only one I'll ever want for the rest of my life. Even if you would've never remembered me, I'd still be in love with you."

Ouch.

"Just checking." I blush. "But none of this stuff is going to make me any less awkward. It just feels right and wrong in here at the same time. Does that make sense?"

A wicked grin paints his lips. "You can wear my things if it makes you more comfortable."

I can't help but to match his smile. Being around Jake is just so *easy* that it's hard to believe it's reality sometimes. A man who's willing to do anything for me, even lay down his life, apparently; I find that completely sexy and unnerving at the same time.

He's imperfectly perfect.

"Bug?" His smooth, deep voice cuts through my brain. "Do you want me to leave while you change?" His large hand extends toward me, and in it is a white t-shirt and blue basketball shorts. "The shorts will be a bit big, but I'm sure you'll be fine. Besides, if you have to take them off during the night, I won't be upset about it." I take the clothes from him and don't bother answering his question, because we both know we're beyond the shyness stage of our relationship.

My body shakes.

Relationship.

"I want to know more about you, too." My voice is rough as I peel off my jeans and sweater. Jake's eyes burn into my flesh as he watches me untangle myself from each article of clothing and slip the white t-shirt over my head. I take down my long, chestnut hair and bite the inside of my lip. "Are you too tired to stay up and talk?"

"No," he growls instantly. "You need to put on those shorts."

The air around us settles, and the silence slips away. He leads me back into the bedroom where I make myself at home on the bed—and it's so comfortable that it'll be hard not to drift off to sleep. I have questions, and I need answers; I'm not about to let the only chance I may have slip through my fingers.

"Okay…" He's still larger than me as we both sit in the bed. "I'm not exactly sure how to make you believe that Michael Cervase was your father other than just telling you—*once again*—to trust me. I can show you all the pictures and videos in the world, but you need to feel it in your heart to believe."

My feet accidentally slide against his leg. "Maybe let's just start from the beginning." I take a deep breath and hold it inside for a few seconds longer than I should. "As far back as you can remember."

"When I was eleven, I met you for the very first

time. You were eight, maybe just turned nine, I don't really remember that part. It was my eleventh birthday party, and you'd just moved in across the street with your parents. You crashed my birthday party with your nanny, Miss Claudine."

There's a twinkle in his eyes when he talks about our past. It's calming to see the light return to his mind and the happiness return to his heart. He sits down so he can look into my eyes as he tells me a story of our life together. I don't know what depresses me more: having an intimidatingly gorgeous man sitting a foot away from me or knowing that he holds a special place for me in his heart that I'm scared to death I'll never quite fill like he wants me to. I let him continue on without interruption; I don't want anything standing in the way of hearing the story of a lifetime.

"And the other kids were taking over the place, acting crazy and destroying the party decorations. But not you. You sat in the garden by yourself; you didn't need chaos to feed your emotions, and it drew me to you. Of course, we became best friends, and my brothers all loved you, too. I know it seems textbook or whatever, but you gotta believe me, Olivia...we had the perfect life."

I sit on my knees and snuggle my body closer to his as he talks. "Then what happened?"

He chuckles. "Puberty happened. I started noticing girls more and stopped hanging out with you as much when I hit middle school. My mother had gone through her second divorce by the time I was fourteen, and your dad pulled you completely away from me after I started going dark. I hated everyone, especially my mother, and I wasn't in the mood to let anyone tell me what I could or couldn't do."

"Sounds like you *were* a bad boy, Jake."

"I guess that's what you'd call it." His blonde curls find the curve of his forehead as he looks down and blushes. "I started hanging out with really bad people, doing really bad things. I wasn't myself, and you desperately tried to help me find my way back, but I resented you for it somehow. You were the best thing in my life, and in my mind, I didn't deserve you so it made me hate you."

"That seems cruel."

He nods. "Now that I look back on it, it was. But when I turned seventeen, everything changed. You came over late at night on my birthday and handed me a note." He leans toward the nightstand and pulls out a folded-up piece of notebook paper from the drawer. His hands shake as he gives me the note; I don't waste any time tearing into it and reading each line several times over.

Jake,

Happy Birthday!

I know we haven't talked in a long time, but I just wanted you to know that I'm still here for you. There isn't anything bad you can do that will make me hate you. I'll always love the person you are, no matter who that person is.

I see you in there, Jake. I see your light.

Never forget that you're not alone.

162

I'll never leave you.
Love,
Lacey Bug

My eyebrows shake when I read the name carved at the end of the letter. I hand the note back to him, and he carefully folds it and places it back into the drawer before shutting it like it's a priceless artifact he's been sanctioned to keep safe from harm.

"That note changed my *life*, Olivia. It's like something shifted inside of me, and I knew that no matter where I go or what I do, you belong by my side. You're my one true love, and no matter how cheesy it seems, it's true."

I lower my eyes to my lap. "Then why didn't we have a happy ending?"

He grits his teeth. "Daddy issues."

"Daddy issues?"

He nods. "Your father hated me for the person I'd become. He didn't want me tainting his beautiful, perfect daughter any more than I already had. I tried so hard to show him that I'd changed by getting better grades and staying out of trouble. But he wouldn't let me see you."

I narrow my eyes at him. "Did you get this from *Romeo and Juliet*?"

He laughs, and my throat burns with fire. "I know it seems like it, but no. We started sneaking around again when you were eighteen. The more time we spent together, the deeper we fell in love. The more my love grew for you, the more I feared that your father was going to take you away from me. Then he surprised me by offering me a job in exchange for staying out of our way."

I smile and try so hard to remember what he's telling me that my head hurts. "That sounds promising. Did you take it?"

He nods. "I was good at it, but he had me shaking people down for money to invest in bogus businesses and such." Jake notices the glare in my eyes. "He stole people's money and left them penniless. I was totally blind to the whole thing."

"My mom always got a sour look on her face when someone asked about her family."

Jake doesn't look surprised. "He was never good to her, not one bit. You were always his favorite daughter out of the two."

"Out of the two?"

A smirk finds his lips. "Paula White is your *sister*, not your mother. Her real name is Carrie Stevenson."

The feeling of my jaw hanging way lower than normal doesn't bother me. I slowly shake my head and try to process everything Jake's been throwing at me.

My mother is actually my sister.

That dream I had really was true.

I guess it never dawned on me what that would mean for every other member of my family if what Jake's saying is true.

He finds my hand underneath the comforter and squeezes, sorrow dripping from his eyes. "You'll need to call her tomorrow morning so she won't worry."

My mother.

He means my *sister*.

A sister I'd never known who took me and tried to save me.

Chapter Eighteen

Three little words

The sunlight tickles my nose before it reaches my cheek. The best part of waking up next to Jake is the warm cocoon he places you in; it's like a safety net of complete tranquility and comfort. His cinnamon breath reaches my nose, and I inhale him into me as much as I can before he wakes up and my dream shatters back into reality.

Olivia White.

That's the girl I know now.

But I don't know how to be anyone else.

Jake's eyes don't open, but he reaches for me and pulls me into his bare chest. He tucks me under his strong chin and holds me against him; his heart beats so hard it feels like it's outside of his warm skin. I snuggle next to him the best I can and wait for what seems like hours.

***

Why can't I scream? The pain in my head feels like someone's drilling into my eye sockets with a power drill. The light hurts even worse, but the panic that sits in my chest as people come into view is what's making my heart weak.

"She's awake!" a girl with bleached hair says. She's around my age and dressed like she's just come home from clubbing. Her mini-skirt rides her thighs, and the crisscrossed, skin-tight navy blouse she's got on looks like a piece of cellophane around her torso. "Hey." She waves her long fingernails in front of my face. "Can you hear me?"

"Jessie, get out of her face!" Another woman in the room snaps her fingers. Deep down, I think that...maybe she looks familiar, but everything hurts too much to care. "What's going to happen to her?"

"Here," a man says, "take this envelope. Michael has secured new identities for each of you. You'll be living in Silver Lake, California. There's a decent-sized suburban home there that isn't in his name anymore. He gifted it to Miss Claudine's estate years ago, and her sister has agreed to let you live there as long as you need."

"Is she in danger?"

He shakes his head and hands a large yellow envelope to her as well. "That question remains unclear. We don't believe she's in danger now that Michael is in prison. We don't have any reason to believe whoever sabotaged the brakes wanted her dead."

The woman walks slowly to me and smiles down into my open eyes. "Then why are we moving her?

The whole point was because she was in danger, and now you're saying she's not."

"There are still people out there Michael has bankrupted and who could very well take matters into their own hands like this person did. You have to understand, this embezzlement runs very, very deep. He owes a lot of money to a lot of people."

A man comes up next to the woman and hugs her from behind. They look like nice people, the generic kind you find in a picture frame before you buy it. "What about money? We can't exactly have real jobs."

"Michael's made arrangements with Miss Claudine's estate, and you'll be taken care of. There's also Lacey's trust fund, but that's frozen until the Feds decide otherwise."

The bleached-haired girl sighs. "I think we should keep her."

"She's not a dog, Jess," the man scolds her.

"She's my sister. We have to help her. I tried helping, and look what happened. Maybe without Michael being the puppet behind me, I can do more good than harm to her. What's our background story?" She opens the envelope like she's done this before. "The White Family. I'm Paula White, you're David White…" She turns to the man and smiles. "…and you're Caitlyn White."

The girl groans. "Such a lame name."

"And Lacey is…Olivia White."

"I like that name better. Can we switch?"

The woman shakes her head and looks at the man, who hugs her. Silently, they have a conversation as the feeling comes back into my skin, *and I start to scream in pain; my voice finally finds itself, and it deafens the room.*

"My head!" I scream. "Help me, my head!"

A man in a white coat rushes into the room and injects a liquid into the IV, making the pain subside slowly over the course of a few minutes.

"How's that?" He pats my shoulder. "I need to clear the room to examine her, please."

"I'll stay," the woman speaks up. "She's my sis—she's my daughter."

The man in the white coat nods. "Everyone else, out."

Before they can leave, there's a scuffle outside of the doors, and the man who hugs the nice woman opens it and closes it behind him again.

I hear someone screaming. It's a man's deep voice…and he's scared and desperate.

"Lacey! Lacey! Lacey!"

***

"Olivia?" Jake shakes me out of my dream. "Are you okay?"

It feels like there's a thousand cotton balls shoved into my mouth. I can't speak—or even begin to explain what the hell I just dreamed. I just want to enjoy waking up next to him.

"Just a dream," I breathe out slowly. "No big deal."

He doesn't believe me, but he doesn't say it out loud. "It's nearly ten already." His wide yawn makes me smile. "Do you want to call your mom?"

Now it feels weird when he calls her that. "You

mean, my sister?"

"I know you're confused—"

I push myself away from him and plant my feet on the floor. "I'll call her now." I trot off to find my phone inside my bag where I left it in the living room. The house is so warm and inviting that every room I shuffle into does something magical to my soul. Jake's feet slide across the floor behind me as I open a door to the sunroom, and his arms wrap around my waist.

"I'm sorry I upset you." His lips find the delicate skin beneath my ear. "You should call her when you're comfortable. I shouldn't be pushing you to do it."

"Thank you. What's this room?"

He clears his throat and slides around me, his hands never leaving the curve of my hips. One arm waves around, and his lips open to flash me a toothy smile. "This is your sunroom." He chuckles and rubs his jaw. "Your mom had one at the house you grew up in, and when I bought *this* house, I had it specially designed for you."

My cheeks flush. "Sounds like I had a pretty cushy life."

His eyes narrow. "I got out of that business with your father and did something constructive with the money I made. I didn't need my trust fund because I was smart with the money I earned—don't discount what I've done here."

I haven't seen the scary side of Jake in a while, but this is proof that it hasn't dwindled away. He notices that I'm nervous and takes a step backward, shaking his head.

"I wasn't discounting what you've done." I glare at him. "What's with the scary face?"

Jake doesn't look amused. "I have a problem." He sighs and lets go of my body to sit down in a leather chair next to us. "When I was younger and into things I shouldn't have been...I developed a serious anger problem. But you pulled me out of it, Olivia...you *saved* me."

Whoa.

That's a lot of pressure to put on someone.

"Before I make the call, I want you to know that," I sit down in a chair and look back up at him, "—even though I don't remember a lot of what you tell me, that doesn't mean I don't believe you."

He kneels down in front of me and runs his thumb along my bottom lip. "Oh, baby, if you only truly remembered how much I fucking love you, then it would help take some of your pain away. I looked for you for an entire year, and you were under my damn nose. I intend on making every day of your life special, Olivia. You can count on that."

A smile creeps across my lips. "You're pretty special too, Jake."

He blushes and looks down at the floor. "I'd hoped when we met again that everything would go back to normal, but I'm happy that it didn't. I love Lacey Cervase, and I love Olivia White. A name is just a name."

I snort, pretending to be offended. "Is that right?"

He laughs and kisses my jawline with grace. "That's right. It's easy to love you, baby." His lips find my collarbone, and he nips at the skin as I giggle beneath his weight now pushing me into the chair. What am I doing to myself? Why am I stopping myself from getting what I want for once? Putting aside the sadness of living a lie…I deserve to be happy with someone like Jake. He's real and genuine and completely into me too.

He finds my eyes, and the hunger reaching for me paralyzes my bones. "Tell me more of the story, Jake." I find a soothing voice and inject it into words. "We left off with who my real father is, but nothing else."

He sighs. "I don't like talking about him, but you deserve more, I agree."

I raise my eyebrows and wait. Once he realizes that he can't get out of it, his breath billows from his lungs, and he kneels in front of me, both hands on either side of my thighs.

"Okay, let me think. When you were fifteen, we started seeing each other. Everything was hot like fire, and we were so inseparable that my brothers often teased me about it. I don't think you remember any of them, do you?"

I shake my head and lower my eyes to my lap in shame.

"Don't do that." He tips my chin back up. "There's nothing to be ashamed of. You didn't do this."

I wipe a tear from my eye. "But you hold guilt because of it."

"Trust me, baby, if I could take it all back, I would. I would still have you, and everything would be like it was before. Even if I don't deserve you."

My arms snake around his neck, and I don't have

to pull him down to kiss me because he's already halfway there. When our lips meet, everything else melts away. He notices the feeling too, so he pulls away from me, and a sexy grin appears on his lips.

"We're getting distracted."

I blush. "I'm sorry, that was my fault."

He laughs, and the heartiness of it makes my heart feel full. "Never apologize for kissing me...*never*. I'll never apologize for wanting you, because I can't help that I do."

Jake's eyes get dark as I squirm in my skin. "Olivia, you *are* allowed to have your own thoughts."

"My own thoughts aren't mine, are they?" I blink a few times to try and suck the tears back into my eyes. "I thought my life was a mess before, and now it's just an even bigger catastrophe."

He sighs and pulls me out of the chair, placing his body beneath mine and putting me onto his lap when he sits down where I was moments before. "Let's just get one thing straight right now, okay? I know it's hard to trust someone you don't know and your instincts are screaming at you to run. For all you know, I'm some crazy fucking psychopath feeding you lies to reach my own end game."

He notices my eyebrows rise. "If at any time this is too much for you or you don't feel safe around me, you take the set of car keys hanging next to the front door and your car is the garage. You take it and run if you want."

The lump inside my throat wants to come out and play, but I smash it back down into my chest cavity as fast as I can. I don't want Jake to see just how naïve I really am—regardless of how much truth is smeared across my damn face. "I have a car here? Like, my beat-up Mazda is in the garage?"

His copper blonde curls shake side to side; the laugh he puts into the air makes me snap my legs together in hopes he doesn't notice how completely spent I am on him. "No, like your car before that car, I guess. You have the matching Mercedes to mine...only in a deep blue color. It's been sitting in there since..." His gaze falls to my lap. "Well, you know."

All I can do is smile like a damn idiot. "Yeah, I know. Maybe I'll take it for a spin later. Is that okay?"

When our eyes lock together, I want to climb out of the deep fire pit I've flung myself into. "Yeah, baby, that's okay. I'm just glad you're home; this house missed you."

I snicker. "How can a house miss someone?"

"She missed you fussing over her is what I mean. The wood floors in the kitchen miss their special cleaning days, and that fireplace over there..." He gently squeezes my chin and pushes it toward the cold and empty fireplace. "...misses you lying naked in front of it."

Fire.

The fire in his eyes is taking me over, and there's not a damn thing I can do about it. Not that I really want to. I've given up putting that wall up against Jake because I know he's not here to hurt me. The last thing on his mind is how to push me away when he's fought so hard to find me again. I'm starting to sound like him, but I don't care. If he says it's the

174

truth…then it's the truth. Still, I feel guilty not calling my mother—*or sister, whoever she freaking is*—and letting her know that I'm okay and Jake hasn't run off with me.

"I have to call my mom." I pull my phone out of my pocket. "Can you give me a few minutes alone?"

He kisses my forehead before standing up to leave the room. When he's gone, the air gets cold, and it's really noticeable to the point where my skin has chills. It's funny how much of a hole Jake creates when he leaves a room, and I take note to put that in the category of things I completely crave about him.

"Livvie?" my mother's voice squeals into the phone. "Are you okay? Where did he take you?"

"I'm in Seattle at Jake's house. Calm down." I yawn and pull my feet up into the sofa next to me. I feel strange, like I'm acting differently than my normal self. "I'm staying here for a few days."

She sighs loudly. "I don't think that's a good idea. It's not exactly safe there for you…"

"No one here wants to hurt me."

"Olivia, you don't know that. What about the man who broke into the house and put a knife to your throat? What if he finds you there…or someone else does?"

"Jake will keep me safe. He won't let anything bad happen to me. I just need some time away from Silver Lake."

"Away from Silver Lake or away from us?"

I don't know how to answer her without hurting her feelings.

"I just wish you would've told me the truth. It's not fun being part of someone's secret and living life like nothing's wrong."

When I find my voice, I wish I hadn't. My mother sits on her end of the phone and cries. After her sobs come to an end, she apologizes a few times and clears her throat. "We didn't know what else to do; we didn't know if anyone was after you, and we didn't know if you'd be safe in Seattle with Jake. You have to believe me, Olivia, we *never* meant to hurt you."

Even though I'm still fuzzy on what actually happened, I stand my ground because she doesn't need to know that I don't know everything yet. "I just need a few days to wrap my head around this. I promise I'll be back," I say, but she's already sobbing again. "Mom?"

She stops and waits a few seconds before answering. "Yes?"

"I know that you're my sister, but I don't know you as a sister. I know you as my mom, and that's what it's going to continue to be, okay?"

If she could scream and jump for joy, I'm sure she would've. "Okay, Livvie," she whispers, telling me she loves me before hanging up. She didn't give me a chance to explain anything else or talk to my dad or Caitlyn, probably because they're upset with me too. I can't think about that—I have to keep my thoughts on what's in front of me.

How exactly did I lose my memories?

"I'm ready to know more. I have more questions." I walk into the kitchen where Jake is hunched over the breakfast bar with a sandwich falling from his mouth. He smiles, and it's heartwarming as pieces of meat fall back down to his plate. "I want to know why I can't remember anything."

He coughs. "Is that a question, though?"

I glare at him. "Jake, why can't I remember anything?"

He swallows the large bite and puts the sandwich back down but looks at it like it's the saddest thing he's ever been through. "Okay." He smacks his hands together. "Toward the end of everything, your father—Michael—he started barking up trees in a lot of the wrong places. He'd taken money from some pretty influential people and squandered it, and they weren't happy."

I sit down next to him and take the sandwich from his plate. His eyes grow wide when he sees me shove the sandwich into my mouth, letting the delicious meat tickle my taste buds. I laugh through the mouthful of food and put the sandwich back down. "Sorry, were you still eating that?"

"You—did you—what the hell?" He laughs and snatches the food back from me. "Yeah, I'm eating that, you little sneak. You were always stealing my food, and I don't know where you put it in that tight little body of yours." His eyes glow as he inhales another bite of the food and hands it back to me.

"I just wanted a taste."

Growling, he puts the sandwich down and twirls me toward him so he can have a better shot at me. "Funny, that's the same thing I've wanted for over a week now."

"Jake—"

He holds up his hand away from me. "Okay, okay. Back to the question. So these people that he owed all this money to wanted it back, of course. He wouldn't give it to them—or couldn't maybe, I don't know—but a few of them were linked to some pretty fucking bad situations in Seattle and around the country. I'm talking mafia-style people, Olivia."

I lick my lips and fixate on his mouth.

"So someone came to me and asked for information on where he would be that night, and I told them. You gotta understand that by that time, your father was pissed that I left my job with him and pissed that I didn't want to help him clean up the mess he created. He came here and forced you to go with him and told me that I'd never see your face again in my life. I didn't know what else to do...I thought he was alone in the car by that time—"

His sobs soften as my body wraps around his and holds him as close to my heartbeat as I can get him. His long fingers clutch to the back of my t-shirt, and I let him cry as much as he needs to, because from the moment I met him, I could tell he's held it in for a long time.

"I never meant for you to get hurt. I thought they were going to rough him up and scare the money out of him. I never thought..."

He buries himself in my hair to let the rest of it out. "I may not know much before Silver Lake, but the way you are with me now? I'll never believe that you'd intentionally hurt me. Not for a second. I don't need memories to know that you hold a deep place inside my heart."

This.

This is all it freaking takes.

The sadness in his eyes gets replaced with an intense fire fueled by desire, and I know it's only a matter of seconds before he gives into it. Jake is like a ticking time bomb—you never know when he's going to go off and surprise the hell out of you.

His lips reach mine, and the whole freaking world explodes. Jake kisses me with frustration and confusion, but I don't let it stop me from taking what I'm hungry for. As his lips glide over my skin, it's like they're returning home, and it's an electric celebration. His rough, warm hand grips the side of my neck gently as his teeth nick the soft flesh of my collarbone.

And then he says it.

Three. Little. Words.

"I love you."

Speechless—and not understanding why since it's not really a shock that he feels this way—I stand in front of him with my mouth open and eyes wide. "If I say it back, it doesn't mean the same to you as it does to me."

Jake's eyes darken. "You have no fucking idea what it means to me."

"And you know what it means to *me*?"

"Enlighten me. What *does* it mean to you?"

I don't know how to answer his question. I know that deep down somewhere in the pits of my soul, there's a lock with the name "Jake" on it. I've never questioned what he means to me; I've only questioned what he *meant* to me. I can't see myself the way he describes this loose and carefree girl who was loved by all and had beauty dripping from her every pore.

No.

Not Olivia White.

I'm awkward and annoying—sometimes—and okay, maybe a little naïve if we want to split hairs on this. I want things I can't have, and usually I can't even get the things I don't want. I flutter by and watch the people around me evolve into better versions of themselves like a long, long movie.

But no.

Not Olivia White.

Not me.

But I do love him.

A lot.

Chapter Nineteen

Say it

Jake

She wants to fucking know everything so damn quickly that it's making my head spin.

It's not that I don't want to tell her everything, but...

I don't want to tell her everything.

And I haven't.

I haven't told her I love her so much it fucking kills me inside.

I haven't told her that I've dreamed about her every single night since I've met her.

I haven't told her that there isn't anything I wouldn't do for her.

...Well, maybe I *have* told her that one.

As I impatiently wait for her to say "I love you" back to me, something bad is triggered inside of me, and I know I have to make it go away. She doesn't deserve this version of me...fuck, *Lacey* didn't even deserve this fucking side of me.

The beast.

When she doesn't say it back, I drop my hands from hers. "I'm sorry." I take in a deep breath and wear my guilt on my sleeve. "Don't think that I don't love you, because I do. I really, really fucking do all the way into the deepest parts of my heart. I know you inside and out, Bug. I'm still figuring out this version of you, okay? I know that sounds fucking horrible, but it's the truth. Don't—" I pull her chin back from looking away so she can see the truth in my eyes. "Don't do that. Don't turn away. I am completely in love with you, and there's nothing that's ever going to change that. Not a horrible fucking father, not an accident, and sure as hell not something as silly as a fucking name. I'll call you whatever you want...just don't ever leave me again." I can tell it's startling her how intense I'm getting.

I know, baby. I'm a fucking monster.

"I'm ready to know more." Her small voice finds me. "Jake..." Her hand takes its place on mine, and she sucks in air through her teeth. "I'm ready to know more."

Jesus. I can't take this shit.

Her pouty bottom lip is tucked in behind her teeth like she does when she's nervous.

Her small fingers twirl around her silky-smooth chestnut hair like ribbons.

Her hips call to me; they want me to grab them so fucking tight she can't stand it.

Get a grip, Jake.

Jake. Jake. Jake.

"Jake?" She calls for me through the fog of my daydream. "Hey, are you okay?"

I lick my lips and look at her. "More. You want to know more."

She giggles. Jesus, that's the cutest damn giggle—

"Hey." Her voice lowers, and she's closer to me now. "Focus."

"I'm here." I snap back into reality, but part of me still stays in my fantasy daydream where I'm tearing through her clothes and taking what I need from her.

I really fucking need her.

"Um, okay so…" I try and return myself to a normal state. "I told those people where your dad would be after he ran off with you. You called me and told me he'd taken you to his house, but I never knew you left with him after that. I also didn't know they fucked with the brakes on his car and chased him down so he'd wrap it around a tree."

"I believe you." She puts herself in my lap. The way she curls her body into mine is fucking intoxicating and, to be honest…not fucking fair. "Where's Michael now?"

"Federal prison in SeaTac. About half an hour from here."

Sadness creeps into her eyes. Everything I am…I owe to this woman. She pulled me from a darkness that would've killed me. There isn't anything I wouldn't give to have things back to normal around here where I could look at her a certain way and she'd let me take her on whatever surface we had nearby.

Not this girl.

No, Lacey Cervase was carefree, and sexiness radiated from her skin.

Olivia White is a different breed of addicting. She's cute and small, and even though she's always been that way, now she doesn't have the confidence screaming behind her, making her the carefree person she once was. I like this version of her, though; she's sweet, not tainted by the fucked-up world she was born into.

She also giggles when I touch her now instead of moans.

I *really* fucking like that.

"Jake, I'd like to visit my dad's house and possibly visit him too," she says underneath my chin. I say nothing but just hold her as the afternoon marches on. "I want to see the house in my dreams."

I grind my teeth. "The house was sold with his estate by your sis—mother. I'm not sure if the people living there now will like us meddling around their house, but I can take you to the outside of it if you want. My mom still lives across the street from it."

Shit.

I can't take Olivia anywhere near my fucking mother.

"Okay, let's go." She squeals and bounces off my lap, making my dick vibrate with her.

I clear my throat. "Okay, but only on one condition."

"What is it?"

My tongue runs across my teeth as I carefully

choose my words. "After this and after I tell you the rest of the story, you're free to ask any questions because that's your right and I don't want to take that from you, but you have to agree on trying to live a normal life with me."

"With you, how? Like, move here?"

"If you want, or we can move somewhere in Silver Lake or wherever you want to go."

She thinks about my proposal for a few minutes, but I'm confident enough to let her take her time. I know she's going to go along with this—she has to.

"I don't want to move in with you, Jake," she softly says. "That's a little too much too soon."

Okay, didn't see that one coming...

"Then I'll move to Silver Lake in a real place so we aren't apart." She accepts my answer because she doesn't want to make it into a thing. I know her well enough to know that. "Okay, we should shower and change if we want to get across town before nightfall."

Olivia laughs. "It's only mid-afternoon."

I pick her up unexpectedly and throw her over my shoulder while she squeals with glee. "Baby, you forget that I've lived with you before. I know how long it takes you to get ready for things, and trust me, we won't be leaving for another few hours."

Her round ass is staring me in the face. Literally. There isn't much I can do to stop myself from slapping it and listening to her giggle uncontrollably. At this point, who fucking knows what I am to her, but I know what she is to me.

She's mine.

My everything.

"Are you going to be okay wearing some clothes from the closet? I can run out and pick something up for you if you want," I offer, but she waves me off.

"I'm sure I can find something that doesn't make me feel like an imposter." She smiles.

This is my chance. "Do you still feel that way?"

She nods and starts sifting through the clothes hanging next to us. "Sometimes, yes. Then again, sometimes no. I think you're confusing me more than I already was, and that's not necessarily a bad thing, really. I just wish I could find the key to unlock *everything* and move on. All of this is exhausting, and it's really terrifying finding out your real family was so horrible."

"Your mother, father, and Caitlyn *are* your real family. As pissed at them as I was, I still understood why they hid you away. Your dad was going to take you down with him one way or another."

Her eyes grow wide with fear. "Am I in danger here?"

"No, you're not."

I don't know how to answer her without freaking her the hell out. I can't fucking tell her the absolute truth about what happened to the brakes of the car or she'll never want to see me again.

Olivia takes her t-shirt off and unhooks her bra without hesitation. She knows I'm watching her; the softness of her skin beckons me to reach out and touch it, but I hold back the best I can.

With her back facing me, she braids her long, chestnut hair down the side of her body and misses a few stray strands that tickle her shoulders. The need to race to her and kiss her bare flesh overwhelms me, but I manage to stand my ground long enough for her to slip on another black bra and lipstick-red sweater. There's a chill in the air outside, but in this small room I can almost see the steam from the heat between us. The loose shorts of mine she's got on slide down her smooth legs and find their new home on the floor at her feet.

"Are you purposely trying to tease me?" A growl from the back of my throat finds its way out. "If so, you're doing a fucking fantastic job."

She turns, and her cheeks are flushed. "I wasn't trying to tease you; I thought you'd left." Her blush deepens, and she's so embarrassed that now I feel bad. "I didn't mean to—"

"I'm sorry, I should've left the room and given you privacy," I apologize, taking a few steps back.

She snickers and finds a folded pair of jeans in a drawer next to her. After pulling them on and being impressed that they fit like a glove, her eyes find mine again. "We are literally the dumbest people on the planet—you get that, right?" She starts to laugh, and it's so contagious that I can't help but join her. "We are a perfect match, you and I. Me with my broken past and lost memories and you with your dripping sadness and lurking Hulk anger."

"I'd like to think we're perfect for each other." I slowly move my body toward her, but she doesn't back away once. "And I don't have dripping sadness, Bug. I have some serious fucking need for you to be writhing underneath me, but that's about it."

Olivia snickers, but her eyes stay locked with mine while she bends over to put on a pair of sneakers. "Aren't you going to get dressed so we can go?"

I nod. "I was waiting for you to finish."

I pull off my own t-shirt, and her eyes glue to my skin. I don't think much about the way I look anymore; ever since Olivia found me and pressed me into her heart like a petal between book pages, I haven't found a need to care about what I look like for anyone else.

As she watches me, her eyes trace over my tattoos like she's studying from a textbook. First, she gazes over the tree, then the mockingbird, and then rests on the Roman numerals on my shoulder blade. Out of all the pieces of ink she could ask about, of course that's the one she picks to lock her eyes questioningly on mine about. "What do those numbers mean?" She wiggles her little finger around in the air. "Are those Roman numerals?"

I run my finger along my shoulder blade where the tattoo is. "It says July 12, 2010. The day that I realized I was in love with you." The flush and heat on my cheeks doesn't compare at all to the fire in her eyes when she processes what I've told her. I fucking love it when I surprise her enough and it shows on her face; I also fucking love it when she looks at me like I'm the only person in this entire damn world who understands her.

She isn't wrong.

"That date is special to me, Bug. It's the day my life changed and turned upside down. I couldn't sleep without thinking about you or eat without worrying where you were. I wanted to spend every second with you, and I often did until your overbearing father stepped in."

The dark strands of her hair frame her face and sway when she shakes her head. "Sounds like you were obsessed with me." Her smirk eases my nerves because she's trying to be sexy and funny. Shit, she doesn't have to *try* to be sexy…I'm not the only one who wants her.

"So…" She walks toward me and places a finger on the newfound tattoo. "Are *all* of your tattoos because of me?"

"Yes," I say instantly. "Everything is about you."

"Not *everything.*"

I place my hands on her shoulders to stop her from moving around my body. "Olivia, I want to be with you."

Her cute-ass giggle rings in my ears. "You *are* with me."

Shaking my head, I let go of her shoulders. "No, I mean…you know what I mean."

"Jake—"

The anger rises in my throat, and I told myself a long fucking time ago that I'd never be that person with her. It's frustrating that she can't remember our life and how much we loved each other, and I know it's there…it's deep down in her heart, but it's buried beneath a year of confusion and fear. It's my job to protect her and help her, and even though I've done a shitty job of it lately, I'm trying to make up for it now by keeping her close.

"Olivia, you confuse me every damn day. I love you, and I know you love me…it's just really fucking hard to keep my distance when I know what we had and you don't. But it's my fault and I have to live with that…and I'm prepared to do that."

The laugh she gives me should piss me off, but it makes me blush instead. "Well, you *do* have my life tattooed across your body like a road map to my memories."

"Like I said…everything is about you."

The way she licks her lips slays me. "I don't want everything to be about me. I just want to be normal, and my normal is piecing together what I've missed so I can move on. I know you're part of my life, Jake—there's no guessing about that, and maybe I do have new and old feelings for you…"

Her voice starts to shake, and I know her well enough to recognize what it means.

"Say it, Olivia." I nudge her with my tone of voice. "Just say it."

My fingers find the ends of her braid and play with it. She loves it when I touch her; I can tell. The way her skin moves toward my touch always lets her true feelings shine through. This time is no different as I run my thumb along her pouty bottom lip and bend down to kiss it. She lets me glide my lips across hers for a few seconds before returning the kiss, folding her arms around my neck and letting me pull her so tightly into me that I can barely breathe.

"Say it," I coax her again. "I want to hear you say it."

"If I say it, it becomes real, and I don't want the only real thing in my life to go away," she whispers into my chest. "I don't want *you* to go away."

"I'm not going anywhere, baby. I just want to hear you say it. I want that part of our lives to settle back into normal so everything else has a chance too."

She breathes in deeply, taking in every ounce of air that she can.

She's going to say it.

Please fucking say it.

I need to hear you say it, Olivia.

"I love you, Jake." She burrows deeper into my chest. "I don't know what that means, but I know that now that you're here...I don't ever want to let you go."

My body relaxes, and for the first time in a long time...

I'm at peace.

Chapter Twenty

Goodbye

I wait for Jake to get dressed and realize that I need so many things that I don't have. I need a toothbrush, a hairbrush, and my own clothes, for starters. *What am I talking about?* I know I don't live here—not really—but I can't shake the feeling that it's home, either.

What am I going to do?

He didn't force me into telling him that I love him: I wanted to do that. I do love him, for reasons unknown other than I just…*know*. I just know. I just know. I just know.

Nope. Saying it three times in a row *doesn't* make it any clearer.

"Hey, baby?" Jake calls for me from the bathroom.

I slip on shoes and trot to the open door, where he's grinning at me with a face full of shaving cream and a razor in his hand. "What if the people that live in the house let us walk through? What are you wanting to do there?"

I shrug and watch him continue shaving. I know he's making this small talk because I was out of his view and telling someone you love them for the first time—in this lifetime I guess, anyway—and then leaving them to their own thoughts may or may not be dangerous, especially for someone as heartfelt and sensitive as Jake.

"Do you think it'll help me remember anything?" I ask.

After he finishes shaving, I hand him a towel, and the smile that's been on his face since I said those three little words hasn't faded one bit. "The only thing we can do is try. Let me ask you a question." He leans over onto the sink and comes eye level with me. "Do you *really* want to remember all the bad shit when you have a chance to get a clean break from everything? You can make new memories without your fucked-up dad in them or the accident."

"I want to remember, Jake. I want to remember who I really am."

He licks his lips and brushes hair from my face. "You are who you want to be, Bug. *You* decide that, not memories of the person you once were."

"I'd like to think I'm the kind of person who tries." Our eyes lock together. "What if I get there and remember everything? Wouldn't that be amazing?"

He sighs, and I notice that he's naked—well, naked except for a white towel covering his lower half. Until now, I've been so worried about where I've been…that I'm missing what's in front of me and where I am right now.

Don't touch him, Olivia.

Don't do it.

I reach out and place my palm over his rapidly beating heart. "After we're done with visiting the old house, I'd like you to take me to a grocery store to pick up a few things. We can't stay here without food." I know I'm blushing, but there's nothing I can do about it now that his interest is piqued and he's crossed his long arms over his hard chest, tucking my hand beneath the weight.

Oh, no.

Don't stare.

You'll want him more than you already do.

"Olivia?" The sexy smirk on his lips annoys me. "Something wrong?"

I quickly shake my head. "I'm ready to go— maybe you should finish getting dressed and meet me downstairs? I'll drive." I find a smile and stick it on my lips. Not bothering to listen to his response, I huff and leave the room.

The car keys to my alleged deep blue Mercedes are hanging right where Jake said they would be. Opening a few doors, I find the garage and step inside to a frigid and dark space. Fumbling around, I find the light switch, and my jaw drops to the floor. I'm standing in the empty space where Jake's car must belong, because next to it is the exact car Jake said would be here. My stomach drops, and something clicks when I use the keyless remote to start it and open the door.

Something inside of me tells me that it's going to smell like lavender when I shut the door. Inhaling a deep breath, the flowery scent tickles my nose and releases pleasure into my body. The large garage door behind me opens, and Jake steps into the now-lit space. His jeans hug his body in every place they should, and it makes me lick my lips. He tightens a black leather motorcycle jacket around his tall body, and the maroon sweater beneath it peeks through a bit.

"Why do you wear a motorcycle jacket if you don't ride?" I joke as he gets into the passenger side of the car. He smiles and hands me a jacket; I blush because I'm making fun of him when he's trying to take care of me.

He slowly nods to the front of the garage where two beast-like motorcycles shine light into my eyes from their shiny chrome parts.

"Oh." My cheeks flush with heat harder. "I guess I don't remember that, either."

Jake lets out a slow breath. "I don't expect you to remember anything, Olivia. My expectations of that are very, very low. Not because I think you can't do it, but because I don't want you to."

My eyes narrow at him. "How can I trust you to take me to this house when you don't want me to remember? For all I know, you could lie about what house it really is just to satisfy me."

His seat belt buckles, and his boyish charm hits me like a ton of bricks. "You've seen it in your dreams, haven't you? I love you. I don't want you to ever think like that about me. If you want someone else to take you—"

"I don't want anyone else," I blurt out. "I want you."

Two seconds.

That's how long it takes for his hidden tattooed arms to reach out to me and pull my lips onto his. He's hungry for me, and honestly, after so long of not knowing where I belong in my own life…it's good to be wanted. I want Jake too, though, and that's going to be a problem for me. I can't be the person he wants me to be no matter how much he denies that he wants me to change back to Lacey Cervase.

But I'm Olivia White.

I love hard and don't trust easily.

Except when it comes to Jake Redding.

His fingers find my lips as we part, and he rests his forehead on mine. "The feeling that's in the bottom of your stomach right now? The bubbly, light snapping feeling? That's what you do to me every time you smile at me. That's love, baby, and I never want it to go away again."

Our lips find each other again, and this time I don't hold back. I take everything he's willing to give to me and then some. I don't realize how long I haven't been breathing until he forces himself to sit back in his own chair and lick his lips. "We better get going or I'm going to take you back in that house and we won't be leaving."

A zip of excitement flashes through my body. "We wouldn't want that, would we?" I smirk and put the car in reverse. He directs me through the streets of suburban Seattle until we get stuck at a stoplight that takes forever to turn.

Jake clears his throat. "Maybe we should talk about that."

"Talk about what? Did I miss a turn?"

He laughs, and the light turns green. I start driving through the intersection, and his long fingers tap on the door. "No, we should talk about sex."

Shit! Keep cool, Olivia!

Eyes on the road!

"Sex?" The word trickles from my lips like it's forbidden. "When?"

He laughs at me again, and this time it annoys me. "Uh, whenever you want, baby. I'm open to it right now in a parking lot to be fucking honest."

I pretend to gag, and he frowns. "In a parking lot? Jesus, Jake."

"What?" He acts offended—and maybe he is, but I don't care. "Listen, it's been over a year for me, and I don't know who you've been—"

"Don't even. I haven't had sex with anyone since moving to Silver Lake. You can count on that."

"I didn't mean to piss you off." Sadness lifts his voice through the car. "I was just stating a fact. I won't have sex with anyone but you." His curls bounce on his head as he shakes it violently. "I *can't* have sex with anyone but you."

"*Can't?* How do you know?"

"I just know," he mumbles, and a sour feeling hits my stomach.

My skin crawls. "Never mind. Which way?"

He points in the direction to turn, and the car lurches where his finger stops. "I just want you to know that there's nothing stopping me from being with you other than you deciding when the time is right for us again."

"And if I never decide that?"

A small hitch in his breath pings around the car. "I hope that never happens, but if it does…I'll just have to deal with it, won't I?" The growl in the back of his throat wants to come out and play. "But just keep in mind that telling me you love me back there at the house…that's turned me on a thousand times more than you ever fucking have. There, that's the house."

I stop the car where he's pointing and pull off to the side of the road.

That's the house in my dreams.

He's looking out his window across the street at what I can assume is his mother's house, like he said before. All of the houses around look like mini mansions—ridiculously large properties that take an obscene amount of money to maintain and keep up to your neighbors' standards.

"Is that your mother's house?" I squint to see through the impending moonlight better. "Why is there a for sale sign on the front lawn? Because you refused to give her your money?"

He slowly nods. "I know it sounds cruel."

"I wish I remembered her and what she was like to you so I can understand." My eyes find my lap and stick there like glue. "What was she like?"

Jake hooks his finger beneath my chin and lifts my gaze back to him. His wide lips frown at my sadness. My thumb lightly runs over the right pocket of his mouth, and his frown fades into a smile. Sliding his hand up my arm, he moves my finger to the center of his lips and kisses it gently.

"I don't want you to ever feel ashamed of your

memories, baby. It's not your fault, and you're trying." The smile deepens on his lips. "I know you're chasing someone you used to be. That's not you anymore, and that's okay." His copper blonde curls fall on his forehead as he nods toward the house across from his mother's. "That's where you grew up. It doesn't mean you belong there now, understand?"

"I get it, Jake. I'm glad you're here with me."

He winks and kisses my finger again. "There's nowhere else I'd rather be."

I take a deep breath and look at the house we're here to see. It's so big that three of my parents' houses could fit inside comfortably. A long, dark circle drive runs in front of it and tall, gray pillars look like they're holding up three tall stories of house. The large window in the lower level—that looks like it's where a living room would be—catches my attention, and I can't take my eyes from it.

"Anything familiar?" Jake asks.

"Maybe." I open the car door to get out. He races out of his side and meets me on the sidewalk before I shut my door. He holds out his hand, and I take it immediately without a second thought. There's no cars in the drive, and it doesn't even look like anyone lives here at all. The air is so silent that it creeps me out, but I stop in front of the window once we walk close enough to it and peer in.

The room is empty.

"Huh," I gruff. "I guess no one lives here."

Something that sounds like heels clicks on the walkway behind us, and a tall, blonde woman in a sparkly evening gown crosses her arms over her chest. "What are you two doing here?"

Jake growls. "We're leaving, Mother. Don't worry."

Jake's mother. She snarls her red-painted lips at me like she wants to rip eyes out. "How dare you bring her back here after what she's done to you...what she's done to this family!" Her whisper is so harsh that it hurts my heart. "She's nothing but a manipulative, controlling little beast just like her father!"

"Don't fucking talk to her like that." His voice is a low warning. "Olivia, don't listen to her."

She scoffs. "Olivia? Is *that* what you're calling yourself now? I see right through you, you little wench. I know you're putting on an act; I know you remember everything. I watched you drag my son through the mud and muck with your dirty father, and I'm not going to sit back and watch it again."

"I don't even know you!" I explode at her. "I don't know what you're talking about!"

The woman's laugh rattles my insides. "You know damn well what I'm talking about. Sit there and pretend you don't remember, that's fine. My son told me the truth, and you're lucky I'm keeping my mouth shut about it."

"The truth about what? I barely remember anything!"

Her eyes narrow, and she stares directly into my soul. "My son's love for you weakened him. You took advantage of his weakness for you and played him right into the hands of the devil, didn't you? Please, don't disrespect me and stand there like you

200

don't know what he did for you!"

Jake's body starts to shake. "Shut the fuck up! Don't say another word!"

"Tell me." My voice finds her through the screaming.

"Jake cut those brake lines because he thought it was the only way you two could be together. You're just a girl...I tried telling him you weren't worth the consequences, but he didn't listen."

My focus goes to Jake as tears stream down his face.

"*You*?" My legs shake, and I want to run. "It was *you* that cut the brakes? It was *you* that did this to me?"

The world spins so fast that I can't catch my breath. My feet feel like they're floating, and before I know it, the arguing stops and they both look at me with heavy concern in their eyes.

"Bug..." Jake slowly walks toward me with his hands in defense mode. "I can explain."

"You lied to me." My body rattles with rage. "*You lied to me!*"

Before he can answer for himself or catch me, my legs take me back to the car, and I'm able to shut and lock the door before Jake can reach me. He doesn't look angry as he pleads with me to open the door and let him inside, but I'm not about to do that.

"Bug, let me in." He rests his forehead against the glass. His brown eyes meet mine, and I almost do what he asks before my instincts kick back in. "I'm not going to hurt you. You know that, right?"

I purse my lips. "I'm going home."

"Okay, let me go—"

"Home to Silver Lake. Don't follow me. Don't call me, and don't show your fucking face there. I don't want to see you anymore, Jake. You were the one person who I trusted, and you lied straight to my face!" I crack the window a little so he can hear me better. "You told me it was someone my father owed money to! It was you...what kind of a person—"

Jake nervously looks around. "I know I'm a monster. I shouldn't have brought you here."

I laugh so loud that it echoes in the car. "I shouldn't even be here with you!"

"You don't mean that—"

"I mean it. I take back everything, Jake. I can't love someone like you."

Jake sighs and tries the door handle again. "Please, baby, don't leave. I can't promise that I won't follow you back to Silver Lake...I can't do that." His pleads get louder, and I see tears in his eyes. "We can move anywhere you want to move. We can leave everything behind. Just don't tell me goodbye, Bug."

I don't blink.

"Goodbye, Jake," I say and hit the gas pedal, leaving him a broken mess on the sidewalk.

He wanted me to fix him, and I just broke his heart for a second time.

Chapter Twenty-One

Blame

The drive back to Silver Lake went much quicker than I thought it would. Maybe it's because I was seething the entire way home; my mind is teeming with questions that I want to bombard my family with. There's no way I'm telling them about Jake's secret; they already hate him enough on their own without adding fuel to the fire.

Jake's been calling me nonstop since I left him broken on the sidewalk, but not once did I care to answer. I trusted him, and he lied to me. Everyone always lies to me, and it's going to stop right now.

I know I have a good half an hour head start before Jake, and I know he's on his way. There's no doubt in my mind that he isn't going to listen to me and stay away. Knowing him, he's probably racing down the freeway as we speak, white knuckling the steering wheel and cursing into the wind.

Home.

There's my parents' house, lit up and waiting for

me to come back.

Not wasting any time, I slam the car into park in the driveway and throw myself out onto the pavement. I want to rip my clothes off because they make me feel like an imposter, but as I reach the front door and it opens on its own, my thoughts shift and my mother's face meets me just a few feet away.

"No more lies. I want the truth." I grit my teeth, and she looks defeated. They all know that they've been found out as I brush past her and see Caitlyn and my dad—or whoever he really is—sitting with their heads down in the living room. My body whirls back to my mother—sister, whatever—as she shuts the front door and locks the deadbolt. "No need to do that. I'm not staying long," I growl as she steps into the room.

She crosses her arms over her chest. "Look, I think you better sit down and take a deep breath before we start explaining. You ran off with Jake, and we were left to worry about you."

"Are you blaming Jake for this?" my voice booms. "This has nothing to do with him!"

"The hell it doesn't!" she screams back. I've never heard her raise her voice to this level before, and it's a little off-kilter. "It's *his* fault you were in that car, because you weren't even supposed to be with him! *He's* the reason those thugs cut the brake lines, and *he's* the reason they knew where and when to do it! Don't you see, Olivia? You've trusted him wrongly once again!"

They don't know the truth.

There's no way I'm telling them anything.

204

"Leave Jake out of this!" I look around to Caitlyn and my fake father.

My father—or brother-in-law, I guess—speaks up. "Make no mistake that we've treated you like our own this past year, and we've enjoyed having you. The reason we don't have any pictures together is because there aren't any. We didn't know you as Lacey: We only know you as Olivia. Do you think it's fair to treat us like this when we've done nothing but try and help you?"

"We turned our lives upside down for you," Caitlyn chimes in. "I left my life in Seattle behind so I could protect you from what happened."

This all sounds like blame to me.

They blame me for loving Jake and trying to be happy.

They blame me for all the chaos.

They even blame me for their choice in taking me in and keeping me safe.

"I don't know what you want me to say to that. Are you looking for a thank you? I'm not going to thank you for lying to me for a year! You made me feel crazy and forced me to see Dr. Ross when everything was true! I've been squirming in my own skin, trying to find my real place in the world, and you people have known about it all along!"

"I'm not going to apologize for keeping you safe, dammit!" My father—what do I even call him now?—raises his voice. "We did what we had to do to take you away from all of that and give you a better, more fulfilling life. We aren't sorry for that."

The air in the room grows even more tense. Three of us are frothing at the mouths and Caitlyn sits next to her father with tears in her eyes. I feel sorry for her for being dragged into this, but she sort of comes with the package since she lied to me too.

"I want the whole, true story," I demand. "Now."

"Michael Cervase got into some bad business deals and started getting death threats," my mom says. "Before the accident, he came to us and asked us to take you away so you wouldn't get hurt. You found out and ran to Jake, who tried to hide you and keep you safe on his own. But Jake has a temper problem, as you probably are well aware of now. He wouldn't let us take you, so we had to take you by force. Then he called the people looking for your father and told them where he'd be. They cut his brake lines to his car after you returned home, but he didn't know. He was taking you out for dinner to calm you down and talk about things, but the brakes went out and the accident happened before he got the chance."

My mother comes up next to me and almost puts her hand on my shoulder but decides against it. "So we had our chance when you woke up in the hospital and didn't know where or who you were."

Caitlyn wipes her eyes. "I left Jake a note, though, so it's not like he didn't know you were gone."

The rage building inside of me intensifies everything. The fact that they are sitting here defending themselves is pissing me off. I can't be mad at them for trying to help me. At the same time, though, they kept my life a secret from me, and if Jake hadn't found me, who knows when—or if—they would even have told me the truth.

And the fact that they blame everything on him pisses me off more.

"You don't know Jake like you did before." My mom sits down on the sofa next to Caitlyn. "You didn't know what he was capable of then, and you sure as hell don't know now."

I try to defend Jake's innocence. "Jake would never hurt me. I know he sure as hell didn't cause this to happen."

"But would he hurt someone for you?" My father raises his eyebrow. "Sam Collins ended up in the hospital with a broken jaw and broken arm—any idea how that happened?"

"Sam said he was jumped, but then he told me he thought Jake was behind it because Sam played a joke on you." Caitlyn smacks her lips. "Why would Jake do something like that other than having a serious anger problem?"

My eyes burn through her skull. "Sam tried to attack me at work, Caitlyn. Whatever happened to him, he had coming." My mom's head shakes. "*What?*"

"You still think Jake can do no wrong."

"Jake is the only person who believed me!" The swelling in my chest deepens, and I have to calm down before my heart explodes. Where do I go from here? How can I just keep on going like nothing has happened? I left Jake, and now—judging from the looks on the faces of the only family I know—they want me to leave them too.

"We took you in because you're my sister and I love you." My phone buzzes in my pocket, and right about now is when Jake should be pounding on the door, demanding that I speak to him. I ignore the vibrations and listen to her. "Since the day you were born, our father doted on you and loved you more. Of course, we're nearly twenty years apart and have different mothers, but that never stopped me from wanting to be part of your life. Michael, though, he didn't want me anywhere near you. I broke free from his grasp to marry your dad—uh, David—and Michael didn't like it. David wasn't wealthy and didn't benefit our family any financially, so he wrote me off and never spoke to me again until he needed my help taking you in."

"I don't trust you." I glare at her. "All three of you are liars."

"Wait right there." David holds up his hand in protest. "You're being cruel, and that's not fair. We didn't have to take you and run. We didn't have to make sure you were safe. We did that because you're our family and that's what family does."

"I can't trust any of you. I'm leaving." I turn to go back to the front door. "For a year you've been lying to me. I'm glad Jake found me, or else I would've never known where I really belong."

"And where is that?" David calls after me.

"Anywhere but here." I jerk open the front door to step outside. I hit something hard, and the cinnamon scent washes over me.

Jake.

"You're just in time." I push him out of my way. "I'm not in the mood to talk to anyone right now, Jake. Go home."

He takes my arm and swings me around to face him. "You don't get to do that. You don't get to throw a fucking tantrum and run away. You don't get to tell me you love me and then fucking throw me away like a piece of trash on the street."

"Yeah? How about the secret you've been keeping from me? How could you do that to me? How could you be the one that takes everything from me?" My hair blows in the wind and whips across my cheeks. "How about a life you should have but can't because you can't remember it? My memories were stolen from me, Jake! I can't even be scared or mad at you properly because it's like it happened to someone else!"

Jake's voice gets low. "Are you afraid of me, Olivia? Do you think I did it intentionally to hurt you?"

"No." My breath is quick and hard to catch. "No, I don't, and that makes everything worse."

Caitlyn bounces outside and shuts the door behind her. Jake seethes so badly that I can nearly see steam coming from his feet. She notices his anger but still stands her ground no matter how scary he's being.

"Olivia, please. I know you don't think you can trust anyone right now, but..." She looks back at Jake and slightly nods. "Trust *yourself*. You have to trust yourself."

"Trust myself?"

"She's right." Jake clears his throat and steps next to her. "We should go before the cops show up from all the screaming you just did."

I snort. "I have more to give if you'd like some."

Jake blushes all the way down his tattooed collarbone. "No fucking thank you."

They have to give me some room to breathe. I close my eyes and tilt back my head, letting whatever I want flow through my brain like rainbow ribbons of light. I have to be smart about this and trust myself…because that's really the only person I can rely on to get me through this.

"I just heard from one of my friends," Caitlyn says. "Sam was behind the attack on you; he was the one who told the junkie there was money in the house. He's out to get you, Livvie. Ever since you turned him down, he…hasn't been the same."

Jake's fists clench together tightly. "How can he do anything with broken bones?"

My eyes snap to him. "How did you know about that? Do you have something to do with that?"

Jake doesn't answer; his eyes are glued to the ground, and he's ashamed of himself.

"Were you followed?" Caitlyn turns to Jake. "Do you think anyone followed you?"

He shakes his head, and the tousled copper blonde curls fall to the side. "No, I don't think so."

Caitlyn frowns. "You better get her out of town, just in case. Have one of your brothers poke around to make sure it's safe to come back."

Jake listens to her plan, and they act like I'm not still standing here with my eyes closed.

Shutting the world out.

Trusting myself.

Chapter Twenty-Two

Tattered hearts and blue skies

I thought that when I finally found out the truth…I would be happy.

Sadly, nothing's what it seems.

Wanting so badly for my life to turn into some sort of weird and fabricated fairy tale was a stupid mistake…but it was a mistake I'm glad I made. I'll never be unsure of my feelings for Jake no matter how hard I try to push them deep into my mind. Still, the protective bubble he's put around me needs to break soon so I can breathe and interact with other people besides him.

Okay…so what we've been doing the last two weeks isn't exactly interacting.

I've basically been ignoring him and making him sad.

His brown eyes darken as he looks across the kitchen table at me. Jake's been doing a fantastic job of letting me have my space, but I know it's getting harder for him each day he has to endure it.

If I'm being completely honest, I'm having a hard time keeping my hands to myself. I want Jake more than anyone, and saying that the feeling of needing to feel his heartbeat next to mine is growing…is a serious understatement.

Today is no different.

He's been acting cheekier and more exuberant the past few days. I've wondered why we've been living in this rented condo for two weeks—forcing me to quit my job at the YMCA and leave everything I actually remember behind—when one of his brothers is supposed to be making it safe for us to head back to Seattle so I can visit Michael in federal prison.

Jake sighs loudly and shakes my thoughts. "Okay, I'm done with this shit." His hands find the table, and he places them palms down. "I'm tired of you ignoring me and acting like I'm not here. I love you, Olivia, and you love me. We need to talk about this."

My eyes narrow at him. He's chosen to start walking around without a shirt on, and it pissed me off at first, but now it's getting too hard to resist the deep, dark lines of the tattoos that tell my story.

I groan. "Fine. What do you want to talk about?"

He licks his lips. "How do you feel about me after knowing what I did?"

"Why did you cut his brakes? Were you trying to kill him?"

It's clear that Jake doesn't even know the answer to this question himself. "I wasn't thinking, baby. You didn't come back in an hour, and I thought he'd forced you on a plane somewhere. I thought you were gone, and I didn't know where…"

"I believe you." The words startle both of us. "Jake, I believe you, okay? It's weird to know you'd do something like that—even for me—but I don't fear you."

"Baby…" His voice lowers, and he snakes his body around the table to sit dangerously close to me. "I know you're confused and hurt, but I can't take this anymore. I need you to keep talking to me…I *need* you."

He wants me to kiss him, but I'm not there yet.

Instead, my fingers find my mockingbird tattoo on his arm and gently run over the black ink. His skin trembles when I touch him, and I kind of like it that he's having trouble containing himself over a three-second touch. I let my fingers fall down his arm and stop, gazing at the artwork laden on his skin that I hadn't noticed before.

"What's this one?" I blush as Jake finds my fingers with his and tangles them together. I don't pull away because it doesn't feel right to pull away. "Is this one for me, too?"

He nods. "I got this the day after you told me I wear my heart on my sleeve. It's also the day after I lost you, but that doesn't matter anymore."

I examine the ink around his arm; the tattered form of a heart haunts me as my fingers run over his smooth skin. It makes me sad to look at it, like there's so much emotion and sadness wrapped up in one little harmless tattoo.

"It's a broken heart." I find his bright brown eyes. "That doesn't sound like a good memory, Jake."

Jake's laugh is so hearty that it makes my head feel fuzzy. Something about his broken heart tattoo and his laugh pops my mind into another place. He snaps his fingers in front of my face. His eyebrows furrow in intrigue; it takes a few seconds for the clouds to clear from my vision for me to fully see his face. I don't care what anyone says anymore: I'm Olivia White…not Lacey Cervase.

Olivia White wants Jake more than she can stand it.

Somehow before either of us realize it, our lips are locked together, and we don't have a care in the world. I settle my body on his lap as he leans back in his chair, moaning into my mouth when I nick his bottom lip with my teeth.

The moment his hands find the small of my back and touch the bare flesh, the frustration built up inside of Jake unleashes with a fury. He grips the back of my hair and tugs backward, making my chin tip toward the ceiling so his lips can suction against the soft flesh of my neck. He trails his mouth back up toward my lips and opens his eyes so he can look at me.

"I need you." He kisses my jawline. "I need you to survive."

I bite my bottom lip as he trails his mouth down my neck again and pushes the collar of my yellow blouse aside. He kisses my collarbone, not daring to go past the fabric of the thin material covering my torso in fear that he won't be able to control himself.

I don't want him to control himself.

I want it all; I want everything he has inside of

me.

"It's not fair to you if we fuck." His cinnamon breath reaches my nose and hovers inches from my face. "I don't want to pressure you into anything when you're like this."

"Like what?"

He grips the back of my head to keep me steady because he can feel me pulling away from him. "Confused, angry, and pissed at me."

His lips linger over me for a few seconds to let me think.

All I can think about are the blue skies above us through the skylight as he tips my neck further to the ceiling.

Blue skies and the tattered heart on Jake's sleeve.

The heart I left behind.

I'm getting what I want for once.

He slides his hands around my waist and squeezes; I lean forward to let him bury his face in between the softness of my breasts as he unbuttons my blouse and lets it fall off of me onto the floor. His hands slide around each breast; there's nothing I can do but tip my head backward where he wants it and moan loudly into the air once his lips start suctioning around each nipple and he tugs lightly with his lips.

His sexy chuckle finds me in the abyss of pleasure. "I take it you don't care how I feel about taking advantage of you?"

Licking my lips, I close my eyes and grip the back of his head. "No talking." I blow a long breath out. "I want this."

He rips off my leggings and shakes the torn

garment onto the floor, and I'm left with nothing but a pair of silk panties, sitting on his lap beneath his aggressive touch. I like it that he's a little scared to be with me because I'm feeling the exact same way—although I'd never admit it to him. There's a few moments I come in and out of pleasure waves and he's taken off his pants and tight, black boxer briefs with one swoop of his arm. I giggle and it's like gas to his engine; he revs beneath me and vibrates my skin as his legs tremble.

"Jesus, Olivia." His hands find each side of my ass, and he roughly grips the flesh between his fingers. He slides his fingers around the bottom of my thighs and raises me in the air, and everything kicks into slow motion. I look down and the sparkle in his eye sends a wave of ease over my body, so when he pushes inside of me I can enjoy every bit of him and not worry about a damn thing.

And I don't.

Not as his tall body cradles me, wraps my legs around his torso, and I ride him in the chair.

Not as he picks me up and bends me over the kitchen counter.

Not as he parts my legs with his tongue and runs it over every inch of space I have between my thighs.

And *definitely* not as he stands behind me, gripping me and wrapping his arms around me like ribbons of sexual warmth and pleasure.

The bedroom I've been staying in is dark; I can still see the look in his eyes before he reaches ecstasy. It's the clearest I've ever seen him. He buries himself in my hair and slows his hips into a rhythmic motion. Something comes over me, and suddenly it's like I'm hungry for everything I can get my hands on...and I want it all.

My legs wrap around his body, and he follows my moves, lying on his back and letting me slide on top of him. I know I've slept with Jake, but to me...it's my first time with anyone.

He's not exactly *small*, either.

Somehow I know what to do and where to place my legs; he sits up and catches me, running his hands up my sides and breathing so hard that it makes easing back onto him much more tantalizing. I feel him getting close so I start moving up and down until he reaches for my neck and pulls me down to kiss his lips. As we both cry out at the same time, the room gets a little blurry, and it's a few minutes before either of us can speak.

Jake brushes the hair from my face and kisses my lips again. He's weak, but he's waited so long for this that in his mind he's ready to go again. I drink him in and hardly care that I'm sweaty and naked on top of a man I'm supposed to love and barely know.

Olivia! Stop ruining it for yourself!

"I love you so fucking much." He tips his head back. "That was literally everything I thought it would be and more."

My smile hurts my cheeks. "I'm glad I could help you out."

He swiftly rolls over and tucks me underneath him, pulling out of me and not giving a damn that we didn't use a condom and he never bothered asking me about birth control. Luckily, I'm just bad at remembering things from my past and not my present, and I've never missed a pill…even now that we've been living miles away from home for two weeks.

"Look at that," he mutters, looking toward the window across from the bed. "We've been in here for hours…it's already nightfall."

I follow his eyes, and they lock onto the dusky night sky outside.

I know this didn't fix Jake's broken heart completely, but I'm open to trying now.

The blue skies are gone.

But the tattered heart remains.

Piece by piece, I'm going to help him mend it as I put the pieces of my life into place, too.

Right now, though, we're exactly where we should be.

"Jake, tell me about my real mother." We lie together, naked and both falling fast asleep. "What happened to her?"

He yawns and wraps himself around my body. "She disappeared about ten years ago."

I wait for him to elaborate, but instead, he stays still and silent. He runs his thumb alongside the outer part of my hand as he holds it. When it gets too much to ignore and he can feel my resistance, he knows he can't hold me off any longer.

"No one knows what really happened but Michael," Jake adds, taking in a deep breath.

I purse my lips in the darkness. "She's in my memories sometimes. Her name is Sabine; do you think we can find her?"

Jake shifts his weight to pull my body into his as

much as it can fit. "We can try, baby." The warmth of his whisper tickles the stray hands around my ear. "I'm sure she'd be proud of the woman you've become."

The woman I've become.

Now that's even more cruel.

Chapter Twenty-Three

Home

"Wake up, baby," Jake whispers into my ear. "I have some good news, but you have to wake up to hear it." His singsong voice isn't something that's comforting when you're woken up from a deep sleep after having the best sex of your life. I'm hungover from a second round, and we didn't bother getting dressed before we passed out from exhaustion.

I'm still naked.

Opening one eye, I see his boyish grin looking down at me; he's also still naked. His tall body hunches over to look at me and make sure I'm awake before he playfully slaps my bare ass with pleasure. He starts to run his hand over where he spanked me, and I know I have to get out of this position or I'll never get to hear the good news.

Rolling over isn't a good idea, either. His hand lands directly in between my legs, and I have to snap them together and sit up before he can slip his fingers inside of me. Pouting, he retracts his hand back to his own space and acts offended.

"What's the good news?" I smile brightly.

"Noah called me, one of my brothers?" He waits for me to catch up before continuing on. "Sam was arrested. He confessed to staging the entire break-in to scare you because…get this: He recognized you as Lacey Cervase and tried to get revenge for his older brother, who invested money with Michael."

Without warning, I start to laugh. It grows and grows until it's filling the entire room, and Jake looks at me like I've finally lost more than just memories. He waits for me to tone it down before raising his eyebrows at me. "What the hell was that?"

"People…" A hiccup leaves my throat. "People are so gross, Jake. I mean, seriously. What is wrong with people? Why are they such monsters?"

His jaw clenches. "Some people just can't help themselves, Olivia."

"I wasn't talking about you. I don't want to even think about that right now. The fact that I know what you did and I still slept with you speaks volumes about the person I've become."

Jake laughs. "That's my girl, always the first to point out the flaws in herself before anyone else."

A lightbulb goes on in my head.

"I'm tired of chasing someone I *used* to be. I'm ready to just be myself, whoever I want that to be." I wrap my arms around his neck and smile. "I'm ready to give being Olivia White a real chance."

I jump off the bed and, to Jake's disapproval, start putting on clothes. Not minding that he's still

221

stark naked—and it's making me wet in the mouth to look at his tall, naked body sitting inches from me on the bed—he watches me like he's seeing a movie for the very first time. I drop my t-shirt on the ground and he's there within seconds to pick it up and hand it back to me with a sexy grin on his lips.

"Why are you in such a hurry?" he asks. "We have to wait for a flight to Seattle, baby."

"I'm not in a *hurry*. I just want to get the day started."

He laughs loudly. "You do realize it's nearly noon, right?"

"Shit." I look at the clock on the wall. "You let me sleep all day?"

"After what we did last night, we *needed* it." He snorts and realizes that I'm serious. "Sorry, I didn't know Noah would call with the good news or I would've gotten you up sooner."

I make a disagreeing noise and leave him alone in the room to get himself dressed. I open the fridge and rummage around for something to drink. When I open the milk carton and tip the cool liquid back into my throat, Jake makes a disgusted face when he rounds the corner to see what I'm doing.

"Do you *have* to do that?" He smiles and takes the carton from me, putting it back into the fridge. "When we move back home, you have to stop that."

Home.

There's that word again.

Jake notices my reservation about the word and takes a step backward to give me some space. Once his body hits the island cabinet, he hops up on it and looks down at me with concern in his brown eyes. I can't meet his gaze for long or I'm going to fall into his trap of cinnamon and whiskey and whatever else he's going to use against my already weak defenses.

Jake Redding is a part of me and he knows it.

"Do you want to talk about that?" His head cocks to the side. "Going home and what that means?"

My hair falls around my face, and I don't bother pushing it away. I want to hide…no. I want to run and hide and be a baby about this. I don't want to face reality and what that means. I know I'm going to have to choose between Seattle and Silver Lake, and ultimately that means I'm going to have to choose between being with Jake or…not being with him.

I sigh. "I can pretend I don't know what you're talking about, but that isn't fair to you." He smiles because what I'm saying is true. "I don't know how to not confuse you when I'm still so confused, you know?"

"Bug," he breathes out his air so fast it blows my hair back a little. "What you have to understand is that I'll do whatever you want to do. If you tell me to fuck off, then that's the way it is. If you want to be with me in Seattle, same thing. I can't expect you to have the same *exact* feelings you had before when you don't even *know* yourself from before."

Well, okay.

"And I hope to fucking God you don't tell me to kick rocks, but if you do, I'll find a way to deal with it. I'm a grown man and I can take care of myself, but make no mistake…" He slides off of the counter and bends his neck to look into my eyes, careful not to touch me and spark something else between us. "You keep me alive in ways even I don't understand. I need you and I want you, but I love you enough to see that you need some time and space."

"Jake…" I instinctively take a step toward him. "It's just hard to know how I feel when my mind feels like a bumper car arena and no one knows how to drive."

A smile creeps on his thick lips. "I know, baby." He kisses my forehead, and I think he's going to wrap me in his long arms and make everything okay like he does…but instead, he opens the fridge and takes out a carton of orange juice. After eyeballing me and dramatically taking a glass from the cabinet, he pours the orange liquid into the glass and takes a big, comical gulp.

My eyes narrow at him. "Really funny you are."

His laugh is so innocent that it humbles me back where I should be. I'm getting into my own head again, and that's going to lead me down a path I don't want to be on anymore.

I *want* this.

I remember that I want this.

I really, really want his orange juice lips on mine.

Now.

"Olivia?" he says my name wrapped up in confusion. I focus on his lips and the sexy, wicked smile that's painted on them as he realizes what I'm coming after. Jake will never push me away, and that's something I can count on. His body freezes with the fridge still open, the dark ink of his tattoos reaching out from the skin that I see around his t-shirt. I run my gaze over each of the tattoos that I know are mine—or made *because* of me—and that excites me more.

Jake's body is a road map of my life.

He moans as I touch him; I run my fingers up his neck and around the back of his head so I can gently tug him down to kiss me. Our lips meet, and it's different this time: he's hungrier than he's ever been, and this is going to be trouble. As he devours my mouth, he lifts me up onto the counter and parts my legs with his body like he *belongs* there.

He *does* belong there.

"You are so fucking intoxicating," he breathes into my mouth. "Everything about you sets me off."

I giggle, and it's not a normal Olivia giggle. This one is more sweet, sultry, and laced with poison that plays to Jake's emotions. He squeezes my thighs and groans as his phone starts ringing in the next room. Of course he wants to ignore it, but I can't let that happen. I have to get out of this condo and back to a life I'm at least a little familiar with.

"No, don't move," he warns me and points playfully at my nose. "I'll get that. You. Don't. Move."

He runs off to grab his ringing phone. He doesn't bother coming back as he answers it, but the tone of his voice carries into the kitchen, and it kills my good mood.

"Yeah, we're coming back as soon as we can. I'll tell Olivia to get packed up."

"Yes, her name is Olivia now. That's what we call her."

"No."

"Okay, fine. If we fly, we can be back by morning. We're in L.A.—can you set up the flight?"

"Thanks. Bye."

I find him in the bedroom with his head in his hands. It takes a few seconds for me to decide what I'm going to do, but my fingers find the back of his head and I gently play with his curly hair to let him know I'm here for him.

"Hey, we have to leave soon."

"I heard. Is everything okay?"

When he looks at me, there's wetness forming in the corners of his eyes. "Michael has been cleared for visitors. He's asking for you."

The stress forms lines on Jake's forehead as he crinkles it and thinks. It's my job—as whatever I am to Jake—to help take some of the burden from him. I'm not a fragile little bird; I have to think of something I can do to help him without making things worse.

"We should pack up. Take things you need and I'll send for the rest." His low voice finds me through our darkness. "It's time to head home."

Home.

Where everything is going to change.

Again.

Chapter Twenty-Four

Prison blues

"You okay?" Jake snickers as the small plane lands on an even smaller runway. He sure doesn't spare any expense when it comes to air travel. One of his brothers—Tyler or Noah or whoever—arranged for a private plane to carry us from L.A. to Seattle. It seemed like days that we were in the air, but when Jake unbuckled my seat belt and pulled me into his lap to sleep, time sped up; before I knew it we were about to land and he'd placed me back in my seat with my buckle returned to its place around my body.

I stretch my body. "I've never flown anywhere before."

He stretches his long legs out in front of him and yawns. "After all this bullshit is over, I'll take you wherever you want to go. We need a proper vacation."

I want to be like Jake.

I want to try and wash away all the bad things

happening around us to make room for the good things we can dream about. I want to be careless and aloof and see the brighter side to life. I want to be free from the chains that drag me down into a deep abyss of confusion.

But I'm still Olivia White.

I worry.

I try and fix what's broken.

"I'm ready to visit Michael."

Jake nods. "I figured as much. Noah's already called ahead to let them know you'll be arriving soon. Visiting hours aren't over for a few more hours."

My hand fits perfectly in his as he leads me down the staircase and onto the tarmac. A car waits for us several feet from the plane, and a short man with a black suit on smiles and nods toward me as he opens the door for Jake to place me inside.

The drive from Seattle to SeaTac is exciting and new for me. Deep down I know I belong here, but I bask in the sensation of seeing things for the first time. The high-rise buildings and bustling city streets are much different than the suburbs of Silver Lake. I like the busyness of the people walking around with important things to get to and places to go. It makes me feel like I'm not standing still anymore.

"Ready?" Jake pats my leg and sighs. "We're here."

"Where?" I crane my neck to see through the window on his side of the car. The gigantic prison looms over us, casting a shadow over the car. "Is that it?"

"That's it. The Fed-Pen," the driver of the car says. "You want me to wait, man?"

Jake hands the man two hundred-dollar bills. "Wait for us, yes. I'll double that when we come out." The driver looks impressed and clicks his seat back a few notches, ready to settle in. Jake sticks his hands in his pockets and pulls everything out but returns his wallet to his front jeans pocket. "Make sure you don't have anything but your ID on you when we go through security."

"Like what?" My voice shakes. "Like weapons?"

"Anything that can be considered a weapon, Bug. All you'll need is your ID, that's it."

I follow his directions and hand over a tube of cherry ChapStick, rolled-up earbuds, several pieces of wrapped hard candy and a folded-up note. "What's this?" He holds up the paper and shakes it.

Playfully, I shrug. "Open it later and find out."

He blushes and takes his wallet back out, placing the paper inside before putting it into his jeans again. He takes off his motorcycle jacket—no doubt because of all the zippers and metal detector triggers—leaving it in the backseat.

"Earrings, baby." He points to my ears. I take them off and hand them over—the same with my necklace and mood ring too. When we've got everything packed way in our luggage, Jake reminds the driver of their deal and takes my hand.

The prison haunts me already; the slate gray pavement beneath my feet tricks me into thinking it's moving so I'm frozen where I stand. Without saying a word, Jake runs back to the luggage and retrieves a headache pill and small bottle of water.

"Thanks." I take the pill and swallow it down before sipping the water. "This is gonna be stressful enough without having an earth-shattering headache in there."

"Take a deep breath, baby," Jake coos. "You can do this. I'm going in with you."

"I thought he only asked for me?"

He smiles and squeezes my hand. "I'm not letting you do this alone."

Security isn't as awful as I pictured in my mind; thankfully Jake knew not to take anything but our IDs in so the process went smoothly. We're escorted down a few hallways before coming to a stop in an open metal doorway without a door attached.

The deputy escorting us frowns. "You have twenty minutes with inmate #4982-C0541." He looks at the paper hanging on the wall next to the doorway to make sure he has the right number. "There's a deputy in the room and the inmate is shackled for your safety. There will be no touching and that includes: no hugging, no holding hands, no kissing, no physical contact of any kind. You will sit across from the inmate and keep your hands folded in front of you. You will not raise your voice; you will not give the inmate anything. You will not agitate the inmate, and you will not sneak anything out of the prison. Do you both understand me?"

Jake nods. "We get it."

"Miss?"

"Sounds pretty self-explanatory."

The deputy's frown deepens. "You would think

so, Miss. You are free to enter; the twenty minutes starts now. I will be back for a three-minute warning."

I waste two minutes standing in the doorway, deciding if I really want to go in.

Eighteen minutes left.

"Baby, are you going in?" Jake whispers.

My legs start to move, and they carry me through the threshold of the doorway. The room is small and sterile; a metal table sits in the middle with three metal chairs. The man with the gray hair from my dreams sits with sadness in his cold gray eyes as he watches me approach him.

"Sweetheart," he greets me. "How are you, Lacey?"

This is the first time anyone's every greeted me by that name directly; I admit, it doesn't feel good. His accent is soft around his voice when he speaks; his voice is weak and tired.

"Jacob." He nods at Jake. "I asked to speak to my daughter alone, yet here you are. Why am I not surprised? You don't know when to leave well enough alone, do you?"

My head hurts; the pill isn't helping me.

"Don't." My throat is dry; it's hard to swallow and not choke on the dry air. "Don't speak to him like that. If you want me to stay, you don't talk to him like that."

Michael nods. "Have it your way, then. I understand you've started gaining memories back?"

"Some of them."

"That's fantastic. The doctors said it wasn't likely you'd recover. What's changed?"

Finally, I sit down across from him. Jake continues to stand; he places his hand on my shoulder for comfort. "I started having headaches and dreams. Then Jake found me, and I figured out the truth."

Michael hangs his head. "I'm truthfully sorry about how things have turned out, love. I never meant for anything like this—"

"Is this why you wanted to see me? To plead your case?"

He looks surprised. The lines on his face are darker than in my dreams; the time he's spent in prison hasn't agreed with him. He was never a large man, but being in this place...he's withered into almost nothing.

"I wanted to see you because you're my daughter. And yes, maybe I wanted to plead my case...not for forgiveness, but for you to understand this was never my intention."

"People never intend to hurt other people, Dad." The words come out of my mouth before I realize it. It doesn't feel wrong so I don't correct myself. "You out of all people should understand that."

Fourteen minutes left.

"What's that supposed to mean?"

The deputy in the corner pretends that he's not listening, but we both know it's part of his job. Jake still stands next to me and squeezes my shoulder as Michael narrows his cold eyes at me, waiting for me to explain myself.

"Where's Sabine?"

A fire rages in my head, and he comes in and out of focus.

"Is she okay? What's happening to her?" Michael frantically calls out. "Jake, what's going on?"

Jake sits down next to me and brushes back hair from my face. He places a hand in the air for the deputy to stand down from tending to me. "Do you need to leave?"

"No, we still have twelve minutes."

His hands find my shoulders, and he massages them to relieve some tension. "The headaches she has, they aren't normal headaches. They incapacitate her sometimes."

Michael frowns. "Oh, Lacey—"

"My name is Olivia." I correct him. "Olivia White."

"Right." The shackles on his arms and legs clink together. "If I tell you about your mother, will you promise that you'll come and visit me again?"

"Just tell her about her mother," Jake snarls.

My head starts to throb, and it's only moments from exploding. "I promise."

Jake looks over at me with worried eyes. "Olivia, you don't have to do that."

"I want to. I'll come back and visit you." I turn back to Jake and frown. "Twenty minutes isn't enough to get through want I need to get through."

Eight minutes left.

"Sabine lives in Maryville, just under an hour north from here. Her name is Sabine Christensen now, and Lacey—sorry, Olivia—don't be alarmed if you don't get the answers you're looking for. Your mother is a very…complicated woman."

Jake snorts. "Complicated woman? That's a nice

way of saying she's bat-shit crazy."

"More like an emotionless robot."

The deputy from before returns to the open doorway, and it's our three-minute warning.

"Olivia." The way Michael says my name sounds like a made-up word. "Don't forget to come back and visit me. I'll be here for the next ten years, eight with good behavior. I want to tell you everything, love; I can't make up for what I've done, but I can help you with your memory."

One minute left.

Michael starts to move his hands toward mine but decides against it. "I love you. You are the most beautiful and perfect daughter a father could ever ask for. I'm sorry you've had such a shit life, and even as much as I hate that Jake is here with you, he's the only one that can take care of you the way you need to be. He's always been that rock for you no matter how much I tried to stop it."

"Sounds like a compliment." Jake's eyebrows rise.

"Time to go, guys." The deputy peeks his head inside. "Thirty seconds."

"I love you, Olivia." Tears fall down Michael's cheeks. "Always remember that I love you."

Jake kisses the side of my head and stands up, walking toward the door to give me ten seconds of privacy.

"I love you too." I'm surprised the words came from my mouth. "I don't forgive you, but I don't hate you, okay?"

He chuckles through his tears. "Okay, love. You let Jake take care of you. That boy loves you more than I've ever seen anyone love another person. He'd do anything for you."

"You have no idea." I smile. "Take care of yourself, Dad."

Jake reaches out for my hand and turns back to nod at Michael. There's a level of peace inside of me that resonates until we go back through security and slip into the backseat of the cab. The headache that pounded against my skull has faded into nothing.

After giving the driver the address of his house, Jake leans back and wraps his arm around me before pulling me into his chest.

"Let's go home," I say. "I'm ready to go home."

Chapter Twenty-Five

Carnival

Jake

The woman that flutters around me in our bedroom at the Seattle house is someone I never thought I'd lay eyes on again. Olivia isn't just the girl I used to love…she's the woman I can't fucking live without. We've only been back in Seattle a few days—and the first day was a little rocky—but I can't help thinking that we don't belong here.

Olivia *doesn't* belong here.

I can't be without her.

Laughing as she takes silly selfies of herself with the new phone I got her, she pulls her body onto mine and sits in my lap in the green, oversized armchair next to the fireplace. My dick gets hard thinking about the night before and the amazing sex we had on this very chair, but I can't be inside of her every single moment of every single day.

No matter how fucking badly I want to be.

"Smile!" She giggles and presses our cheeks together. We both look into the camera, and I plaster the biggest, warmest smile on my face I can muster. The bullshit with my mother and Olivia's father is weighing down on me, but I can't—and won't—let her see me worry about it. It's over, but it never really fucking feels like it's over.

After inspecting the picture and smiling in acceptance, she places the phone down on the table next to us and takes my head into her hands.

"Jake Redding, you need to stop worrying so much." She crinkles her adorable nose. "Haven't I told you a hundred times that you have nothing to worry about?"

I sigh and pull her into me, wrapping my arms around her curves. "I don't want to think about that. Let's do something fun." A wicked smile spreads on my face as she swats me away, and we both laugh the biggest, purest laugh we have. "I don't mean sex, although I'd never turn *that* down."

"There's the city carnival downtown." She holds up a flyer. "I saw this in the phone store earlier today. Wanna go?"

I make a sour face. "Sorry, baby. Clowns really aren't my thing."

Snuggling her body into my lap, she places her head over my heart. "Please? We could be that really cheesy couple that runs around to all the games and you can try to win me the biggest, most ridiculous stuffed animal they have."

My eyebrows rise. "Are we a couple, then? We haven't really talked about that."

Her thighs tighten around my legs, and the only

thing I want right now is to thrust upward—

"I thought we were." She laughs and pushes her lips onto mine. "Let's not dance around the subject like middle schoolers, okay? I want to exclusively be with you." She playfully gags and kisses my cheek.

I play with her silky, dark brown hair between my fingers. "Okay, then, we won't dance around it. You're mine, and that's that." The softness of her skin underneath my fingertips entices me into a dark place I really don't need to be right now for both our sakes. She does things to me that even I don't fully understand.

I can stay like this forever.

Touching her is lethal to my mind, though.

One touch and everything's done and over with for me when it comes to her.

I close my eyes. "If it means that much to you, we can go to the carnival."

"Really?" She jumps off my lap. It takes everything I have not to reach out and grab her to pull her back into my vortex again. "Okay, I'm going to take a shower and get ready."

And she's gone.

I'm left alone in the bedroom to worry. Just because Sam's crazy fucking ass got picked up doesn't mean it's over. In order for him to pay for what he's done, she'll have to go back to Silver Lake and testify against him. I told Neal to take care of it, but that's the way it has to fucking be, and I haven't had the heart to tell her yet. She shouldn't have to face her attacker a second time.

"Jake!" Her voice squeaks with fear from the

bathroom. "Come here, hurry!" Several quick emotions wash over me, and I half-expect to see someone standing in there with her but she's alone.

Catching my breath, I look at her sitting on the edge of the bathtub with her feet extended in the air.

"What's wrong?" I look around the room.

She dramatically points toward the opposite corner from where she is. "There's a spider!"

I see the small spider where she's pointing, and a warm feeling washes over me. Without hesitation, I swoop down and grab the insect and rush it downstairs and outside. Normally, I would've smashed the shit out of it, but with Olivia watching, this was the better thing for her to see me do. When I return to her, she's started the shower, and the steam tickles my nose when I enter the bathroom.

"It's gone, baby."

The door to the shower opens, and her wet head sticks out. "Thanks, he surprised me. You probably think I'm such a baby for that."

I shrug. "It helps that you're cute."

Her smile widens, and she returns to the shower before letting me see her blush. Oh, but I fucking *know* she's blushing in that steamy shower...naked and wet and...

I have to get the hell out of here.

After sniffing myself to make sure I can dress without showering, I'm dressed in jeans and a sweater, and I pull on my boots while I'm waiting for her to enter the room. I think about how she's going to walk back in to me...will she be naked? Wrapped up in a towel? *Wet and inviting*?

Jesus.

Take a deep breath, Jake.

There she is.

"Sorry, I didn't take any clothes in with me." She blushes, and her naked, wet body glides across the room. Her tits bounce as she walks, making my mouth water because my lips want to suction themselves around her erect nipples. Her skin is so damn soft it makes my brain melt inside my skull, and it's really, *really* fucking hard not to touch her as she passes me several times. First, she pulls on panties and hides her ass from me. Next, she clasps a bra around her tits so I can't see those anymore, either. Finally, the jeans and silky olive-green blouse clutch against her skin, and everything I dream about is hidden from me.

But that's perfectly fine.

I know it's all mine and only for me.

"Jake?" A giggle wraps around her voice. "You okay?"

I lick my lips. "Fine. I'm fine. Ready?"

She nods and pulls on her sneakers, ready to go. The innocent smile on her lips humbles me as I grab the keys—and grab her hand—ready to get into the car and go to the carnival.

I go because she wants to go; I go because I love her, and if going to a carnival makes her happy, then we'll stay there all night until she's had enough.

I still really don't fucking like clowns, though.

The bright lights of the carnival invite us into the parking lot, even though it's midday and sunny. I park the car and run around to her side to let her out like a gentleman; she notices and kisses me on the cheek; everything around us just seems so sweet and simple that it's hard to realize that it's not. Our lives aren't sweet and simple, we have forces working against us, and it pisses me off that anyone could want to even hurt Olivia at all. My mind wanders to Sam and how he tried to hurt her, but I took care of that, and she'll never know what happened if I can help it.

"Oh, look!" She squeals with delight and tugs me toward a row of striped covered booths where the carnival games are. By the time we've played the area three times over, she's got an arm full of stuffed animals and a wide smile on her face. "I'm hungry. What should we do with these?" she asks, holding up her prizes. "Should we find some kids and give them away?"

"I don't think walking up to random children and giving them toys is acceptable, baby." I laugh and take the car keys from my pocket. "I'll run them to the car and we can donate them to a hospital or something tomorrow. You go ahead and figure out what you want to eat, and I'll be back."

It takes me less than five minutes to get to the car and back.

But now she's gone.

Vanished.

***

Olivia

Reading every sign for every food truck at the carnival is a task. My stomach grumbles as I walk

241

past the root beer floats and cotton candy stand, and then the funnel cake takes my nose on an entirely different ride. The scents of the carnival food trigger my brainwaves and send them into a frenzy.

Hold on.

Something isn't right.

My head hurts a little, and my vision gets hazy, so I find a picnic table and sit down. I'm sure Jake will come looking for me soon, so staying put will be my best option. I can't see five feet in front of me without my eyes watering. I hold my head in my hands, and it feels like something is snapping like firecrackers in my brain. The bright lights are affecting me more now; my brain feels like it's slamming against my skull so it can escape.

"Livvie?" a familiar voice says. "Hey, Liv, are you okay?"

I squint up at them.

Brant!

"What—what are you doing here?" My mouth manages to move, but it hurts my head worse.

He leans down and gets eye level with me while the girl he's with scoffs and puts her hands on her hips. "She's my friend," he says to her and brushes the hair from my face. "Hey, Liv? Can you hear me?" He raises his voice, but all I can do is fall into his chest and groan in pain. Without saying anything else, Brant lifts me up and starts to carry me against him with his date in tow. I need to tell him that Jake is here and he's going to be looking for me, but I can't open my mouth to speak because I'm in so much pain.

A man in a uniform stops us and asks questions

that Brant can't really answer.

"What's wrong with her?" the man demands.

"She's my friend, and I found her like this. She has head issues, I think," Brant answers.

"What's her name then?"

"Olivia White."

The man in uniform steps closer and raises his voice. "Olivia? Olivia White?"

I'm able to raise my head enough off Brant's chest to acknowledge my own name, so the man is satisfied and steps back to his original stance.

"Does she need an ambulance?"

Brant shifts his weight to hold me better. "Man, I don't know, okay? I literally walked up and found her like this. I can take her if you'd just let us go."

After a few seconds, the man steps aside and lets Brant carry me out of the carnival and into the parking lot. "I'm glad I found you, Liv. What are you doing in Seattle? Where've you been for the past few months?"

I groan so loudly that people walking into the carnival stop to stare. "Jake." I let his name escape my lips. "Jake is here."

Brant stops and looks around. "Where's Jake?"

"My...Jake." I close my eyes and take a deep breath. "I have a phone in my pocket."

Brant finds his car and places me gently inside. Nervously looking down at me, he fishes inside my jeans pockets for my phone and pulls it out. "Okay, let's call Jake." He breathes in and out deeply before making the call.

I hear Jake's booming voice on the phone as Brant speaks to him. Seconds later, he comes bolting from the carnival with fear oozing all over the pavement as he skids on his knees to pull me close. "I was so fucking scared. What happened?" He looks up at Brant for answers, and I let him tell Jake whatever he wants because my head hurts so badly that I can't stop him.

"Can you drive us to the hospital?" Jake asks him.

Brant agrees and gets into the driver's seat while his date slides in next to him in the passenger seat. Jake tucks me inside fully and climbs into the car, but before Brant can start it and pull out of the parking lot, something snaps inside my head, and the pain drifts away to the point where I can stand to open my eyes without burning my eyeballs up.

"Wait." I breathe heavily and blink a few times. "We don't have to go to the hospital. I'm fine."

Jake shakes his head. "No, you're not. You need to go—"

"I don't want to go," I growl at him and narrow my eyes. "I said I'm fine. Let me out."

Before Brant can fully stop the car, I jump out, and Jake follows me. Brant gets out to watch, but his date has had enough drama and chooses to sulk inside the car. After catching up with me and swinging me around to face him, the fear in his eyes fades; he brushes my hair back from my face to get a good look at me.

"It's just a headache." I swat him away. "That's all. Let's go back to the carnival."

For a few seconds, I know he wants to argue with me. I know he wants to take control and whisk me away to get my head checked out, but the pain has gone away and my vision is coming back piece by piece. Even the dark edges of my life tattoos on his skin look brighter than before when my vision fully shifts back into a normal state.

Jake sighs and looks back at Brant, who shrugs his shoulders and places his arms on the top of his car. "Are you sure you're okay?" he says when he looks back down at me. "Maybe we should just go back home and rest."

"I'm fine, okay? I'm lucky Brant found me—"

Brant comes around his car and stands next to Jake. He's not much smaller than him, and Jake's copper blonde curls swaying with the light breeze and Brant's sunshine-colored shaggy hair make them look like long-lost brothers. Jake crosses his arms over his chest, and Brant shoves his into his pockets. But they both have looks of concern on their faces.

"You were basically unresponsive, Liv," Brant says. "I had to carry you out of there."

"I know that. I was there. It was just a headache."

They look at each other again as if they are silently having a conversation about my life. They don't get to decide what I do. Only I do. "Look." I put a smile on my face although my head still feels a little fuzzy. "Let's all go back into the carnival and eat some food. I need food. Feed me, Jake." I smile devilishly and bite my bottom lip. "Feed me."

He knows this isn't fair, but he takes the bait anyway. "Fine, but afterward if you feel funny at all, you're going to the hospital."

"Yes, sir."

Jake blushes and takes my hand before turning to Brant. "Thank you for looking after her. I'm lucky someone found her that cares for her. Can we treat you and your date to a dinner of carnival food as a thank you?"

Brant laughs and looks back at his car, and it's empty. "Well, looks like she hightailed it out of here, so if you don't mind me being the third wheel…"

Jake pats him on the shoulder. "Park the car and we'll wait for you."

The camaraderie between them is heartwarming, and for the next two hours we hit every food booth in the carnival, and our time together ends in laughter and friendship. Brant drove up to Seattle from Silver Lake because his date—who took a cab back to her parents' house in town—grew up here and wanted to come back for the carnival.

I never knew Jake could be such a loving and warm person to someone he used to see as a threat, but he's changed. I mean really, *really* changed. The scary person I met again months ago just isn't there anymore.

Maybe—somehow—I managed to fix him after all.

Chapter Twenty-Six

Phoenix

"Are you sure you want to do this?" Jake's eyebrows rise. "Baby, just because I have tattoos doesn't mean you need to mess up your perfect body and perfect skin…" He kisses my fingers one by one. "I'm not saying don't do it. I'm just saying…*think* about it."

I'm already sitting in the chair at the tattoo parlor, ready to go.

"Jake, I'm doing this. Now help me figure out what I'm getting. What about a unicorn?"

He frowns and makes a gagging sound. "I wouldn't be able to have sex with you staring at unicorn." He pretends to shiver; he laughs as I smack his shoulder because it's the only part of him I can quickly reach.

"A unicorn it is, then."

"It's a good thing I'm in love with you or else you'd be in so much trouble for your little fucking attitude," he growls in my ear. "You have two hours before your appointment with Dr. Ross. You better choose something."

The pictures and sketches on the wall are all amazing, but not for me. The black binders next to me have one-of-a-kind artwork, but none of that speaks to me either. Jake reaches his long arms for another book, letting my hand fall and brush against his inner thigh on purpose.

"Nice." I snort. "Classy you are."

He shrugs and pretends to be innocent. The next book he hands me is smaller than the rest and purple instead of black. The pages are thicker and the designs are darker and more eclectic. Jake points to a few as I pass them, but once I turn the next page over, the dark red and black lines of a palm-sized phoenix call to me.

"That's the one." My fingers hit the plastic over the page. "A phoenix gets reborn from ashes. It's perfect."

Jake's brown eyes find mine and soften. "Have I mentioned how proud I am of you for coming this far? You're pretty fucking remarkable, Olivia White."

"Oh, my first *and* last name, you must mean business."

His sexy laugh sends chills down my spine. "Oh, I think I've more than proven that I mean serious business when it comes to you." He presses his lips on mine and gently parts them. The tattoo artist knocks on the door, and we quickly part; Jake rubs my lip gloss from his lips as the man enters the room and introduces himself.

"I'm Romero. Did you find one you like?" His

long, dark braided beard ends at his chest. I show him the phoenix, and he nods. "That's one of my brand-new ones, good choice. Shouldn't take too long. You stayin', man?"

Jake takes his phone from his pocket. "Are you okay if I run a few errands?"

"What errands could you possibly have in Silver Lake?"

"You'll see." He winks. "If you want me to stay, I will. It's your first one, baby."

I wave him off. "Go run your errands."

"Take good care of my girl." Jake kisses my forehead and leaves the room as Romeo salutes him. He's gone the entire time it takes to put the bird on my shoulder—where I finally decided I wanted it—and when he steps back into the room, he examines Romero's work and smiles.

"That's really fucking amazing," he compliments the artist. "Maybe I'll stop in before we leave town and get a new one. Thanks, man."

Romero nods and pats my other shoulder. "I'll meet you up front and get you a few things, okay?"

Jake helps me up from the chair and wraps his arms around my waist. "We only have twenty minutes to get to Dr. Ross' office. You ready?"

"I'm ready. I'm glad I did this before we went there. I already feel more in control of my life."

He lightly kisses my lips. "I'm glad you decided to keep going by Olivia…I think it's sexy. I also think that tattoo is sexy. It's turning me on."

"Jake," I warn him. "You just said we have twenty minutes to make it to Dr. Ross. We can't—"

The fire in his eyes reaches for me and consumes

whatever defense I have.

"What if Romero comes back in?" His body pushes me against the wall next to the door. Spreading my legs apart, he unzips his jeans and puts me gently on my feet. His fingers find the clasp of my jeans and unhooks them, roughly pulling them from my legs and onto the floor.

He turns me to face the wall, and a package crinkles behind me. With one hand, he grips my hair; he wraps it around his hand and pulls, making my head tip backward. A satisfied grunt comes from his throat as he kisses the side of my neck and spreads my legs with his, pushing himself inside of me.

My moans echo in the room; it's a wonder no one comes rushing in to see what we're doing in here. With each deep thrust Jake pushes inside of me, the world melts more around us.

"Jesus, Olivia." He breathes heavily and starts to thrust into me so hard that the wall starts to shake. It's not until he carries me to the chair and sits down with my back against his chest that my eyes can focus again. My body bounces against him, and he clutches my sides, pushing me up and down to his pleasure. Jake cries out into my naked shoulder and wraps his arms around me for a few minutes to catch his breath and let his heart rate slow down.

My throat is dry; I half-expect puffs of smoke to come out when I speak. "We're definitely going to be late for my appointment."

***

Dr. Ross sits in his chair and waits for me to enter the room. The disappointment he feels is apparent as he continuously checks the clock on the wall. "You're late."

"I know, I'm sorry." My fingers smooth over my hair one more time; Jake and I paid for my tattoo and raced across town just to still be fifteen minutes late. "This won't take long."

"I hear your dreams were true after all. Are you here to ask if I knew?"

The familiar squeaky brown leather sofa is probably the only thing I'll miss about coming to this place. Dr. Ross doesn't have his signature yellow notepad this time; I guess that's something I'll miss too.

"Did you know?"

He shakes his head. "I'm afraid I didn't. Although, if I had, I wouldn't have been able to tell you."

"I know that. I wouldn't blame you if you kept it from me. I know you were just doing your job. Which is why I'm here."

"You want to try being hypnotized again."

My cheeks flush. "Is that okay?"

Dr. Ross smiles and pushes his glasses on the bridge of his nose. "Tell me everything first and then we'll see what we can do. What exactly did you find out, Olivia?"

I take a deep breath and tell Dr. Ross the entire story from beginning to end. I start with moving to the house across from Jake when I was nine and end with getting my phoenix tattoo—I leave out the sex with Jake part. By time I'm finished, it's been over an hour, and Dr. Ross sits on the edge of his seat like he's watching an intense movie.

"Good Lord." His hands cover his mouth slightly. "How are you dealing with everything? Let's talk about that."

"I'm just taking one day at a time. Jake's been a big help, and he's been really patient with me."

He shakes his head. "You truly are a remarkable young woman."

"Can we try hypnosis now? Jake's waiting for me, and it's a long drive back to Seattle."

Once he's set up and puts me into a sleep, it's hard to focus on a single memory since I've been storing so many in my brain. What was once empty is now starting to fill.

***

"What are we doing here, Mom?"

Sabine puts her finger to her lips and shushes me. She told me we were going shopping for school supplies, but instead she's dragged me by my hair into an old office building that smells like moldy cheese. She pushes me down into a cold metal chair and points her skinny finger in my face.

"Stay fucking put. Don't move. Understand me, Lacey?"

I nod. "Yes, Mom."

"If you move one fucking muscle, you'll regret it."

"Yes, Mom."

She straightens her blouse. "Good. I'll be right back."

She's gone for hours. No one comes into the building, and no one leaves. I'm alone, and there's nothing I can do but stare at the white walls and walk around the empty offices. When darkness starts to fall outside, I search the rest of the building for her.

She's not here.

She left me.

I wait another hour and realize she's really gone.

The air outside is warm, and it makes me thirsty as I start to walk in the dark along streets I've never been to before. I don't know where I am; I don't know where she left me. A few car lights pass me by so quickly that water splashes on me from small puddles created by the light rain earlier today.

"You lost, little girl?" a woman screeches from somewhere in front of me.

I think I'm imagining things.

"Hey, you there!"

My legs start to pound against the pavement, and I run as fast as I can. There's woods around me now, and strange sounds come from the trees. I walk forever; my feet hurt when I reach a diner on the side of the road.

Starlight Drive-In, *the sign says.*

The door is hard to push open, but I manage to get it far enough to fall inside. Several chairs scoot across the floor after I hit the hard floor; several pairs of hands reach for me and lift me into the air like their savior. It's hard to focus on who says what, but they shove a straw in my mouth and the cold water trickles down my throat, reviving me enough to shift my eyes around.

The waitress wears a pink dress and white apron.

The truck driver's hat is green and says, "Truckers do it better."

The man in the suit has hair like Dad.

Dad.

"I need to call my dad."

The waitress—her nametag says Bev—sits down across from me. "Sweetheart, you just fell into our door at one a.m. What's your name, baby?"

Her southern accent is nice and welcoming.

"Lacey."

"What are you doin' out here this late at night, Lacey?"

I don't want to tell on Mom; she'll get in trouble.

"I ran away from home."

"And now you wanna call your dad to come get you?"

I drink more water and drum my fingers on the table. "Yes, please."

"Do you know his number?"

I nod. "I know it. Do you have a phone I can use?"

Bev gestures toward the bar, and a white table phone sits on the end. All eyes are on me as I scoot from the booth and reach it, dial Dad's number, and he doesn't answer. I call him four times before he picks up and snarls. "Who the fuck is this?"

"Daddy." I start to cry. "Can you come and get me?"

"Lacey? Sweetheart, where are you? I thought you were with Mom?"

254

If I tell him what happened...

...I can't lie my way out of this one.

"She took me to a building and left me there. I walked a long time and ended up at this diner. I don't know where I am. I'm scared, Daddy."

Michael inhales and exhales slowly. "Is there an adult around?"

"The waitress, her name is Bev."

"Very good, darling. Put Miss Bev on the phone and you sit down and order whatever you'd like, all right? I'm on my way to get you."

"Okay, Daddy."

"Lacey?"

"Yes?"

"Be a brave girl for me, okay? This is the last time your mother will ever hurt you, I promise. I'm sorry I let you down. I'll always protect you from now on. You can count on me."

I wave Bev over and hand her the phone; I go back to the booth and open the menu, looking at my choice just like Dad said. When she hangs up the phone and returns to me, there's sadness on her face, and I know Dad told her everything.

"How about some chocolate chip pancakes, whipped cream, warm maple syrup, and a sundae? Your daddy will be a few hours."

The truck driver and man in the suit go back to their own booths but keep a close eye on me as Bev tousles my hair and runs off to get my goodies. My stomach is so full that I can't finish the sundae, and I feel myself starting to drift to sleep.

The man in the suit takes off his jacket and wraps it around me; I lie down in the booth and sleep until the bell on the door rings and I feel Dad's arms around me. He thanks everyone and cradles me in his arms. Bev whispers a goodbye to me and tells Dad she'll pray for him. He thanks her and takes me back out into the dark early morning and places me in the backseat of his car.

"Hey Lacey Bug," I hear Jake whisper.

"Jake?" I yawn and find his shoulder, snuggling into it. He wraps a blanket around us and leans his head back onto the headrest, returning Dad's gaze in the rearview mirror.

"Let's go home, kids," Dad says and pulls the car onto the dark roads.

Jake holds my hand under the blanket. "What are you doing here?" I whisper.

"Your dad called my mom and asked her if I could come with him. He thought you might need me right now."

I smile. "I always need you, Jake. You're my best friend."

"I love you, Lacey. You should go to sleep. We can talk about everything tomorrow."

I kiss his cheek, and his arm rests on my shoulders.

"I'll never need anyone more than you, Lacey Bug."

***

Dr. Ross makes me promise to come back and spend more sessions with them when I can. I don't have the heart to tell him Jake and I plan to move away from Seattle someday.

Jake waits for me in the car; he's talking on the phone but hangs up when he sees me emerge from the doctor's office with a pale face and wet eyes.

"What happened?" he asks when I get into the car. "Olivia, what—"

"You never told me how you and Michael came to get me when my mom left me in the middle of nowhere."

Jake's face pales. "I didn't want you to know. I'd hoped that memory wouldn't come back."

"You can't do that. You can't pick and choose what you want me to remember, Jake. It doesn't work like that. I don't want any more surprises, okay?"

"Okay, Bug."

I cross my arms over my chest. "Let's go home. We have a long drive. You can make it up to me."

"I'll never stop trying, baby." He smirks and starts the car, heading for Seattle. "You don't want to visit your parents or Caitlyn while you're here?"

"They've already moved back to Seattle for now. I think they're moving to the East Coast."

He knows I want to leave Silver Lake and never look back.

And I don't.

The red phoenix that glitters on my shoulder made me feel better for the first few days that things started to settle down, but honestly, nothing has really been *settled*. Just because I know that I'm not crazy to think I'm living someone else's life doesn't make anything clearer.

I know I'm Olivia White.

That much I know for sure.

Whatever that means, of course. Honestly, I don't even have a straightforward answer to what it means. Who knows exactly who they are, really? Even Jake struggles with trying to be someone he thinks he needs to be sometimes, and it's hard to see him hide himself to try and be the man he thinks I want him to be. I just want him to be Jake—the intense and sensitive man that holds the key to everything I am or ever will be. There isn't a minute since I realized I fell in love with him that I didn't want to spend every waking minute with him no matter how much he annoys the shit out of me sometimes.

Most of the house has been packed up or sold off—thanks to Caitlyn's help as she stayed here with us before they left for South Carolina—but we've yet to decide where we're moving to after the dust settles. For now, we're in limbo, and it's not a foreign feeling to me to not know whether I'm coming or going.

"Good morning, baby." Jake kisses my forehead. "Noah just called me."

The coffee tastes fantastic on my tongue. "Did he find Sabine?"

"He found her." He sighs and takes my hand into his, leading me into the living room. "If you want to contact her, I'll take you to meet her. If you don't, that's fine too. That choice is yours and yours only. No one can sway you on that decision."

"I don't want to meet her. She didn't want me then, and I doubt she wants me now. It's not going to change anything, either. Not really," I answer almost immediately. I've given it some thought since Michael told me her name and the truth about her, and deep down I know I can't trust anything he says, but something just...fits. Not to mention she abandoned me in the middle of nowhere without a second thought.

Jake notices my reservation and sits down on the sofa with worry in his soft brown eyes. "Are you sure about that? I don't know much about her, Olivia. I wouldn't bother with her, but it's not up to me."

"There's really only one other way to make up my mind—ask my mom about it."

He nods his head and leaves the room after kissing my forehead. He knows I should be alone for this, but it's hard for him to leave and not take charge of making sure he's there for me. I take the phone from my pocket and dial my mother's number—*the one that actually treats me like a daughter*—and wait for her to answer. I hadn't talked to her in a few weeks, so when she answers, the surprise in her voice startles both of us.

"Livvie?" Her voice cracks. "Is everything okay?"

"I'm fine," I answer straight away because I don't want to waste any time. "We found Sabine."

She sucks in air through her teeth. "How was that? Are you okay?"

She's so silent that I have to check the phone screen to make sure the call didn't drop. After a few long seconds, she sighs and chuckles. "I hardly knew your mother. After my mother divorced Michael when I was eleven, she kept me from him for a long time. It wasn't until Sabine came into the picture a few years later and he married her that I met her." Jake peeks his head back into the room to make sure I'm okay. I wave my hand at him to come in, and his lean body relaxes next to mine; he hands me a wine glass with a dark red substance inside.

"Thought you might need this." He kisses my fingers.

I zone back into the phone conversation and take a drink of the wine in my hand. "What was she like?"

"Your mother?" It pains her to say it out loud, but she knows there isn't another way to talk about her. "She was...young. Twenty years younger than Michael. I hated her because Michael was finally fighting to be a part of my life, but when Sabine entered the situation, things changed."

I nearly choke on my wine. "You mean, when I came along."

"No, I was excited for you. I was sixteen and about to be a big sister—I was excited. Things changed when Sabine found out that you existed. Something shifted inside of her, and she became colder and more deflective. She always hated having me around, even if it was for just a weekend."

Licking the excess wine from my lips, I frown. "Did she ever love me?"

"I'm sure there was a time that she did. I don't know what to tell you to make things better, Livvie. You were raised by a nanny because she couldn't bother. She never held you or changed your diapers. When you fell and broke your arm on your tenth birthday, she didn't take you to the hospital. Jake's mother had to do that because Sabine refused."

My eyes widen with disgust. "Jake's mom did that?" He notices his name, and his ears perk up. "I thought she hated me."

"She may hate you now for taking her son away." My mother laughs into the phone. "But she always treated you like one of her own when you were younger. Things got weird for a while, and no one knew where Sabine was, and that's when Michael told everyone she disappeared."

I finish the glass and hand it back to Jake; he notices that I need more so he kisses my forehead and jumps up to retrieve it. "What do you think I should do?" I ask. "Do you think I should try and contact her?"

My mother sucks in air through her teeth like she's put her hand on a hot burner. "That's up to you, Liv. No matter what, me and your dad are here for you, and so is Caitlyn. We're your family, no matter who else comes into the picture. Think about it and do whatever your heart tells you to do."

"Life only gives you one mother." I slap my hand over my mouth.

She doesn't seem surprised. "Life gives you whatever it thinks you need and can handle. You needed a mother, so life brought me to you. Sure, you had some tragic times before we got there, but can you honestly imagine it any other way?"

"No."

I almost feel her smile through the phone. "That's nice to hear. Trust yourself, Liv—you're the only one that you can fully trust with every ounce of yourself. I'm not saying you can't trust Jake, but he can't make this decision for you."

When we hang up, I don't feel any better than before I called her. When Jake comes back with more wine, his face twists in confusion when he looks down at me.

"You okay, baby?" He hands me the glass, and my hands shake.

I swig it all down and look up at him with tears in the corners of my eyes.

"We're going to Maryville."

Chapter Twenty-Seven

Sabine

The last thing I remember about my mother is her leaving me behind. It's different...I shouldn't say I remember, because I don't. Just because these dreams are actually memories resurfacing doesn't mean anything. The feelings that should be there in the memories just...aren't.

Jake notices I'm frustrated but gives me space. That's really been my saving grace since the first day waking up in the hospital; the patience he tries so hard to have is endearing.

Taking daily medicine hasn't completely taken my headaches away, but they are few and far between. There are days where I feel more like myself—Olivia—than anything else. There are also days where I'm completely off-kilter and opposite of myself, which I assume is the person I once was—Lacey.

My life is confusing.

Even before my accident, my life was confusing.

But Jake always made it better.

His fingers haven't left mine since we left Seattle; the copper stubble on his face has turned into a thicker, fuzzier patch of a shadowed beard. I like the way it feels on my fingertips; the coarse hair pricks against my skin when I touch his face.

"We should've called before driving up here." Jake's voice rumbles through my brain as I look outside at the passing scenery—which isn't much to even look at. The dried-up ground passing us by looks like it's been burned and forgotten. "Don't you think we should've called first?"

I laugh. "Are you nervous about meeting *my* mother? Have you met *your* mother? How bad could this one be compared to her?"

"Fair enough." He laughs with me and follows the GPS line toward the address we mustered up online for Sabine. She's changed her name, but the connections that Jake still has were able to figure out exactly where she is.

It's a strange feeling, though—trying to find someone who doesn't want to be found. It's an even stranger feeling trying to find someone who abandoned you as a child…literally. I guess I take comfort in the fact it wasn't on the side of the road or in the middle of the woods.

On the long drive, Jake and I have been through every possible scenario *including* the ones where Sabine clearly doesn't want to be found and screams at me that I'm a waste of space and to leave her alone. I don't much care for that one, but I can't be naïve in thinking that she'll welcome me with open arms. I don't think I'm even looking for that, honestly. I think I'm more looking for closure on a life I can't remember so I can start living a life that was meant for me with a clear conscience.

"Bug, you forget that I have actually met your mother." Jake turns the car and parks on the side of the street. "I knew her when she was around. Not well—she pretty much kept to herself and didn't care about our side of the street, but I still knew her from coming around you."

We're parked on the side of a wealthy suburban street with children playing outside of a few houses and people stopping to take a peek at us intruding on their picture-perfect neighborhood. "Do you remember what she was really like, though?"

"I already told you, she was cold and quiet. She hardly ever spoke two words to me, and I never saw her even do anything motherly. Your dad was always the one at softball games, parades, and talent shows, baby." I don't want to believe that, but it hurts Jake to tell me the truth so I have to be diplomatic about it. He waves at an older man who stops walking his dog to glare at us because he knows we don't belong here. "We're here. It's that house over there…you ready?"

Three small children play around the plush green lawn of the mini-mansion he points to: two boys and a girl. They look like they're all under the age of ten; the boys both have dark hair like me, but the little girl has golden blonde curls.

Before I think about it, I step from the car, and Jake has to rush to keep up with me as I barge onto their front lawn. The oldest boy puts his siblings behind him and crosses his arms over his chest.

He's not afraid to defend his siblings; I find that admirable.

"Who are you?" he demands.

"My name is Olivia." I smile and try to diffuse the tension. "I'm looking for Sabine Christensen. Does she live here?"

The boy narrows his eyes at me. "I don't know you, and I don't know a Sabine."

"Mommy's name is Sabine, Jeffrey," the little girl says. "Daddy's name is George."

The older boy frowns at her. "She's stranger. Don't tell her our names, you idiot!"

"Don't call her an idiot." Jake tugs at my shirt to warn me to back down. "That's not a nice way to talk to your sister."

The boy snorts. "You can't boss me around. I'm telling my mom."

"Jeffrey!" A woman rushes from the front door of the house and places the kids behind her in defense. It takes a few seconds for me to be able to look directly at her, but when I do, it's like looking *directly* into a mirror. She has the same thick, Hershey bar-colored hair and long, thin nose as me. She's a little taller than me, but even Jake squeezes the back of my shirt because he realizes he's looking at me in thirty years. "Who the hell are you?" She glares. "I've already called the police."

"I'm Olivia White."

She looks confused at my name. "Keep away from my children." Before she can usher them inside, I grab her hand, and she hisses at me. "You need to leave. You shouldn't be here!"

Jake steps up to my side. "Exactly why shouldn't

266

she be here?"

Sabine knows she's been caught, and it takes her a few seconds to figure out what she's going to do. After whispering to her children and ordering them to go inside, we watch the three of them reluctantly stomp back into the house.

Jeffrey looks back at me and waits until his siblings go inside. "You're my sister, aren't you?"

Sabine frowns. "Your sister is inside. Now go."

"I hear you and Dad arguing about her all the time." He shoves his hands into his pockets. "I first heard you last year on New Year's Eve."

"That's when I had my accident." I look at Jeffrey, and he smiles. "What did they argue about?"

"Dad wanted to see if we could help you, and Mom said no."

Sabine grabs him by the arm and marches him inside. When she returns, all three children start peering from the living room windows.

"You had the opportunity to help me after my accident but said no?"

Her chest heaves up and down as the weight of what she's done presses down on her more with each second that passes by. "I don't have to explain myself to you. I left you a long time ago, and as far as I'm concerned, you're no longer mine."

A chill runs down my spine, but it's too late to turn back now. "What are their names? My siblings."

She doesn't rush to answer me. "Jeffrey, Steven, and...Lacey."

Ouch. Right through my chest.

"*Lacey*? You named another child after the one you left behind?" My throat is dry, but I can't stop myself from raising my voice. "How can you be a mother to these children and not to your first one?"

She looks nervously around at her neighbors and joyfully waves them off to let them know she's okay and I'm just some crazy person on her front lawn. "I think you need to get back into your car and drive back to wherever you came from." Her eyes find mine, and they are cold and as unloving as they can be. "I don't want any trouble from you or your deceitful father, you understand me? I'm someone else's mother now."

My lips are on fire. "You're not a mother. Don't even say that. A mother doesn't take her child hours away to abandon her. A mother doesn't skip town and never look back. A mother..." I take a step forward and let the anger take over my body. "...doesn't disappear."

She laughs.

Laughs.

Jake holds the back of my shirt so I don't pounce on her. "You left me in that abandoned office building, alone and scared. What kind of monster does something like that?" I wipe the excess spit off my mouth that escapes when I'm spewing my hate for her right in her damn face.

"I knew your father would save you like he always did."

"Why didn't you just run away from home like a normal person?" My voice echoes in the air. "Why did you have to drag me hours away just to abandon me? Do you get off on being cruel?"

Sabine pales. "You were such a clingy little thing. You'd never let me go anywhere or do anything alone. You wouldn't let me leave, so I took you with me and waited until you slept and didn't know where we were to leave you. It's not like anything bad happened to you."

Rage fills my entire body. "Not like anything— what? You're fucking kidding me, right?"

"Lower your voice. I don't want my neighbors knowing about you. I'm better off if you didn't exist to these people, okay?"

"Look, she's only just found out about you and didn't hesitate in wanting to meet you to complete a part of her life she's lost." Jake closes in on her, and his tall body is intimidating. I know the look in her eyes when he towers over her; his aura suffocates you in the worst and best of ways. "But you're fucked in the head if you think I'm going to let you speak to her like that anymore. You'll speak to her with respect."

"What is it that you want from me?" She looks at me, trying to ignore him standing over her. "I haven't seen you in over ten years."

First question.

"Why *did* you leave?"

She answers instantly. "I was young when I married your father and then we had you shortly after. I never got the chance to be a young wife or finish living life before you came along. I never wanted you. He forced me to have you. I fell in love with George, my husband now, and you know the rest."

Second question.

"You didn't want to be a mother then, but now you do?"

"I love my children, all three of them." Her cold stare freezes my heart. "This conversation keeps going around in circles. You're here thinking I'll hug you and we'll be mother and daughter, and that's not happening."

Jake tugs on the back of my shirt. "Baby, you're not going to get any closure here. Maybe we should just go." He nods toward the street, where two police cars pull up and the officers make their way toward us. "I'm not going to call your mother and tell her you were arrested."

"At least she'll care more than my real mother." I glare at Sabine. "You could have taken me with you."

"I didn't want to."

Stop doing this to yourself, Olivia.

"But you could have."

The officers stay back and listen when she holds out her hands for them to back off. "I didn't want to take you with me. I didn't want you. I *never* wanted you."

I didn't want you.

I never wanted you.

My hand rises to slap her across her face, but Jake stops me just in time. He mumbles something to the officers about us leaving and wraps his arms around me in a reverse bear hug so I can't move.

"I hate you." I spit fire at her. "I'll never forgive you, and I hate you with everything I have left inside of me. I'm glad my father didn't tell me about you before now."

She shrugs and walks back into her house like it's no big deal. Jake places me in the car and goes back to speak to the officers, who eventually get back in their cars and leave. When he climbs back in next to me, he starts the car and drives out of Maryville without saying a word. Once we find a small diner on the outside of the city, he pulls in and turns off the car in silence.

"How can someone be like that?" I hold my head in my hands. "How can you just throw someone away like a piece of trash?"

His hand finds mine, and he takes it. "I don't know, baby. I couldn't imagine anyone not wanting to even be around you. You're the best thing that's ever happened to me, that's for sure."

I want to smile, but I can't. "I mean, what kind of a monster does something like that? I know I should be something other than angry, but I guess not remembering her helps with that. I don't know what I was expecting, coming here."

He kisses my fingers, and a wave of relief washes over me. "You were thinking that you wanted to know your mother and see what she's like. There's nothing wrong with that." He brushes the fabric of my shirt off of my shoulder and smiles at the red phoenix staring back at him. "This is the person you are. You've risen from the ashes of tragedy. Don't let Sabine ruin that for you."

Then it hits me.

None of this matters.

Michael and Sabine don't matter.

What they've done to me doesn't matter.

Jake matters.

271

What we have matters.

"I love you, Jake." He takes my chin in between his thumb and index finger, parting my lips with his and letting me taste his cinnamon tongue.

"I love you, Bug, more than anything." He breathes into my lips. "You're the only person I'll ever need in my life. You mean something to me, and that's the best feeling in the world, meaning something to someone, right?"

I blush and chuckle. "Are you trying to fish for a compliment?"

He laughs and starts to back the car out of the parking lot. "Have you decided where we're moving yet?" I know he wants to change the subject so he doesn't tear up, and I'm okay with that. I haven't given much thought to where we would move, and honestly it doesn't even matter where we go as long as I wake up next to Jake every morning.

"You choose." I pull up a map of all the states on my phone. "Keep your eyes on the road and point."

He laughs and rolls his eyes. "You want to me choose where we spend our future by simply pointing to a map? What if I choose the worst place on the planet?"

"Then it will be the worst place on the planet and we'll share it together."

His finger pops out into the air, and I guide him to the screen and where he touches starts to zoom in and I turn the phone so he can't see where it lands.

"So where are we moving?"

"Kansas."

"Kansas it is, then. You and me, Bug. Forever."

I lean my head back on the headrest and look at

the passing scenery outside the window. It's the same things we've seen coming in, but now it just feels different. Life feels different. I can't change my past, but I can make sure my future is everything I want it to be.

Jake held the pieces of my past on his skin and in his heart.

Now he holds the pieces of my future at the touch of his fingertip.

"I'll tell you when we get there." I smile and open the window to let the crisp air inside the car. He doesn't complain because he knows I'm washing away everything that's happened in the past few months so I can let it go and be who I want to be.

The accident doesn't define me. What happened to me doesn't define me. Jake doesn't define me, and Michael and Sabine sure as hell don't define me.

I define myself.

I choose who I want to be.

Who I'm truly meant to be.

I am Olivia White.

Chapter Twenty-Eight

A year later

The air hovering over the backyard full of friends and family is thick with love and laughter. The Midwest sun showers down on us and fills our bodies with warmth and the best feeling of being content that I've ever known.

It's been a year since Jake and I left Seattle for a quiet, suburban life in Kansas with a picket fence, friendly neighbors, and everything cliché that comes with it. He sold off all of his businesses and invested in some business opportunities that apparently are making him money. I try and stay out of that business since I know nothing about it—and really don't care to.

I got a job at the local YMCA because I felt the need to give back the time that I'd wasted in Silver Lake. No matter how many times Jake tells me it wasn't my fault...it was. I owed it to myself to try and be a better version of myself, whatever that meant.

The phoenix tattoo on my back helps to remind me of what I'd lost without knowing I'd even lost it. There's something comforting about knowing there's a piece of you floating out there in space and time that someone can grab at any given moment just to have something comforting to hold on to.

And then there's Jake.

He has so many pieces of me that it's hard to keep track of.

The dreams have slowed down, but they're not completely gone. I have some now and then; some are repeated memories I've already seen, and some aren't. The headaches aren't completely gone either, but the ease that Jake instills inside of me helps with that tremendously.

Sometimes we'll talk about what our life was like before the accident; he'll tell me stories and answer whatever questions I have without hesitation. When we met—this last time—I knew that Jake Redding was connected to me somehow. Little did I realize that he's my past, my present, and my future. There's something about his tall frame and curly copper blonde hair, muscular arms and ripped chest that holds a special place in my heart. But that's all just visual. There's many more things—I learn something new about him every day—that make up the compound of Jake Redding that entice me more than a set of strong arms can.

The unspoken love that Jake holds for me is the warmest feeling I've ever experienced. After everything all of us have been through, it's hard not to take the first thing I can and run with it. I've had to block any feelings for my real father that muster themselves up inside of me just to make room for the people in my life that haven't put me in harm's way.

I haven't spoken to Michael Cervase since I visited him in the prison. He's tried to contact me while rotting away in a jail cell, but those efforts have stopped after the fifteenth time of me rejecting his phone calls and throwing away his letters.

Jake's even flown Brant out a few times to visit, but I think it's more of a silent obligation he feels he owes to Brant for helping me more times than one. Last time, he brought his new girlfriend out to meet us, and they stayed for a week to relish in the suburban Midwest life with us. After the week was up, she was itching to get back to the big city of Dallas and leave our little town behind her in the dust, taking Brant with her. I haven't heard from him since then, but as long as he's happy, I'm happy.

And then there's Caitlyn and our parents.

Well, my sister and brother-in-law. I still call them my parents because it's all I can remember them as, and it just feels right and fits.

They are in a corner of the backyard, drinks in hand and smiles on their faces as Jake walks up to them and engages them in a conversation. They moved to South Carolina, but for this special occasion, they flew in to celebrate with us just like the dozens of other people chattering and laughing around the plush, green backyard.

"Hey, you," Jake whispers behind me, and it startles me. "I'd ask if you were okay, but that seems like a silly question." His smile warms my heart as he steps around me and kisses my lips. "Are you having a good time? You haven't really spoken to anyone."

I let my lips spread across my face. "Just taking it all in. Life's changed so much these past few years that it's hard to appreciate it for what it is."

He makes an agreeing noise and snakes his arm around my waist. "And what do you think life is all about? I'm sure you have an excellent answer."

I know he's mocking me, but I don't care. The fact that he appreciates what I have to say, no matter if he agrees with me or not, is the real point to focus on. "I think everyone has a different purpose in life, and we don't just have one; we have many. Like for instance, you and me."

His eyebrows raise, and he waves to one of his brothers. "You and me, huh? What's my purpose in life, do you think?"

A giggle escapes my throat as he tickles my side. "To be at my beck and call, of course." I laugh and let him playfully groan and tug me into his arms for a bear hug. Some people in the crowd make cute noises and clap when Jake puts me down and kisses me. I knew we would be on display today, but it's weird to have dozens of pairs of eyes watching and waiting for you to do something adorable.

"Hey, you two." Noah, one of Jake's brothers, walks up to us. "Jake, didn't you want to make a speech or something?" He winks at his brother and nods toward the concrete patio where a microphone has been set up for use. "Everything's ready, man."

Jake takes my hand and kisses my fingers before leaving me with Noah, who puts his arm around my shoulders to keep me in place. Jake clears his throat when he reaches the microphone, and once everyone gathers around to hear what he has to say, his eyes meet mine, and for the very first time, his entire face blushes red and he's suddenly at a loss for words. His hands shake as he reaches into his jeans pocket and pulls out a folded-up piece of white paper, ready to read whatever is on it.

He clears his throat and tries to calm down. "Hey, everyone, I, uh…I just wanted to start off by thanking everyone for being here. It means a lot to Olivia and me that you care enough about us to join us today." He nods in my direction, and it's my turn to blush from the pairs of eyes that are fixed on me again. Noah laughs and takes his arm from around my shoulders. Apparently, he's confident that I won't run from anything now.

Jake nervously laughs and looks at the paper in his hand. "Okay, so I just wanted to say a few words about the one person in my life that has always been there for me, no matter what sort of trouble I got myself into. She's the only one that tried to bring me out of the darkness when I got so far deep that I didn't care if I made it out alive. I was a fool to deny her, but once I let her into my heart and soul, that was and continues to remain the best decision I've ever made in my entire life. Being with Olivia has made my heart full of emotions that I never thought I was worthy to feel. I was in a bad place before Olivia found me and held on. We all know that she was born Lacey…"

A lump forms in my throat when I hear that name every single time.

"…but to me, she's Olivia, and most of you just see that as a name, but to her, it's much more than that. She lives and breathes kindness, and without her, I wouldn't be the person I am today. I owe her much more than just my life. I owe her my freedom. I owe her everything and anything I can possible give to her because she chose to love me not only once, but twice."

The crowd coos, and Jake takes a glass of champagne from a passing waiter's tray while Noah fetches one for the both of us and hands mine to me. "So let's raise our glasses to this incredible woman that rekindles the pieces of me that I never thought could be fixed. Let's raise our glasses to the woman that has touched each and every one of our lives in a positive and unforgettable way."

Jake's eyes reach mine, and tears stream down his cheeks. "Let's all raise our glasses to Miss Olivia White and the fact that she agreed to let me make her my wife. I love you, Bug." He brings the glass to his lips quickly so others will follow suit before they realize that he's crying.

I dodge all of the arms flailing around me to swoop me into a hug so I can make it to Jake first. He catches me as I run to him, and our lips mesh together so soundly that nothing is going to keep us apart.

"I love you, Jake," I breathe into his lips, and he smiles.

"Thanks for fixing me, Bug." He laughs and swoops me up to carry me around the backyard so everyone can congratulate us on our engagement. "Thanks for sticking around to fall in love with me again."

"Jake Redding, I wouldn't have it any other way." I smile, and our family and friends surround us with smiles on their faces and love in their hearts.

I wouldn't have it any other way.

Bonus Chapter One

Six months

Jake

The constant ticking of the clock on the wall pisses me off. The green paint on the wall underneath the clock pisses me off. The way the bed looks without her in it pisses me off, and the fact that it's been six months since I've touched her skin really fucking pisses me off.

Everything pisses me off.

"I fucking miss you, Lacey. I don't know how to be normal without you," I whisper into the darkness. The room is cold; it has been since she left. I don't know what the fuck I'm talking about...she didn't leave. Her hand was forced; they played to her emotions and got her to leave with them. She wasn't in danger; I was supposed to keep her safe. I didn't know I had to keep her safe from them too.

My heart burns.

I hate everything.

Fuck this house. I'll burn it all down.

"Jake!" Noah's voice echoes through the halls. "Where are you?"

I want to scream and tell him to fuck off, that I don't want to see anyone right now. This is all my fault; what kind of fucking monster nearly kills the woman he's in love with?

Me. Jake Redding, that's who.

Noah turns on the bedroom light and stands in the doorway, surprised. "What the hell are you doing in here, sitting in the dark?"

"Did you find her?"

He shakes his head.

"Then fuck off."

"Jake, this isn't the end, okay? Whatever Michael did with her, he buried it deep. There's people out there he still trusts, and he used them. It's gonna take some time, brother."

My fist slams on the bedside table. "I don't have any more fucking time! It's been six months, Noah. Six. Fucking. Months! You know how I get without her! I need her, Noah! So go out there and fucking find her!"

"I have another lead. I was coming to tell you. I'm going to Miami."

"It better be to find my fucking lifeforce and not take a fucking vacation."

Noah shakes my shoulders. "Would you calm the fuck down? I get it, Jake, you love her. I love her too. We all love her. Lacey is special, man. Everyone knows that. What I can't do is magically make her appear, okay? I'm doing the best I can."

"Find her, Noah."

He sighs and releases me, leaving me alone in the bedroom. The problem with living in this house without her is she's everywhere. Her perfume lingers in the bedroom on the bedsheets where I can't even sit without thinking about her naked body beneath mine. Her sneakers are still where she's kicked them off underneath her vanity; I can't bring myself to move them.

Her purple toothbrush. The bottles of Merlot in the wine cellar. Her sun room. The dying maple tree in the backyard.

Lacey is my heart.

I can't survive without a heart.

Every room I walk through has something to remind me of her, and I can't take it anymore. From the moment I laid eyes on this girl, I knew she was the end of the world for me. The love in her eyes when she handed me the note that changed my life forever on my seventeenth birthday was so real and pure, I didn't stand a chance.

I still don't stand a chance.

She makes me better; I don't have to be the beast when I have her.

But I don't have her.

When I find her, she won't want me anyway. She'll know that I cut the brakes on the fucking car and tried to kill him. There's no denying what I've done, and she's going to fear me again. I haven't seen fear in her eyes since the day I told her I never wanted to talk to her again.

***

"Jake, this isn't you. You're better than this. Come home with me."

Lacey tugs at my arm, and for a split second, I do want to run away with her. I've always wanted to run away with her; there's no question about that. She's been everything to me from day one. That hasn't changed.

I've changed.

I'm a monster now.

"Lacey, go home. I don't want you here."

She gets knocked back a few steps and looks stunned. The group of friends I've been running around with aren't exactly decent people. Lately, we've taken to lurking in the woods smoking pot for the time being until we can stir up new trouble around town.

"What's this we've got here?" Larken Brown, the self-appointed leader of our group and total fucking scumbag, stops to stroke Lacey's hair. "Who does this one belong to?"

Lacey grits her teeth. "I belong to no one."

"Me," I speak up. "She's mine."

Larken's eyebrows rise. "Better get this one in line, Jakey Boy."

Once he moves on, I grab her wrist as tight as I can. "Lacey, go the fuck home. You stay here and I can't protect you for long. This isn't the place for you."

"Or you, Jake. Please, I love you. Come home with me."

I can't look into her sad gray eyes. "I love you too. Go. Home."

Larken makes his way back around and hears

what I say to her. He claps his hands together and starts laughing loudly, making a big scene. "Look at all these pretty ladies out here tonight! Who wants to drink my special punch?"

The fear in her eyes when he stops in front of her kills me.

This is gonna fucking cost me big time.

I reach over and grab Lacey by her waist and throw her over my shoulder as hard as I can. She whimpers from the blow, but I don't care. I have to make it look believable so nothing bad will happen to her. Larken watches me stomp away with her and throw her into the backseat of my car.

"Lacey, kiss me." I lean over her and try not to cry. "You have to kiss me."

"What is happening here?" she cries into her hands. "You're just a kid, Jake. What are you doing here with these guys?"

"Larken gets fucked up when he's drunk. He won't touch you if I am. He doesn't like someone's sloppy seconds."

Her eyes darken. "That's disgusting."

"His words, not mine. If he thinks you're with me, he won't hurt you. I told you not to come after me, Lacey. I don't want anyone to follow me. I just want to be alone."

"Why? What's so bad that you want to be alone?"

"I'm just so fucking angry all the time I can't trust myself to be around you without hurting you. I've done things you would be scared of me for."

She leans up and kisses my lips, and my skull nearly explodes. I've thought about kissing her *before, but this is…different than I thought it would be.*

"Take me home, Jake," she says. "Take me home, and when you're ready, I'll be there for you."

I want to kiss her again, but I can't.

"Promise?"

"Promise."

***

Noah comes back into the house; his boots stomp against the hardwood floors. He waits for me in the kitchen, giving me the space I need to cool down and have a rational conversation about things.

"Michael had some accounts in Miami that were closed down not long before his arrest. I think that maybe he hid her there with the money," he says and hands me a hot cup of coffee. "Remind me again why we're looking for a girl who doesn't remember any of us?"

The hot liquid burns my throat, and I need it to feel alive.

"We owe it to her to find her and bring her home."

"For your sake or hers?"

The cup clinks on the table as I lose my focus and nearly drop it when he says this.

"Whatever gets her home."

Bonus Chapter Two

One year, six days, four hours and nine minutes

Holy shit, there she is.

I can't believe Noah actually fucking found her.

I'd given up hope; a year has gone by, and I knew life was punishing me by keeping her hidden from me. Now, here she is: wafting around an upper-middle class suburban backyard with four too many flutes of champagne swimming around her veins.

She's still as gorgeous as the last time I saw her.

I want to call out her name, but she won't answer to it. Noah found out the truth, and Lacey has no fucking idea who she is or where she's from. She doesn't remember her fucked-up life, and she doesn't remember what I did.

Look at her. She makes me fucking smile, and I'm sure I look like the biggest fucking creep here. That includes the guy with the buzzed head that's hitting on her. Fuck that guy; I'll pulverize him if he touches her in any way other than a nice one. How

287

can I bump into her without freaking her out?

Shit. There's Caitlyn. I fucking remember her, though we've only met once.

***

"Who the fuck are you?"

"You don't know me." The girl with the bleached hair stands at my doorstep. "My name is Caitlyn. I just wanted to tell you that Lacey is safe and we're moving her tomorrow."

I haven't fucking slept in weeks. Is this girl even real? I reach out and poke her shoulder, and she looks surprised and scared. Her body is solid, and she sways backward a little, bouncing right back to her position only a few feet in front of me.

"Where the fuck is she?" My voice vibrates in my throat. I grab the girl's arm, and she squeals, looking around the darkness for help. "Tell me where you took her."

"I didn't take her anywhere, please...it's for her own good right now..."

Half of me wants to pull the girl inside and lock her away to exchange her for Lacey. I know I can't do that without repercussions, and I've already become the biggest fucking monster I've ever been. Reality sets into my bones, and I fall to my knees, hugging the girl's legs and pleading with her.

"Please bring her back to me...I need her...she's everything..."

The girl pats my head and cries with me. "I'm so sorry, Jake. I shouldn't even be here. I heard my mom talking to my grandpa about Lacey and how much you mean to her...I don't know where we're going, but I just wanted you to know she's safe."

"Is she okay?" I look up at her and see Lacey in her face a little.

"She's with family. She's fine. She's having headaches a lot and can't remember who she is or anyone around her. I asked her about you today, and she had no idea who you were."

I want to fucking die.

"Why are you doing this to me?"

"Did you get the note I left you? The one explaining where she was?"

My legs allow me to stand; even though I'm much taller than her, I feel so fucking small. "I got it. I read it. I didn't fucking like it."

"I just wanted you to understand we're not doing this to hurt you—we're doing it to save her. She needs to be in a place where she can heal, and she can't do that here."

A car pulls up and honks the horn. "That's my friend. He's giving me a ride back to the hospital." The girl puts her hand on my cheek and frowns. "You need to move on, Jake. I don't know when, or if, she'll be back. I know it hurts..." She looks back at the car and wipes a tear from her eye. "She's not the only one leaving someone she loves behind. My life's been uprooted too."

"Then don't do this," I plead. "Don't take her. Stay here with her and help her."

"I can't." She shakes her head and takes a few steps backward. The man steps out of the car and crosses his arms over his chest—in a defensive stance in case she needs help.

That sorry fucking bastard.

He's losing someone he loves, too.

"Just promise me one thing."

I shake my head. "I can't make any promises to someone who's taking the very reason I fucking breathe from me."

She sighs. "Don't come looking for her, Jake. Don't confuse her any more than she already is. All you'll do is hurt her more, and if you do that, she may never recover."

"You expect me to just...let her go?"

The girl looks into my eyes and nods. She backs away and joins the man in the car, and he speeds off, leaving me a broken fucking mess on my doorstep.

***

I can't fucking let her see me. If Caitlyn sees me, it's all over. She'll pull Lacey from me and disappear with her again; I just found her after an entire year of searching.

One year, six days, four hours and nine minutes, actually.

Lacey looks disturbed by the buzzed-headed guy talking to her. I laugh to myself because even though she doesn't remember me or what she felt for me...this guy doesn't stand a fucking chance. It was one of the things I hated most about being in public with her...the countless number of eyes following her wherever she would go. She's gorgeous—anyone can see that—but now she's looks different, yet the same. I wonder why they didn't change her looks when they changed her name?

Her long, dark hair is pinned up the best it can be; it's so thick that she's always had trouble keeping it up and out of her face. I never minded, though; I like brushing it back behind her ears.

Did he just fucking push her?

I put my bottle of craft beer on a table as I walk calmly to the guy who's now joking around with his buddies and talking about Lacey. They pat him on the back and motivate him to touch her in ways that only I should be fucking touching her.

"Got a problem?" the buzzed-headed guy snickers.

A smart-ass smirk forms on my lips. "Yeah, I do. See that girl over there?" My head bobs towards Lacey, who's taking two more champagne flutes from a waiter's tray and guzzling them down.

"Olivia? Yeah, what's it to you?"

My hand wraps around his wrist, and I squeeze so hard his eyes bug from his skull. None of his pansy-ass friends help him as he writhes beneath the pain I'm inflicting purposely on his skin. "Leave her the fuck alone, you hear me? She doesn't want you—don't fucking talk to her like that again."

The buzzed-headed guy laughs. "I'll do what I fucking please. Now let go of me or you won't like what happens to you."

I pull the guy until he's inches from my face; the fear in his eyes brightens, and his friends disperse around the backyard, not wanting any part of this confrontation. "You definitely won't like what happens to you if you don't leave her alone. Take this as your first and only warning, jackass."

I release him a little too hard, and he falls into the bushes like he tried to do to Lacey before. He sputters as I walk away, threatening me and causing a scene, but I'm already inside the house looking for where she's run off to.

"Jake!" a man's voice booms in my direction. "Nice of you to make it, son!"

Stan Burrows—the man I invested money with so I could attend this party—motions me over to his group to introduce me. I make nice and shake hands and let the others get bored of the shiny new guy before averting my attention to Caitlyn and Lacey as they have a small argument in the foyer. Caitlyn leaves her and returns to her own group of friends, leaving Lacey alone with another glass of champagne. She teeters a bit once she's outside, and the dress she's wearing—that tight little black dress that makes my fucking mouth water because I know what's underneath—slides up her thighs as she falls down in to the grass with her head in her hands.

This is my chance.

I'll walk up to her, and if she doesn't know me, I'll put on the charm and win her over.

The only way this is going to work is if I make her fall in love with me again.

How did I do it the first time?

Several old men are staring at her from the bottom of the lawn; they nudge each other and point at her slightly open legs. I snarl at them and rush to her side, ready to defend her.

I stand in silence, inches from the person I love most in the world, and she doesn't have a clue who

I am or why I'm hovering over her.

She needs me, though. She needs me to wipe the sadness away from her heart.

I need her to come home.

Taking a deep breath, I sort out what I'm going to say to her, but the way she sways lets me know that all that champagne has gone to her head and she's drunk. She always has been a lightweight.

Speak, Jake! Talk to her! Don't let her go away!

I clear my throat softly and take a deep breath.

Here goes nothing...

About the Author

I live in Kansas City with my husband and our son, Ryker. I have been writing for over a decade, I started out writing songs and music and then realized that those stories were too short for the tales I wanted to tell, so I switched to writing books and articles, which then blossomed into writing contemporary romance and fantasy novels. I am in indecisive person at heart, I love coffee more than a Gilmore girl and my most favorite time to write and create is during a rainstorm (with coffee!).

I love hearing from those who read my stories, I love to hear how much people relate to each character and how they are rooting for their favorites to succeed! I don't only create stories, I create entirely new worlds and people that come to life

Facebook:
https://www.facebook.com/authornickyshanks

Twitter:
https://twitter.com/nickyshanks84

Instagram:
https://www.instagram.com/authornickyshanks/

Goodreads:
https://www.goodreads.com/user/show/68847149-nicky-shanks

Wattpad:
https://www.wattpad.com/user/NBenson

Join our Reader Group on Facebook and don't miss out on meeting our authors and entering epic giveaways!

Limitless Reading

Where reading a book
is your first step to becoming
limitless...

LIMITLESS PUBLISHING *Reader Group*

Join today! *"Where reading a book is your first step to becoming limitless..."*

https://www.facebook.com/groups/Limitless Reading/

www.ingramcontent.com/pod-product-compliance
Lightning Source LLC
Chambersburg PA
CBHW052024240626
47153CB00006B/1943